SEP 0 0 2007

DATE DUE

DEMCO 38-296

HALLELUJAH CITY

HALLELUJAH CITY

TOM LaMARR

University of New Mexico Press
Albuquerque

© 2007 by the University of New Mexico Press
All rights reserved. Published 2007
Printed in the United States of America

12 11 10 09 08 07   1 2 3 4 5 6 7

Library of Congress Cataloging-in-Publication Data

LaMarr, Tom
    Hallelujah city / Tom LaMarr.
    p. cm.
    ISBN 978-0-8263-4041-2 (alk. paper)
1. Fathers and daughters—Fiction.
2. Cults—Fiction.
3. Redemption—Fiction. I. Title.
    PS3562.A4217H35 2007
    813'.54—dc22

                        2007008234

DESIGN AND COMPOSITION: *Mina Yamashita*

For Bud and Hobbes

Acknowledgments

Once again, it pays to have smart friends and relatives. Big thanks to Timothy Hillmer, Bill Collister, Robert Garner McBrearty, Mark Lamprey, Mark Kjeldgaard, Lucia Fiori, Chet Hampson, Robert Ebisch, Juliet Wittman, Dave Crowl, John Collister, Bill Jones, Luther Wilson, Maya Allen-Gallegos, David Gallegos, Karen Palmer, Debbie Korte (several seasons past due), Darrin Pratt, Janis Hallowell, and Marianne Wesson. Finally, I'm indebted as always to Anne for her patience and Alison for providing perspective.

◆

CHAPTER ONE

Surprised didn't begin to cover it. No, surprised is what Scott Chambers would have been if his daughter had phoned him. But this—seeing her standing on the small front stoop, her feet hidden by a frayed duffel bag that indicated she might be staying—this was Columbus sailing off the world's edge, or Newton watching his apple float, suspended in air.

"Mary." He waited a few seconds before unlocking the storm-security door, a few more before pushing it open.

"This is it," she said, looking past him. "Everything we've waited for."

"Right," he said. "End of the world." He moved toward her, stopping close enough to reach out and touch her shoulder, something he nearly did. The door's metal knob dug into his elbow. "You'll excuse me for hoping you came to your senses."

"The city had no need of the sun, neither of the moon; for the glory of God did lighten it. Tonight, Dad. When my name is called from the Book of Life, I will *let go* of my senses."

"I see." A Volkswagen bus was parked at the curb, light in color, possibly white. He couldn't tell much more in the darkness. "But why in God's name are you here? If you really still believe. I know you didn't come to save me."

"The Teacher gave me a mission." The Teacher was Daniel Hawker, leader of Mary's cult. Of all the people inhabiting this world, he was the one Scott Chambers saw as least deserving of air, food, water, and sleep.

"Wait—Hawker wants you to save me? Seriously?"

"I must try to give sight to one of the blind."

"And you chose me?"

"The Teacher did the choosing. Maybe—" She lifted her bag. "Your blindness stood out."

The retired stenographer in the house directly across from Scott's peeked out from between her blinds, carving a sliver of flickering blue, the light from her TV. Ms. Brearty. Always calling roof and glass repairmen to her house for estimates on work she'd never do.

"And you have—what—five hours to pull this off?" he asked.

"My mission is to *try*." She walked around him and into the house and placed her bag on the hallway carpet. "You're the one with five hours. Clock's ticking."

He started to say, "Doomsday just seemed to sneak up on me this year," but chose instead to think before speaking. "I'm glad he sent you home. Whatever the reason."

"That's funny," she said without smiling. "Sending me home. I think you're forgetting that's still a few hours away."

Scott shrugged. Come midnight, this nonsense would be over. Hawker's mask would fall to the floor, transforming him in Mary's eyes into the lying, manipulative megalomoron that everyone else had always been able to see. This final scene had been scripted months before—when Daniel Hawker crowned himself "the true End Time Messiah"—and given its inevitability, Scott could endure watching his daughter affect an IQ one digit short of her real one. He would try harder not to agitate her. *Just be glad she's here.*

He asked if she was hungry and followed her to the kitchen. "I could make you a sandwich. I still have those pickles you like." As she took a seat, he wondered how well she'd been eating at the compound; she seemed so much thinner than he remembered. The news reports made it sound as if all the cult members, with one probable exception, had toiled away the daylight hours. Yet, Mary's appearance was that of someone who avoided all manifestation of labor—along with daylight. He thought of junkies he'd seen on TV, of vampires and rock stars. But what made him reach for his mint-flavored Maalox tablets was that she still looked so young. Hawker had stolen a child—and damn well knew it.

"I'm sure you already ate," she said while he sliced her sandwich into perfect halves.

"I wasn't expecting company." The knife slipped across his index finger, and would have hurt like hell had it been sharpened in the last twenty years. "I never stopped thinking about you, Mary," might have come next, but he wasn't sure if he'd spoken the words or merely thought them. He handed her the plate, then watched as she closed her eyes and prayed in an iron-gray whisper, "Daniel . . . Holy Father . . . bless this, my last meal on this last of nights." Her words came out in hard straight lines with nothing but space between each sound, unpolluted by warmth or vulnerability. "All food is a gift. Some gifts bring joy. Others bring challenge and strength." He searched her face, came up empty again. His daughter's personality had gone into hiding, the way blood reacts to a winter's chill, abandoning one's extremities to protect the heart and brain. "Tonight we join—"

◆

With eight dollars still wadded in her pocket, Mary wished she had stopped at Pizza Paradiso. A Paradouble Two-Slice Platter would have left change for cinnamon sizzlers and chocolate-chip cookies, once basic food groups she'd gone without knowing for nearly three years. Not that the Teacher forbade desserts. As He once said, *My Father gave you five senses that you may fully enjoy creation.* But the sweets in Hallelujah City just didn't taste that sweet, and they always involved some kind of fruit, usually cherries or apples. In three years, she had not once glimpsed cheesecake or brownies or soft, cool cookie dough, except when she was dreaming.

Her dad stood by the sink, clearing his throat. She forced down another bite. Ham and Swiss, cold, on store-brand wheat. Miracle Whip as opposed to mayo. Certifiably predictable, she thought. His diet is still determined by what's on sale that week. Maybe if she'd brought home coupons for salvation. *Save thirty cents on your next Rapture.*

"Sometimes I can't believe you," she said.

"I'm just glad there's *something* you can't believe," he responded, "even if it has to be me. A little skepticism wouldn't hurt you."

"No question. I can see it's done wonders for you."

The phone rang and her father grabbed it. "And how is that of interest to me?" he said sharply after listening a few seconds. "I see. But she's in Minnesota. And this is not Minnesota." Mary couldn't hear the other voice, only its effect. "No, no, and last of all, no." He cleared his throat for emphasis. "Don't call again."

His right hand covered the mouthpiece as he hung up.

"Who was that?" she asked.

"Someone claiming to be an author. Said he was writing a book on cults."

Mary knew who it was. Adrian Hummel. She was impressed he'd tracked her down.

She was just about to get up when her father took the place across from hers. "So, convert me," he said. "You don't seem to be in any hurry." This was not his usual spot; at least it wasn't when she lived there. He always sat at the head of their small rectangular table. There were three chairs altogether, one seat too many, with none at the foot. It had been that way for as long as she remembered. "I'm waiting," he said.

If her dad was a master at hiding his feelings, his fingernails gave him away. They had been chewed down to nothing, chewed without mercy. And if his face didn't show emotion, it did provide a record of wear. His cheeks were collapsing like sinkholes, a process that had clearly gained momentum in her absence.

He had red marks on the bridge of his nose from the reading glasses he must have worn all day at work. But that was most of the color she saw. His hair had frosted over like a Minnesota field, its brown completely gone, and some of it had not survived the seasonal change. Even his moustache seemed thinner, though this had to be from excessive trimming. Drying up—that's what he'd been doing while she was gone, like he'd skipped a few years and landed in his fifties.

"Twenty minutes, Dad. There's something I need to do upstairs."

"The ticking clock?"

"We've got time," she said, already on her feet.

"But your mission." He was pointing at his wrist; she didn't see a watch. "Aren't we under a deadline here?"

She thought she detected the beginning of a smile, and wondered if he understood that he had inadvertently called her bluff.

For while everything Mary said was true, it wasn't exactly the truth.

CHAPTER TWO

The Son of God had allergies. That, for Adrian, said it all. When it came to spectacular frauds, Daniel Hawker was the real damn thing. What Son of God had allergies?

That noted, there was one point on which Adrian dissented from the majority of God Boy's detractors. Adrian wanted Hawker to be right, in that he wanted the world to end without further delay. It would save him a lot of trouble.

Who would have thought that writing a book would be so much harder than coming up with an idea for one? Who would have thought it could demote you to serf, which was precisely how Adrian's creditors, agent, and editor saw him? Alone in his room at the Valfaard Inn, he stared down a TV that hadn't once worked in the two years he'd been there.

His business cards read, *Adrian C. Hummel, Author.* So did the contracts he'd signed for his agent and editor. Which would have been fine had he written a book. As it was now, he had notes everywhere, on scraps of tissue, legal pads, and memory sticks. He had cassette tapes recounting his talks with Mary Chambers and one other disciple. He even had a title, *The Last Days (And Then Some): Inside the Cult and Mind of Daniel Hawker.* But he didn't have the one thing he'd promised his publisher: the view from within. (Well, that and five hundred pages.) An interview with Hawker could rectify the problem. *Exclusive access,* the thought made him smile, to the extent he still could. *Hawker's story, in his own words.* He pictured the four-color dust jacket. *After two years undercover . . . After a series of candid face-to-face conversations . . . Author Adrian C. Hummel takes you inside the mind of cult leader Daniel Hawker as events unfold . . .*

With or without the world's imminent demise, time was running out. He needed to get to God Boy soon, before Hawker did something horrendous and unoriginal, like host a mass suicide with only one willing participant. As Adrian's mother would have put it, having recently applied the cliché to Adrian's situation, Hawker had painted himself into a corner.

Adrian's laptop, stationed on the small round table near the front window, got tired of waiting for attention. He caught a glimpse of the screen saver, a photo of a car he once owned, just before the monitor went dark. Earlier that evening, the computer had yielded some useful information, courtesy of a website that sold "personal private data" to anyone with a credit card. (He had thirteen.) There, Adrian had located a phone number for Scott P. Chambers, 48, father of Mary Elizabeth Chambers, 21, residing at 1225 Turnbolt Drive, Aurora, Colorado.

The Chambers girl had been Adrian's last reliable contact inside the cult, right up until Hawker's hypocrites kicked her out of the compound. Though it was little more than a hunch, Adrian felt certain the girl had gone to her father's house in Colorado.

What *private_I.com* hadn't told him was that Mary's old man was a jerk. The first three times Adrian tried the number, Mr. Chambers didn't bother to pick up on his end. When he did, on try number four, he curtly dismissed the caller, denying that Mary was there.

"You don't understand," Adrian had cried as the line went dead. "You don't understand."

The girl from Colorado could get him to God Boy; this was the one thing Adrian continued to believe. She could help him gain Hawker's trust. He just needed to get her back to Minnesota first.

He heard what sounded like trucks going by out front. SUVs, he assumed, Chevy Suburbans, the black ones driven by federal agents. He'd been seeing more of these on Main Street in recent days, just as he'd been hearing more helicopters at night.

"Idiot," he said in a whisper. "Should've told him you were a cop. Or a deprogrammer. I can help you, Mr. Chambers. I can help you with your daughter."

He returned his attention to the dead TV's screen. The dark green mirror favored silhouette over detail, and this favored Adrian. It wasn't that he was a bad looking guy; he just wasn't especially good looking, with his plain dark eyes and plainer nose. His cheeks hadn't always been this puffy. He'd gained forty-one pounds since checking into the Valfaard. Add a pair of wire-rim glasses, and you'd be looking at the face of middle management, of director, or comptroller.

He did have good hair—make that perfect hair. Lustrous, thick brown with just a hint of gold, he got this from his dad, the lady-killer. Adrian had always been proud of his hair, even when it worked against him during his first months in Trappers Point, Minnesota. To the locals, good hair meant TV newsman. They didn't like TV newsmen.

Adrian sneezed (dust—one of two allergies shared with Hawker) and walked to the dresser where he kept his bottles of caffeine pills. He would try the number again in the morning. The way his luck was going, the world would still be here.

CHAPTER THREE

Seated on the toilet with its cold plastic seat, Mary was thinking she might just stay in her father's upstairs bathroom till the Cleansing commenced. It wasn't simply that she wanted to hide. She would use the time wisely, use it to pray she was still among the saved. Cher Balser had been right. Mary deserved her exile.

And yet . . . if Mary could have undone one thing from the past few weeks it would have been—*Forgive me, Daniel*—getting caught. She could still hear Cher going off like an air-raid siren. "A lowly disciple should not be alone in the Inner Sanctum."

The scene had seemed surreal, and only in part because Mary had been fast asleep seconds before, dreaming of chocolate-chip cookies the size of pizzas. She should have been in her own bed, in her own trailer, but had obviously drifted off after pleasing Daniel. So much for telling herself, *I'll rest a few minutes. Then I'll get up.*

Cher paced the room in an agitated state, a lioness circling her prey after days without food. "She has corrupted the Most Holy Teacher! She has caused shame to rain on our city!"

Dozens of candles, rising from the floor on simple holders, no two alike, painted the walls and ceiling in a fuzzy, living orange. A subwoofer crackled like thunder in the distance, having run out of musical notes to produce when Daniel's CD came to an end. "You must cast her out, Lord," Cher screeched. "She's a virus of sin." Cher kicked over a candle. It must have gone out before hitting the carpet.

A dog ran into the Inner Sanctum. A young English sheepdog that may have been Daniel's favorite, it barked a few times before dashing back out. Mary wondered if Cher had done something to scare it. The Teacher owned a number of pets, including a potbellied pig and some cats nobody ever saw. Mary loved the dogs, having wanted one when she was growing up.

The next yelps came from Cher. "Banish her now! Banish her now!" Mary cowered near the headboard of Daniel's king-size bed, knees to her chest, wrapped in a blanket that didn't smell fresh. The Teacher surprised her by saying nothing.

This set the pattern for what remained of Mary's stay in Hallelujah City. For ten days Daniel took no action, while Cher took her case to anyone with ears. Mary walked, ate, and worked with eyes pointed down, afraid to receive the looks the others must have been giving her. Finally, with three days left to ascendant bliss, the Teacher called her aside. "We cannot have discord at this crucial time."

They stood outside on a path where the snow had been stomped down to form a dirty, solid pavement. This narrow trail led to the Inner Sanctum, more specifically to the back door that opened to a kitchen. It was early Saturday morning. An icy fog hung in the air, a wall of blindness, achingly bright.

"There are some I cannot trust," He said next. "I must keep them in my sight.

"As for you, my Lamb, I have a special mission. There is a doubter you wish to rescue from the world . . . No, no, don't speak. Your mind has not yet accepted this truth. But I see it in your heart."

She would never contradict Daniel—though she had no desire in mind *or* heart to rescue any doubters—and this kept her from asking if there wasn't another unspoken reason. Mary feared something had changed, something much, much bigger than getting caught by Cher in the Inner Sanctum. If her suspicions were correct, the Teacher was being diplomatic. He was showing her mercy by calling this a "mission."

He gave her six twenties and the keys to a Volkswagen bus as old as her father and just about as likely to get a speeding ticket. "You will journey to the place of your old life." Two other disciples would travel with Mary, he explained, each with an assignment identical to hers. She would drop them off at their points of worldly origin, which happened to be towns along the route to Aurora, Colorado.

"These two, like you, have unfinished business in the world."

Braving His eyes, she whispered, "But, Teacher . . . the Cleansing?"

"Your reward is secure."

"Shouldn't I be here?"

"Fear not," He said softly. "We'll be together the instant it happens. In that time without hours, that place without distance."

◆

The talk with Mary did not go well, despite the simplicity of the rules Scott set for himself. There were only two, for Christ's sake: *Keep your opinions to yourself*, and *Try not to upset her.*

Still, he had to say *something*, and after ten minutes of listening to nonsense his daughter couldn't possibly believe, Scott calmly asked, "How do you know he's God?"

"I witnessed two miracles."

"Two? What would that have been for Jesus? A day's work?"

"I *saw* them, Dad. Miracles."

Regretting his previous words, he stopped himself from saying, "Let me guess, he walks on water when it's ten below."

"You just don't get it," she continued. "If you could see the things I've seen. It's hard to find words."

Although Scott couldn't let it show, her composure unnerved him. She seemed so earnest, so certain. They were facing each other across the kitchen table, where she'd made him wait for more than an hour after running upstairs "for twenty minutes." He'd held his tongue when she came back down, keeping her from seeing the frustration she'd caused. "I'm ready," he'd said, trying his best to affect sincerity. "Enlighten me."

That was when she'd smiled, if ever so slightly, while shaking her head. It proved just enough to bring out the slight dimple in her chin. Though others might not have seen it, his daughter was beautiful. The hair that draped her gently freckled face was more red than brown, and the eyes still sparkled, soft green and searching. *So like your mother*, he'd come close to saying as Mary placed a plump white candle on the table, without trying to light it. *So like Liz.* He figured the prop held some significance, but there were bigger demands on his curiosity.

"I still don't get why you came home," he said now.

"I told you. The Teacher decided."

"And with all that's going on, he's worried about me?"

"He's worried about your *soul*."

"And without even meeting me once—"

Her face thawed as impatience flared. Now, here was the daughter he knew. "You're not even trying, Dad." She hoisted the candle up on end, then let it fall back over. "I knew you'd be impossible—that I'd have more luck with the neighbor's cat."

"I've seen their cat out back. I think he's a Buddhist."

"See. The most serious thing ever and you make a game of it."

"Sorry," he said. "No, really." He scratched an itch behind his ear. "It's just . . . maybe I'm trying to make *sense* of it. It just seems—"

"That I should be with the others," she whispered frostily, her eyes pointed down.

"You just pinned down the source of my confusion," he said, leaving off the words *and hope.*

She gave the candle a good hard spin, creating a circle of jittery whiteness. Scott could see it was time to back off, though he wasn't exactly sure what he'd said to make that thin blue vein on her forehead visible. "What is it?" he asked. "Is there some other reason you're here?"

"Maybe it's good you won't listen," he heard her say next. "All you're doing is reminding me how much I *don't* want you yapping at me for all eternity. It won't be that crowded the way things are going. Why can't you just accept that everlasting joy would be a good thing?"

She lifted the candle as she rose from her seat. "Heaven, Dad. Eternity. I wish I could explain it the way Daniel did, but I can't. Not that you'd listen."

Then she was heading for the stairs off the front hallway. "Is that it?" he called after her. "I hardly think we're finished."

"I think we are," she said without looking back.

Returning to the front room a few minutes later, he picked up a book of short stories, took a seat in his La-Z-Boy recliner, and automatically turned on the TV. *I'm not going to let her get to me.* But he didn't pay much attention to his book or the show that happened to be on—one of those World's Most Exploitative Videos specials. Babies attacked by pets or something. Typical weeknight programming. Still, he couldn't be bothered to change the channel.

◆

Alone in her room, Mary was even more confused. Angrier, too. She thought of her father and briefly considered going downstairs to talk with him. Just to be talking with someone.

She tried keeping her mind on the New Millennium and what it would mean, but kept hitting the walls of an imagination housed within a material body. In the words of Daniel, "Man lacks more than words to describe the World of Light. He lacks the senses to perceive such wonder. Vision, hearing, taste—these are but children's toys in the realm of God. You who have not lived in both worlds can no more imagine the other than a seed can anticipate what it's like to be a flower."

She shifted her focus to something more manageable: the end of the world and all *it* meant. No more greed or corruption, sickness or frailty. Likewise death and divorce. *Sorry, not available here.* They'd be leaving some good things, too, of course. Like blue skies, pizza, and online chat rooms. But these were all things—save the occasional blue sky—that she'd gone without in Hallelujah City. In this one respect, she wouldn't have to adjust. She'd been living the end of the world.

"Heaven is a river in the bright morning fog," she whispered, but her thoughts had returned to the problem she couldn't handle, the source of her anger and confusion. She wondered if there would still be a place for her in the New Millennium. After all those months of happily following Daniel's commandments, had she stumbled onto the other path, the one about to end abruptly? "Forgive me for my weakness," she whispered.

Not that the test results packed any kind of surprise. Really she'd known for days. Her bladder had already started to squeeze out her other organs, making her pee every couple of hours. But why had this happened at all with the world about to end? Why had God bothered? There was only one explanation, and it wasn't a good one. She had violated God's trust—and at a time when He had so much on His mind. This was His way of rubbing it in, of letting her know it *did* matter. *"You corrupted my Son."*

She heard her father moving about in the bathroom next door, then back downstairs to the TV. Making too much noise as usual. She caught the lifeless echo of canned laughter, assumed he was watching a sitcom. She knew, too, that if she shouted after him and asked what he was doing, he'd promptly reply, "Reading."

How could she even have considered sharing her crisis with him? He wouldn't have been able to listen. He already hated Daniel. Just imagine the fit he'd throw if he knew.

She cringed, thinking of all the times she'd said, "You're right, Dad." Just to shut him up. She wasn't going to say it ever again.

She picked up her Bible and held it to her chest. *The Gate is open to all. Knock and He shall answer. The Gate is open to all.*

◆

Sitting in his reclining chair, with its back straight up and leg-support tucked in, Scott P. Chambers was seething. Waves of washed-out light rolled over him. Illumination by *Frasier.*

He had known his daughter's secret since the nine o'clock news, about twelve minutes in. Monday was garbage night, same as always, and the discarded wrapper for the home pregnancy test had been buried beneath what seemed to be unused Kleenex in the upstairs bathroom wastebasket.

He'd felt himself reeling, coming to a stop with outstretched hands on the hamper lid. *I am not having a heart attack*, he told himself, refusing to make that wrapper the last thing he'd ever see. *Only three hours. You have to make it past midnight.* It didn't help that when he returned to the news, Hawker's photo was dominating the screen. It was an image Scott had seen before of a handsome self-assured leader with an off-season tan that belonged more on a nineteen-year-old surfer than a middle-aged messiah. His long, dark hair showed no signs of graying, and his smile appeared as a patch of brightness. Scott wanted to know why TV news bureaus always chose flattering shots when there had to be photographs missing the smile and self-confidence, if not the constant suntan.

TELEPHONE INTERVIEW, the caption read, RECORDED EARLIER. COURTESY CNN. Apparently, someone had forgotten to add, THE USUAL HORSESHIT.

"Oceans boil. Atoms collapse," Hawker was saying on tape, his fake British accent more annoying than usual. "All that begins must also conclude. That which was created must now be destroyed. My Father's commandments have become targets for barristers on the hunt for advancement, material for third-rate comedians, and oral calisthenics for so-called believers who covet all and spend Sabbath at the mall. We gave you a world of life, beauty, light. Look at it now. Look at yourselves." When asked if it was true some disciples had left Minnesota, Hawker replied, "We'll be together in that time without hours, that place without distance."

Barely visible near the bottom of the screen, Hawker wore his Keys to Heaven, the indisputably homemade necklace meant to show off a playful, childlike side—or as Scott saw it, a calculating core. Three wide plastic keys, bright and white and blue and red, had been taken from a baby's rattle to form its pendant, six inches south of the suntanned chin.

"Out of time, outside of time."

The seething didn't help, no more so than assessing the facts as Scott saw them. These were his standard responses to anger, but years had passed since he'd been this angry. *Be first. Be sure. Walgreens 1-Step Home Pregnancy Test.* He looked at the TV remote, in pieces on the floor. It wasn't enough. He wanted to break everything he owned, beginning with objects he could never replace and would regret breaking later. The more valuable the better.

"Damn it," he muttered, pushing himself up from the chair. He went upstairs and knocked on the door to Mary's room. "We are not finished." There was no reply.

He opened the door. No Mary.

"We need to talk," he said to the empty room.

◆

His daughter was sitting on a landscaping tie in the next-door neighbor's garden, silhouetted in the faint light of an ornamental lantern, a blanket pulled over her shoulders. He called to her. "Mary?" he called again, louder. She seemed unable to hear. She was talking to herself.

"Come inside," he shouted across the property line where lilac bushes once flourished. "It's cold out here." These words were barely out when he noticed how pleasant the night air actually felt. Mary probably thought she was in the tropics. "We need to talk."

She didn't respond, didn't so much as turn her head. He could still hear her mumbling.

"Goddammit, Mary—"

He stopped, reminding himself that he had a strategy and it didn't involve scaring her into leaving again. *Everything changes at midnight.* He looked up at the stars, thinking he might find perspective in their numbers. Not many were out. He looked at his daughter; the soft orange light seemed fastened to her, as much a part of her as her hair or skin.

He thought he heard her say, "Take me to—" but that was all he made out.

◆

Mary glanced at the watch borrowed from the dresser in her father's bedroom. *10:34.* Not that she'd need it to know the time had come, but she wanted to be ready. She was in the garden, seated on a landscaping tie, a blanket pulled over her shoulders. It was the neighbor's garden, of course—her father would never have gone to the effort of maintaining one—and it was mostly dormant. She made out the presence of buds near the solar-charged lanterns.

"Please, God, take me too." The air was getting colder. "Please, God, take me too." She would spend her last minutes in the world repeating this prayer and staring up at the few stars that bothered to come out in a city sky—basically, the Big Dipper and a handful of hangers on. There may have been fewer clear nights in Hallelujah City, but there sure were more stars. A jet passed overhead.

Then it was eleven—midnight in the Midwest. Nothing. She whispered more rapidly, "Please, take me too. Please, take me too." *Daniel, don't forsake me.*

Twelve o'clock Mountain Standard. "Please, God. Please, God. Please, God." At twenty-five past she finally gave up. Surprised to find water outside that wasn't covered by ice, she tossed the watch into Mrs. Jones' birdbath—and she cried.

Please, Daniel, please. Don't leave me behind.

Walking to the front of her dad's house, she saw that after all these years he'd never found time to fix the latch on the fence gate. The shrubs on the corner tried to scratch through her blanket, like beggars grabbing at Jesus. She closed the front door as gently as possible and removed her shoes. Her father was sleeping; she turned to climb the stairs.

"Mary—"

"Not now."

"We need to talk."

"He never said which midnight, Dad. There are other time zones."

"It's 1:40 in Minnesota."

"You're not safe yet," she said. "Thin ice. Look around you."

The mattress seemed soft compared to her bunk bed in Hallelujah City; it made her feel as if she were sinking. Her thoughts were unformed, hard to hold on to, as she tried convincing herself that what she'd said downstairs made sense. There *are* other time zones. Maybe God's waiting for the very last one. She was thinking, too, about how tired she was—how her brain felt like warm jelly, like when she had the flu. When sleep finally hit, it hit like the end of the world.

CHAPTER FOUR

*D*aniel, *forgive me.* Birds were singing outside. *It's all my fault.*
Her father was testing a new way to wash dishes, clanking them
together till the germs fell off. Though downstairs in the kitchen, he
could have been standing right next to her bed as he emptied his vintage Potscrubber 300. She remembered the name for its irony. When
Mary lived there, the waste of space worked best as a dish rack for pre-
scrubbed kitchenware. It needed to be replaced, had always needed to
be replaced.

The microwave beeped four times, but the warning came too late.
The smell had already found her—the stale transgression of recycled
coffee, at least two days old—like a cat going straight to the one guest
allergic to dander. "The world is still here," she whispered to her pillow.
"There's no mistaking this for Heaven."

She heard plastic wheels on concrete, the hissing of hydraulic
brakes—the neighbor in the house across from theirs racing to beat the
garbage truck. A can bounced into the street, rolled along the gutter. *Still
here. This body, this room.* The cheap pull-down shade discolored the
light, a burnt, or burning yellow. She was lying in her old bed, watched
over by an original movie poster for *Lord of the Rings: The Fellowship
of the Ring.* There was a diploma on her nightstand, white and gold,
Aurora High. Her father had picked up a frame for it. The black clock
radio—the same one she once slapped, shoved, and swore at each stupid
weekday morning—read *7:13.*

All my fault.

"Rise and shine," her father called up the stairs a second time.

Sorry, Dad, she said to herself as she got out of bed, *there will be no
shining today.*

The movie poster came off the wall. *You're not supposed to be here.*

Her diploma, too, went into the trash, a jagged crack dividing the glass. She remembered waking with a start only hours before, thinking, *This is it, time to go.* But she must have been reacting to one of her hallucinations, a *pavor nocturnus,* and one not even worth storing in memory. She couldn't pull up a single detail. Even the brief cold terror of finding herself awake, in this room, was breaking up in her recollection, retreating, like a radio signal on the interstate, western Nebraska, late afternoon. Had she screamed in the darkness? Called out for Daniel? Not that it mattered now, not in the least. Not with those stupid birds singing and carrying on like this was always supposed to be just another Tuesday morning.

On the hardwood floor behind her nightstand, she spied something that had been in her life since she was three, a true-to-its-name Raggedy Ann doll made entirely of cloth, now that both glass eyes were missing. The mop-strand hair was a rust-tinged red. The dress, partly concealed by a plain white apron, was dotted with flowers, springtime colors. Her grandma had owned it decades before. Mary picked up the doll, brushed off the dust, and feeling both foolish and sentimental as she did so, gently tucked it inside her duffel bag. Daniel had taught her to be wary of nostalgia. *The past is one more thing we must not covet.*

Yet, she nearly got down on the floor to look under her bed for Raggedy Ann's left eye. It had still been in place, giving the doll vision without depth, the last time Mary had been in this room.

The grumbling in her stomach intensified. She went downstairs to the kitchen where—big surprise—breakfast was waiting. The cereal looked good, but she knew it was old. Dad stocked up; it was how he shopped. If a sign at the store read, BUY ONE GET ONE FREE, he bought three more than he could possibly consume. Good thing she was famished.

He'd seemed startled when she entered the kitchen, the way he pushed the cabinet door closed, a little too quickly and forcibly. Did it hide something interesting now, along with his phone books and extension cords?

When he turned to face her, she nodded, unable to say, "Good morning." She could tell he wanted to ask her something, probably, "Are you okay?" But he must have realized how stupid this would sound when, clearly, she wasn't okay.

Her father settled for small talk, a familiar retreat, saying, "The mountains are beautiful this morning." There was a window above the sink, the last place in this house where you could still make out a sliver of pearl-white mountain snow, crammed between trees that hadn't always reduced the view. "You can hardly see the pollution."

She didn't think he was gloating; he didn't sound triumphant. But his observations irritated her anyway, and not because Denver's brown cloud was as bad as ever. The Rocky Mountains were one more thing that should not have existed that morning. Like stale cereal and milk. Like small talk.

"Highs in the sixties. There's something you never hear in Minnesota."

Mary got up and swiped a banana from the counter. Coming downstairs had been a mistake, and now she wanted to be invisible, just as she'd been as a teen in this house, her moods and moves unnoticed.

"I see you're still not a morning person," he said as she left the room. "Just like your mother."

Just like my mother who divorced you, she thought. *You really aren't a very quick learner, are you? Does that come with being a morning person?*

She came close to pounding her fist on the fall board as she passed the old piano, *Mom's* old piano, off to her left in the hallway. But restraint kicked in while her arm was in motion, resulting in more of a solid tap. The instrument responded with rolling, muted reverb, the echo from a chord no one had played.

Pausing before she shot up the stairs, Mary patted the wood's smooth finish in gentle apology, knowing this had to be one of the few times the upright had been touched since she lost interest in her lessons when she was fourteen.

"You're welcome for breakfast," Scott whispered, reopening the cabinet to retrieve the business cards he'd been looking at before she came downstairs. These cards contained the names and numbers of nine deprogrammers, only one of whom had screwed Scott before. It was time to forget that now, time to forget that he'd once watched the most highly recommended of the bunch leave for Minnesota with $22,000 in fees and expenses, never to return.

After listening a few seconds to make sure Mary was staying upstairs, Scott picked up the phone and dialed the first number, that of a woman who lived in Fort Collins, forty minutes away. To Scott's relief, she answered on the second ring, and he was able to explain that he needed someone—fast—who could say the right things to his daughter. "Don't ask me why, but she's here." When the deprogrammer started to quote her fees, Scott cut her off, saying, "Please get here as soon as possible."

He gave her directions, and heard what he needed to hear: "I can be there in two hours."

Of course, this still left the problem of finding the right things to do and say until help arrived, neither of which he'd been able to pull off so far. His daughter was obviously shaken and raw—and looking for someone to blame. Good thing he had not left that morning's *Denver Post* out on the table, open to the headline, *Just Another Judgment Day*. Good thing he'd resisted the temptation to point out that the world's end had been relegated to page four, and that the photo this time was indeed unflattering: no bright smile, tired eyes; looking his goddamned age for once.

Scott gathered the dishes and heard the shower come on upstairs. This sound, too, stirred memories from their slumber. But these were more pleasant—a house creaking to life. He reminded himself it was good to have her near. *Try to relax before you blow it.*

He was careful not to run any water so Mary could enjoy her shower. She'd never been easy on the water heater. Besides, it was time he called the office. If he waited much longer, the head clown would be in to pick up his phone. For this call, Scott needed to hear, *You have reached the voicemail for . . .* The advertising copywriting department had already missed two deadlines—and was closing in on three.

Scott didn't have time for a lecture about his "indispensability," a word that never came up in annual performance reviews.

He smiled with relief as the recording started.

◆

Mary turned up the pressure. Cold water only, to cleanse the spirit as well as the body. She could hear Daniel pronouncing these words, but doubted they still applied to her particular spirit.

I tripped up Judgment Day. All for the weakness of my flesh. This was the truth—it had to be. What else would cause God to change His mind? This was the truth, and it was a cumbersome thing to balance on two slight, rounded shoulders.

Though lacking the power to wash deeper than her pores, the cold water was good. A thousand tiny needles pricked her skin; there was no chance of mistaking this for a pleasurable experience. Self-flagellation— was that the right word? All those showers she'd endured in Hallelujah City, where hot had never been an option, made this one more effective. Just knowing she could reach out and turn the knob marked H, knowing it was her choice. *Out of his mouth go burning lamps, and sparks of fire leap out. Out of his nostrils goeth smoke, as out of a seething pot or cauldron. His breath kindleth coals, and a flame goeth out of his mouth.*

Climbing out of the shower, Mary hoped the towel would be scratchy. Thanks to her father's shopping habits, it did not disappoint. She rubbed herself dry until her arms and legs were red from the abrasion.

In his neck remaineth strength, and sorrow is turned into joy in his presence.

She stood before the mirror, brushing the straight auburn hair that touched her shoulders when it was wet. Her green eyes were hard, lusterless, as if her tears from the evening before had washed out all life. Her skin was pink, a pale, splotchy pink—she had so looked forward to shedding it, even without really knowing what would replace it. She remembered a taunt from an older classmate in the Aurora High locker room: Cosmetic surgery required, with lots of cosmetics.

Worst of all, her body seemed fragile—small, ungainly, poorly proportioned—not the kind of thing that would bring down a politician or CEO, let alone God's chosen one. There were far more seductive bodies on the magazine covers at the Walgreens checkout. Or in her high-school locker room. Or, and this was the most puzzling aspect to her, in Hallelujah City. Another disciple—not Cher Balser, but one of her allies—had called her mousy behind her back. Mary had been hurt by that word, after a disciple who didn't like Cher filled her in on the conversation. But now it brought Mary a smile, because it was clear that Cher's ally was no more perceptive than this mirror. Appearances didn't matter. The mouse was a monster, a sexual predator. How could she ever have expected to be part of the New Millennium? She'd never been worthy.

◆

Scott was in the downstairs bathroom, reading the *Post*'s opinion section, when the water stopped running for Mary's shower. He enjoyed editorials—he liked it that people could argue about things that had no direct impact on their own lives, issues that involved strangers, as opposed to family, coworkers, friends—and for years he'd saved that section for last. The radio was on low, and while the NPR commentators usually stayed in the background, today they kept him from fully appreciating page two.

"The Great Disappointment," a woman was saying in a husky deep-purple that brought to mind Maya Angelou. "In 1844 the Millerites waited on a hilltop in upstate New York for the moment when, in the words of founder William Miller, 'all the affairs of our present state would be wound up.' That moment was set to arrive at midnight October twenty-second. Which brings up the problem of October twenty-third. What must it have been like to watch these End Time believers as they descended their mount in dawn's accusing light to live out what Miller himself would later call the Great Disappointment?"

Scott heard the phone ringing in the kitchen, something it would do a full twenty times before the caller gave up. He'd remember to carry the cordless handset with him next time. He didn't need Mary talking to an author in search of an interview, or worse, to a professional deprogrammer who'd misplaced her directions.

The NPR sage had not been distracted. "In recent decades, followers of doomsday prophets weren't given that option. Our latter-day Millerites, Jim Jones and David Koresh, revised the historic precedent by literally sealing off the exits, dispensing murder under one of those big-lie euphemisms, *mass suicide*, thus eliminating the nagging residuals of personal embarrassment and public defeat. Now, all eyes are on upstate Minnesota, waiting to see if Daniel Hawker, the messiah whose résumé includes Disneyland magician and L.A. session player, will follow the original model and let his devotees dwell in disillusionment alongside the rest of their species. Or should we expect the darker scenario?"

No chance in hell, Scott told himself, just as he'd been doing for weeks each time he talked himself out of flying to Minnesota to be near his daughter. Hawker's ego would never permit the rest of his mind to take an action that would deprive the world of Daniel Hawker.

"There is a third possible outcome, cultologists suggest. A small plane has been spotted on a runway near the central bunker, apparently ready to go. The question is hereby begged, Is Mr. Hawker planning to add a new wrinkle by fleeing?"

A man's voice broke in. "We've just received word that a devotee of Hawker is speaking outside the compound. Do we have sound?—"

Scott placed the opinion section on the cabinet top to his right.

After a few moments of silence, a woman spoke, her voice loud and emotional, way over the top. Scott was reminded of the acting in a play he'd seen at Mary's high school. "—message from Daniel, our Teacher and Lord, savior of those who choose to be saved. The doubting billions can expect something big in the next twenty-four hours. This isn't over."

Scott heard Mary descend the stairs and go out the front door.

In a matter of seconds he was standing in his bedroom, wondering why she had taken his watch and not his wallet. But when he opened the wallet, he had an idea where she might stop on her way out of town.

◆

She was able to move quickly because she hadn't bothered to empty her duffel bag. What would've been the point? At 8:16—the King Soopers Sooper Center was only a few blocks from her father's house—she was facing the ATM inside the supermarket, dressed in the same simple clothes she'd been wearing when she arrived in Colorado. A plain white sweatshirt, faded jeans. The Volkswagen bus was parked out front in the fire lane.

She guessed her father's PIN number on the very first try. The four digits of the year she was born. He was so beyond predictable, a living monument to anality. And here, the word "living" was open to debate.

She counted the money, checked the receipt. Three hundred dollars—more than enough to pay for gas and food. And look at the balance. $21,632. Her father could afford to pay for her trip.

The store didn't look busy, so she decided to grab a few supplies. Bread, pickles, two gallon-bottles of water. Then she'd be off.

"Is this yours?" the clerk asked, holding up an apple. It must have been a discard, left behind at the checkout stand by accident, or because it had pushed a previous shopper over the ten-item limit.

"How fitting," she said. "Sure got my name on it."

Back in the Volkswagen bus, she bit into the fruit and wondered, *How can something taste so good on a morning like this?* The parking lot was busy, but she barely noticed the young trainee pushing carts—or the man coming her way across the handicapped spaces. Her imagination had skipped ahead to the end of her journey, and she was looking into the lenses of cameras at the main entrance to Hallelujah City. "I've come to make you understand," she was saying with greater confidence than she'd been expecting to muster. "This was my fault, not Daniel's. I took away your Paradise, like Eve did to Adam." She was trying to come up with a closing line that would please Daniel, who was standing beside her. "I made the infallible fall." He squeezed her hand for support.

Her father yanked open the passenger-side door.

"What's going on here?" he asked.

It took her a moment to respond. "I need to get back to Hallelujah City. I need to seek Daniel's forgiveness."

"You? Seek *his* forgiveness?"

"Don't you see? I corrupted him."

"No, *you* don't see," her father said. "There is no such thing as corrupting a forty-eight-year-old man. Especially Daniel Hawker."

"You just don't know what it's like to believe in something."

"I strongly believe the world is still here."

He climbed in, claiming the front passenger seat. She saw now that he was carrying a State Farm atlas and a bulky winter coat. These he placed on the dash and floorboard.

"What're you doing?" she shouted. "Get out of the car!"

"I'm coming with you. You'll need someone to share the driving. And—" He pulled out his wallet, holding it above the stick shift. The wallet was missing three cards. "I want to see how my money is spent."

This sounded better than the truth, he knew. A second quest had started that morning, one that would take Scott Chambers to Minnesota—and needless to say, Hallelujah City—for the first time in his life.

He was going to kill the holy man.

CHAPTER FIVE

The dark green curtains parted to reveal an icy crust, bright in the light of morning, barely translucent. The window needed scraping again; Adrian couldn't see his truck in the motel's parking lot, or the cabin-like houses facing the two-lane highway that doubled as Main Street in Trappers Point, Minnesota. He reached for the black plastic ashtray.

"Mary," he muttered to the ice that shone without reflecting or revealing, "you've got to get me to God Boy."

Adrian tried singling out a body part that didn't ache, thinking he'd concentrate on that part and feel better. He couldn't find one. Recalling mornings past when he'd been sure he'd bottomed out, he saw now how wrong he'd been, and how much further one could descend.

In Room 17 of the Valfaard Inn, Hawker's prophecy was fulfilling itself in microcosm. Adrian's world had come to an end. How long could it be before "The Teacher" torched his compound? Afternoon soaps would be interrupted by live coverage, and books would appear within weeks, if not days, retelling the story that everyone knew from network TV. And he, Adrian C. Hummel, would be slinking out of the Valfaard Inn at three in the morning to elude his creditors, agent, and editor, cradling boxes of cassette tapes and yellow legal pads in his arms.

His fingers trembled, and he almost expected to hear them rattle, much as his caffeine pills had rattled in their bottle an hour before. Adrian hadn't slept, at least not past the nightmare, which if anything was worse than the usual recurring nightmare that made it impossible to go back to sleep. This one had started as a dream, simply senseless and strange. A baby no more than six months old stood (yes, stood) in a robe of green and gold and colors Adrian didn't know. The baby held out the sun, or a miniature version thereof, in the flattened palm of her left hand. Adrian took comfort from the gesture.

Without apology or segue, the scene changed. A mother cat, gray and black, was giving birth to dozens of tiny, grublike babies. Seconds later, a stream of liquid feces replaced the runaway birthing process. Light brown, the color of melted milk chocolate, the river kept coming, and as Adrian sat up abruptly in bed, he knew the cat had cancer and would soon perish.

Now, thinking back on the dream, Adrian twitched, something he caught himself doing more and more often. *Thanks, cat. Thanks for two hours' rest, total, for the night.* Other people didn't realize how lucky they were to spend a third of their lives in sleep. Take away that escape and life became way too linear. As Adrian vaguely recalled, fragmentary was so much better.

"Mary Chambers," he said as the first frosted pines appeared through the aperture scraped clear by the ashtray. "Where are you?"

◆

He wrapped himself in his cocoon. The liner, parka, ski mask, and gloves would make it possible, if just barely, to survive the block-and-a-half walk to the diner, where he would order waffles and ask Bev, the diner's owner, if she had any news about the compound.

Before he could unlatch the door's chain-lock, the cell phone in his pocket released a flurry of Morse code stutters. The "Newsflash" motif from ancient black-and-white movies, downloaded from some obsessive's website, this was Adrian's ringtone. He threw off his ski mask and gloves, one of which flew across the room and knocked the plastic ice bucket for Room 17 from its place on the counter by the sink to the thin, hard carpet.

"Mr. Hummel?"

A collection agency. No one else called him Mister these days.

"Hello? Mr. Hummel? Is anyone there?"

Retrieving the errant glove, he heard what sounded like the growl of chainsaws coming through the cruelly inadequate cinder-block wall that in theory separated his room from Minnesota's deep freeze.

"Bev," he whispered, sure that what he was hearing was her snow-mobile, headed south to No Name Road. The press didn't know that way into Hawker's compound, or if they did, had not been able to bribe Bev Larsen's stepbrother, Len, into letting them use his property to get around the obstacles in the road. Fallen limbs and piled-up tires blocked a path that was already difficult. These obstructions were not random or coincidental, no more so than that NBC correspondent getting scalded by coffee at the diner. The locals hated the press as much as they hated Hawker, possibly more, and Adrian had been quick to turn this to his advantage. By kissing up to nearly everyone, leaving tips for the maid on his dresser in Room 17 no matter how little she had cleaned up the time before, and eating double-servings of dumplings at the diner, he had managed to dilute the hatred apportioned to him, toning it down to mere distrust and amusement. Adrian had allies, at least to the point they did favors for cash.

For more than a year, Bev had been making runs to the compound, bearing packages stuffed with strudel, blueberry Danish, and other delights she was known for. Adrian helped prepare the boxes, intended for Bev's son, Gunt. At thirty-one years of age Gunt Larsen had joined Hawker's circus and renounced all interest in inheriting a diner, having been swayed by a story that was the source of much controversy in Trappers Point. Alone among locals, at least to Adrian's knowledge, Gunt had chosen to believe that Hawker really had brought a dead dog back to life. (Adrian, not too surprisingly, took the side of the doubters. He'd once impressed a duck hunter from Independence, Missouri, by labeling the tale "apocryphal at best.")

God Boy not only tolerated the arrival of Bev's packages; apparently he welcomed them, thanks to a weakness for double-dark fudge and apple dumplings. He never thought to inspect the boxes, his well-cultivated paranoia having been softened by the moistness of Bev Larsen's brownies. As such, Hawker never saw the letters Gunt crumpled without reading. *My darling son, I haven't changed my will. The diner will still be yours.*

As for the envelopes addressed in Adrian's hand to *Disciple Mary,* hiding notes that made requests such as, *Meet me in the Field of the Eastern Star, Saturday, midafternoon,* all evidence suggested that Gunt forwarded these without once thinking it might prove interesting to open one and examine its contents—or thinking it might be wise to hand one over to his Lord and Savior. Adrian's luck, it seemed, had not left him completely. Here and here alone, he'd found the last trace. The Larsen boy was not big on thinking.

The idea for the deliveries had been Adrian's, but Bev had embraced it from day one, because she saw these visits as a way to reclaim her son—and because Adrian paid her. Typically, the two got everything ready the night before. Holed up in the diner, she baked, he packed, they wrote their respective notes, and when they were satisfied with what they had made she swiped his credit card.

But today was different. Bev had discarded all precedent, leaving without notifying her client beforehand. Adrian understood, of course. Bev needed to know that her son was still breathing—and that Hawker wasn't planning to change this.

Poor Bev. Poor desperate Bev.

Maybe she could get him inside.

◆

Like being surprised by a dozen flashbulbs . . . that's how it felt to step outside. Adrian pulled out his sunglasses, and as the frosty glare turned green, muttered into his gloves, "Florida. Should've kept my mouth shut."

Walking briskly, Adrian saw something he'd never seen before he moved to Minnesota. His breath. It popped out now in short gray bursts. Without slowing down, he read the note taped to the glass of the diner's storm door, just below the Closed sign. Using a black magic marker, Bev had spelled out *BACK IN THIRTY* in big block letters. He jogged around back of the dark log building and straddled the Arctic Cat 9000 he rented from Bev on an as-you-need-it basis. The key was on his chain.

Then he was in the alley, passing the dumpsters and telephone poles. With Bev so far ahead, he'd have to lay off his brakes, leaving him with the steering capacity of a hockey puck. Of greater concern, he'd be mummified by the frigid air, which paid no heed to stocking caps or scarves. As in the past, Adrian marveled that the inventors of snowmobiles had found a way to make the upper Midwest feel even colder. Accelerating as he traded the alley for the icy shoulder of 71, the two-lane highway that took the name Main Street when sauntering through town, it felt as if two cats were fighting, claws bared, for control of his face.

A black Suburban raced by in the other direction, heading north into town. Things were heating up, figuratively of course, just as he'd been expecting.

At No Name Road he took a sharp left, and was immediately reminded why brakes were important. Banging sideways into a hard wall of snow, he was thrown like a rodeo rider, flying and rolling, *ouch, ouch, ouch.* With time enough only for a quick goddamn, he didn't even mess with brushing off snow. He was back on his horse, back on the trail, leaning and ducking to avoid the dangling pine boughs that looked so soft but hurt like hell. A sudden left, another right, and Adrian recalled something that Bev had once said: *They should've called it No Plan Road.* True, one of the diner's ancient regulars had told him it skirted the periphery of a long-abandoned quarry. But no signs of excavation could be seen through the trees, and the route seemed more the result of a bulldozer driver getting plowed at lunch and going for a joyride in the meadows and woods. *What would you extract from a quarry here?* he wondered. *Ice?* He took up his speed on a straight, clear stretch. The pines shot by.

Winter disguised the piles of debris meant to keep outsiders out, throwing wide white tarps across their jagged spines. Adrian took a right, braking this time, while cutting between the No Trespassing signs that marked the start of Len Larsen's detour. Smoke squiggled from the chimney of a log-cabin house, and dogs woke noisily from slumber.

Len, known to fire buckshot at unauthorized guests, was home. The barking dogs were visible now, as were their teeth. Adrian looked at the gas gauge, two-thirds full. Though he paid Len well for the privilege of being on his land, this was no place to stop for a social visit. The under-fed Chows and three-legged Rottweiler weren't asking to be petted, and Len himself wasn't much of a talker.

Adrian didn't see the pine-green helicopter until it was out in front of him. His ski mask and hood, and more so, 140 HPs of growling Arctic Cat had kept him from hearing the chopper as it came up from behind and passed overhead. Was he being trailed? Had the government finally noticed that this route could get you in? But the answers to these questions were no and ditto. The copter kept going, probably returning to base on the far side of Hawker's compound, on farmland owned by banks. No one else around here would have hosted the ATF or FBI, since the locals were even less welcoming to federal agents than they were to the Fourth Estate. Sitting at the Trappers Point Diner, Adrian had heard them referred to as the "Washington Gestapo" and "Big Brother with a bigger budget." But after all these months of not seeing checkpoints on No Name Road (or helicopters tracking suspicious snowmobile activity), he held silently to his belief that the feds' reputation had not been earned.

Back on the road, there was no Bev, not even a distant Bev. He'd never catch her now, but then, it made no sense to stop (and he was in no hurry to further tempt Len's teeth-baring dogs). He came to the fork where he usually turned right on a pair of ruts that snaked in parallel formation toward the compound's most remote parcel of land, the Field of the Eastern Star. But this time he steered left, choosing the road to the lake, and driving more slowly than before due to his unfamiliarity with the route. *Low branch. Duck.* He straightened his scarf, leaned into a curve, primed the throttle coming out. He thought he could see a sliver of the lake, though it could have been a field, cleared of brush. There was a roar from the woods, loud enough to be heard above his own. A second snowmobile slipped from between the trees, stopping sideways, blocking his path. Bev.

She pulled back her ski mask as he sputtered to a stop. "Adrian! Why the heck are you following me? You've never done that before."

"And you've never gone without telling me."

"I can't get you to Hawker. The guards, don't you know."

"I need to get in today."

"I've told you I can't do that. It took a long time to gain their trust."

"One hundred bucks for trying," he said.

"It won't work."

"Two hundred. You know I'm good for it." He figured he'd use his new Home Depot Dream Rewards Visa, barely two weeks old and almost maxed out. She could run it back at the diner.

Closing her eyes, Bev seemed to be thinking, a process that lasted a good eight seconds. She gave her head a few spasmodic shakes, like someone trying to wake from a nightmare. The eyes reopened, warily. "I guess this isn't your ordinary day. Why don't you go on and park Old Slick—careful now, he doesn't belong to you."

Easing back on the gas, he half expected the engine to die, in which case Bev would have been able to hear him whisper, "I *was* being careful with this piece of crap machine I've already bought twice over with the rent I shell out." The way she was watching, he felt like some sixteen-year-old in driver's ed. *Slowly now, son. Keep your eyes on the mirror.* As he climbed on the back of her Ski-Doo 250, repainted cherry red to look brand new, he heard her say, "I still get paid if they stop you."

◆

The lake was alive—and vocal. At different times, he heard what sounded like whale songs, gun shots in the distance, and a dozen stomachs grumbling as one. Adrian couldn't help but think the ice was protesting the weight of their incursion, even as they hugged the shoreline. "Hard to believe it's still frozen in March," he said.

"And how long have you been living here?"

"It wasn't this cold last year."

The ice stretched a good quarter-mile to his left, and looking across its smooth, snow-covered expanse, dark green through his glasses, he pictured sunrise on the moon. Sublime desolation, coupled with a radiance that stopped just short of blinding. The ice grumbled louder. He clutched the passenger handgrips with all his strength.

Coming off the lake, they passed between dozens of thick gray oaks, sturdy old trees that suddenly shouted, "Halt there!" Heavy with reverb, these words came from every direction, and Adrian remembered there were loudspeakers in the branches. "Throw down all weapons! Remove your masks!" Emerging into an open space, he saw two men walking with purpose from doublewide trailers. These were Hawker's sentries, and they were dressed identically in camouflage colors meant for milder seasons when green, brown, and yellow were much more prevalent.

Though this wasn't Adrian's first encounter with the sentries, he didn't think they would recognize him after nearly two years. Gaining forty-one pounds would go a long way toward ensuring that, and these might not be the exact same thugs who had escorted him off the property. Then, the sentries were almost as new to Minnesota as Adrian was. Through a controversial prison ministry in nearby Michigan and Wisconsin, Hawker had set out to recruit the steroid-popping felons that seemed most likely to get an early release. Once they were out, Hawker brought ten or so of the beasts here to work and gave them weapons that had to violate any terms of parole. They all shaved their heads. They had lots of tattoos.

Now, the guards blocked the snowmobile's path. They stood shoulder-to-shoulder, a wide cliff wall of summer vegetation and fertile earth tones. The snowmobile stopped.

"Hey, Bev, what goodies you got today?"

"Why sure, goodies," she said, dismounting.

"The baggage. Who is he?"

Adrian waited for Bev to say he was needed inside, that he had news for Hawker, that he helped make the goodies, something. He waited for her to *insist* he make those last steps with her. "A reporter," she said coldly.

"Bev! I'm hardly a reporter." Adrian slid off his seat and took a few steps toward the guards who once had to be guarded themselves. "I'm an author—"

"Great," said the taller ex-con. "We got a special for reporters today."

"Yeah, you ever play Find Your Way Back?" his colleague, who was wide as a door, asked. "That's where we throw you in the trunk of a car and dump you in the middle of fuck."

"And you gotta . . . you know . . . find your way back."

Hoping that someone inside might hear, Adrian spoke forcefully, "*I am not a reporter. I am an author. I want to tell Daniel's story from his side.*"

The taller guard stepped forward, blocking Adrian's view with a blurred camouflage pattern. "Mrs. Larsen, *you* can go on," he said.

"Bev. Wait."

She didn't wait.

The other guard circled the author, moving in as he did so. He stopped directly behind Adrian, resulting in a closeness most people didn't want from convicts. "You're making a mistake," Adrian said, his gloved right hand tightening its hold on the ski-mask. "If you let me go in, I can help your cause." His parka hood was ripped away. "Hey, come on. If you'd listen for one minute." He felt burning in the back of his neck. A Knife. All the guards carried them. He'd heard this from Mary.

"Stop! Don't—"

"Kill you?" said the guard in front. "Joey here's just having fun. He's good, too. Barely leaves marks. Don't give our enemies a reason to come down on us."

"And don't give reporters nothing to report," Joey added.

"I'm not a reporter." Adrian felt the beginning of tears, but knew better than to draw attention to this development by trying to wipe them away. "There's no reason to hurt me."

"Don't be a baby."

"Or we *will* have to kill you."

Adrian could see it was time to be quiet.

The knife stayed in one spot, a needle in the hands of a sadistic acupuncturist, going just deep enough to make Adrian wish he didn't have nerve endings. He was reminded of high school, of how one class-mate might prick another with a pin while standing in line for hot lunch. The victim had no choice but to endure torture of that degree, because on this one subject, the guards had it right. Run weeping to the principal's office and you were likely to hear, "Don't be a baby." Now that he was learning how it felt to be on the hurting end, Adrian felt sorry he'd ever done the poking, even if Goofy Dan Spurlock had been asking for it that day.

He stood as rigid as possible, not wishing to add any movement on his end. Whenever he assured himself, *I can get through this*, the guard twisted the tip. "Enough!" Adrian finally cried. "Has anyone noticed I'm cooperating?" He felt the knife withdraw before promptly finding a new point to penetrate.

The monster would do this six more times.

Adrian felt warmth on his upper back, wondered how much he was bleeding, wondered how long he'd been captive. At least fifteen minutes, he thought, with thirty being a better guess. He tried escaping into his imagination, but only came up with worse scenarios: the guards getting bored, the knife digging deeper.

The pain lessened, if only for a moment. Both guards were backing off, distracted by Bev's reappearance. The short, heavyset woman who got even less exercise than Adrian most days was running clumsily. Her face was crimson, and as she got closer, he could see she'd been shaken. He could see this because she *was shaking*.

"What happened in there, Bev?"

A whimper. "Help us, Jesus."

Bev mounted her Ski-Doo, revved the engine, and motioned for him to hurry along. He barely made contact with the cold black seat before the machine jolted forward. "Better hold on," she said.

The knife wounds were throbbing again. "Come on, Bev, what's going on? What in hell did you see?"

She wouldn't say, but he knew what she was looking at now—their point of exit on the opposite side of the frozen lake. She aimed straight for it, choosing diameter over circumference. "Bev, don't you think we should stick to the edge?" The engine roared full throttle; the ice bristled and moaned, an equal expanse to either side. Adrian was whimpering too now, but he didn't miss the irony in what he knew must be coming. A full-immersion baptism, resulting in death by hypothermia.

CHAPTER SIX

It was every highway Scott had ever traveled. The alpha-wave hum of tires on pavement, the unchanging horizon.

Even the van seemed familiar. "I used to own one of these when I was in college," he said. "The hitchhiker's prayer—a VW bus. Mine was a sixty-nine. This might be newer."

Mary didn't respond.

"Fish lived in its radiator."

She wasn't listening.

"It ran on D-batteries. Six hundred of them."

A coyote stared back at him from just off the gravel shoulder. Bone-thin and—*Was it silver or brown?*—ambiguous in color. Still as a mound of dirt.

What Scott really wanted to do was restart the argument about his coming along on the trip. For while he was fairly certain he'd won it, he didn't feel like much of a winner. *"The wrong person is angry here,"* he imagined himself saying. *"Wasn't I the one who learned his credit cards were planning a cross-country trip without him?"*

He shifted in his seat. Hard and cracked from side to side, the plastic cover leaving a permanent stripe on his ass had to be as old as the vehicle. The bus still had its original shocks too. It rattled loudly when it vibrated, which it had been doing without interruption since hitting the on-ramp out of Aurora. Worse, it seemed drawn to every pothole and crack, and the slow lane they were in had the Aristarchus Plateau beat for number of craters per square foot. Scott's knowledge of lunar geography came from the catalog page he had recently completed for *Mapping the Moon—An Introduction.* He had used the plateau in a bullet.

His daughter turned on the radio to the All Static, All Hours station —a sound that worked well with the alpha-wave hum, still massaging the neurons in his brain. Briefly, he thought he recognized a singer's voice straining to break through the crackle and hiss. HIGHWAY CONSTRUCTION 1/2 MILE AHEAD an orange sign warned. 50 MILES PER HOUR. FINES DOUBLED. Fairness at last, he thought. If they couldn't reach the speed limit, the limit would come to them.

This was, in fact, the route he had traveled most frequently in his life, at least in terms of long-distance mileage. I-76 to southwestern Nebraska, where it merged into 80-East. Scott's ex-wife Liz had been born and raised in Omaha. This had been the route to his in-laws.

Liz's parents, Gerald and Phyllis Carpenter, had raised three daughters in a single-story house. They were mild mannered, easy to get along with, and rarely in a hurry to move or act—qualities they had failed to pass along genetically. Liz had been ambitious; she disliked inertia.

Especially Scott's.

Liz started at Heritage just before Scott's second anniversary at the Denver-based textbook publishers. But she soon moved up, leaving the ad department for better pay in production editorial. It was the first of several promotions, and by the time she and Scott married, she made double his so-called salary. By the time she divorced him, she no longer drove long distances. She flew. To meet with prospective textbook authors. To represent the firm at trade shows. And to visit her parents in Omaha. Without him.

Yet, there had been those first pleasurable years. When he felt he could teach her things. When she took pride in being engaged to a gifted young writer destined to dazzle the world's fiction-reading elite (despite the inconvenient fact that he had not yet thought of anything worth committing to paper). The two announced their engagement within weeks of *his* surprise promotion to head copywriter. Liz seemed to take pride in her Scott, having no way of knowing he was destined to hold this position until he retired or was demoted back to his original job, or went to prison for murdering the leader of a religious cult.

The Volkswagen swerved to miss the cracked remains of a semi tire and rumbled as it hit the shoulder's rough pavement. Scott saw a green sign. A dark, fading sign. FORT MORGAN 12. His own overworked eyes were growing heavy, just as they did each weekday afternoon between two and three when he'd been staring at his computer screen too long through generic Wal-Mart reading glasses. He needed caffeine. Dr. Pepper or coffee. The horizon was dimming. He thought he heard music emerging from the static, an old Beatles song. FORT MORGAN . . . 12. STRAWBERRY FIELDS . . . FOREVER.

He knew he was dreaming when he saw Liz smiling with no trace of anger. Mary was two. They were singing "Happy Birthday." Just he and Liz.

◆

Mary wanted to shake her father. His muffled snoring was making a good case for sleep—and he'd been making the case for forty-plus minutes. He must have nodded off before Fort Morgan, the fast-food hub of Colorado's eastern plain. The morning was more than half gone; she wished they were farther along. "Heaven is the first star you see on the eastern horizon," she whispered for the first of several times. "Focus on the light; be not distracted by the gathering darkness."

For Mary, this meant concentrating on getting to Daniel to beg His forgiveness, then crawling before the world's press to confess her own culpability. As it stood now, the doubting billions couldn't possibly understand what had or had not happened. To the shallow and self-satisfied, the Teacher had become another tired joke, joining the scores of boastful losers who'd gone before, only to see their Judgment Days, too, pass like shadows at dusk.

She wondered how long it would be before the doubters lost interest altogether. The press would move on, literally, to another story, abandoning their famous "post outside the compound." This last word still made her cringe, still made her want to use the bad words she'd stopped using at Daniel's command. They might as well have called Hallelujah City a prison—they being the reporters and pundits, the arrogant s-heads who should have thanked her that morning for postponing their admission to Hell. Some compound. There was no outer wall, only a four-foot-high barbed-wire fence meant to limit the mobility of cows. From the beginning, Daniel had told Mary and the others they were free to leave, though not without reminding them, "Freedom is what you'll be leaving."

Some compound. The previous occupant had been a third-generation dairy farmer, the previous owner a Savings and Loan in Fairmont. A modest ranch house marked the property's center. With its earth-colored brick and peeling white trim, this was Daniel's most holy place. His disciples, Mary included, had eaten, slept, and offered up thanks some fifty yards away, sharing doublewide mobile homes that had not been designed to keep out the winds of a Minnesota winter.

Her dad coughed, breaking the rhythm of his snoring. Seconds passed without a sound. Were his eyes about to open? She unconsciously held her own breath, compounding the quiet, until finally, the growling resumed to prove he was still sleeping.

Focus on the light.

Yet, he managed to keep distracting her. Asleep, he seemed fragile, like a baby without the cuteness. For a moment, she pitied her father, and for that one moment she wished she could bore through the ice and rescue the soul trapped beneath it. She wanted to wake him by shouting, *God is alive, Dad, more alive than you or me. He is beauty and music, fellowship and grace. He has a sense of humor. He catches colds and has trouble sleeping. This is good news. My God is real.*

There was rain over Sterling, *above* but not *on* the small Plains town. Virga, they called it, a downpour that evaporated before touching the ground. This was the promise of rain, the lost expectation. Streaks of gray hung from heavy clouds like brushstrokes on canvas, applied top to bottom with the paint losing thickness as the brush ran dry.

As the clouds eclipsed the sun, headlights came on in the westbound lanes. *Go ahead, rain already. I'm calling your bluff. Let's see a deluge.* Mary could still taste the air in Hallelujah City, her first summer there. Humid and cool, in defiance of the season. It sure rained a lot then, though it always seemed to stop by the time Daniel was ready for his Sermons by the Lake. Not that the sun ever popped back out—it was usually too late—but the rains did stop. Mostly anyway.

◆

That lake was frozen now, of course, due to a winter that refused to leave the upper Midwest. Record lows and broken pipes; trailer walls that could have been made of paper. Daniel had joked it would literally take the end of the world to get rid of the cold. During the last sermon before Mary's exile, he walked onto the lake to illustrate his message: "Mankind builds its prisons and towers and mansions and malls on ice as real as this—and every bit as fragile. This, then, is the great thaw, the melting of illusion. The end of all days."

She was thinking now about her first weeks at Hallelujah City. Though she didn't like sharing a dinged-up mobile home with eight other women, she savored the attention she got. Daniel made her feel like she was the only one there, and his disciples were all sweetness and light, with none of the jealousy and mistrust she'd witness later. They smiled all the time, called her "Sister." Even hugged her when she finished a chore.

Hard to believe now, but there were times back then when she wasn't so sure. Like when she was told to refer to the trailers as Life Ark Stations . . . or daybreak as "Time to get up." Even the preaching confused her some nights. *He likes to quote the strangest parts of the Bible,* she'd thought—an observation quickly pursued by, *There sure are a lot of strange parts in the Bible.* But then, it was pretty amazing the way the rains stopped right before he gave his sermons. Even more amazing was the music that started when Daniel finished speaking. The sounds drifted and drummed from speakers in the trees, making it seem as if nature itself were erupting in song. Daniel had created this music in a California studio once used by Fleetwood Mac. He'd played every part, multitracking the various instruments, and while these instruments were the creations of man, the music was otherworldly in nature. Soothing, soaring, while the music played there was no doubting. Mary was one with her God, just as she'd been the first time she heard it in Aurora.

On some nights, the disciples with good voices joined in and vocalized, adding *ooh*'s and *aah*'s and other scat sounds as they saw fit. Often, their singing lifted the notes even higher into the firmament, on wings like doves, fluttering bright against the darkness, an effect heightened by the slices of brown mushroom distributed before each sermon. Though bitter in taste, the fleshy fungal meat possessed Illuminary Essence and heightened one's feelings of communal love. These mushrooms grew freely in the woods, but were only to be ingested as prescribed during the nightly gatherings.

As each day blurred into the next, the Sermons by the Lake sounded better and better. "Throw off your notions of culture and religion. These are the products of conquest and coincidence—the ballast of your forebears." Sometimes when Daniel was preaching, Mary entertained daydreams of grand coronation parades, complete with carriages, Clydesdales, and trumpeters. It was something in His voice, in the way He presented each word. "All these can do is cause you to sink."

It helped that Daniel let others leave Hallelujah City, that no one was held against his or her will. *If I'm staying,* Mary could reason, *it must be because I believe.*

It helped, too, that Daniel let His followers do whatever they wanted on Saturday afternoons. Mary could stroll, nap, meditate. She could even, as she'd discover later, slip off to the outlying fields.

There was also the matter of clothing. The Teacher took little interest in it. Most everyone in Hallelujah City wore items they'd brought here, including T-shirts and jeans. Daniel provided the rest of their wardrobes, mostly simple work clothes, blues and grays and blacks. But no one wore anything strange or antiquated, like she remembered from news stories about cults.

This wasn't a cult.

Following one hard Tuesday spent harvesting corn by hand, she told the others in her Life Ark Station, "My old life wasn't important." Privately, she wondered if her other life had existed at all. Her memories were so gray and intangible. When one of the grumblers revealed herself by suggesting, "I think we're being brainwashed," Mary was first to reply, "And you don't think our brains were in need of a thorough cleansing?"

Sometimes it was fun. Like early on, when Daniel baptized three novices a few weeks ahead of Mary in their advancement. His voice boomed as the trio completed their passage to discipleship: "Open your eyes, look toward the sky, your sins like silt have been washed away." But the moment He was finished, He slid His hand across the water, splashing the newly minted disciples, all of whom looked puzzled, an expression Mary must have shared with them. Then Daniel was thrashing away, a kid in a crowded municipal pool, using both arms to fuel the sparkling jets. "Come on," He shouted, His smile stretched to its absolute limit, "my Father wants you to be happy. He has no chosen ones—" The others were splashing, too, and Daniel's face disappeared in the unruly spray. "He saves His love for the *choosing ones*, the ones who choose Him. Share His joy. Welcome to the Family of God."

Mary no longer had night terrors, and may have stopped dreaming altogether. She slept especially well on nights when she'd come up with a question on a spiritual matter that she could ask Daniel the following day. He nearly always found time for her, even with all the new converts. There were ten doublewide trailers by then. An older disciple, one of the Original Seven, had connections to a company that specialized in repossessing mobile homes. The bunk beds came with them, the foldout cots from other sources.

When Daniel wrapped up His sermons by asking, "Are you ready to live and die for glory?" Mary may not have been the one who shouted "I will live and die for you" the loudest. But she was no longer surprised by the sincerity she heard in her own voice.

◆

Scott's dreams were less clear now, skittish and half formed. *A pair of soft-green eyes. Water bursting from the ceiling when his ten-year-old daughter left the bathtub filling upstairs. Familiar voices in conversation . . . or was it, conspiracy?* These fragments vanished as quickly as they appeared, dancing in and out of consciousness like the fences and irrigation systems and rusted-out pickups in his peripheral vision. Like tumbleweeds. Like the very real tumbleweed that had just bounced from left to right across the interstate lanes, whisking him back into the bumpy present.

He looked at the clock in the dash, the predigital clock. 11:10. That would have been Central Standard, assuming it was accurate. A sliver of sunshine warmed his right shoulder—the sky was mostly clear now.

"How are you doing?" he said to his daughter.

◆

Great. Her father was talking again. Only a few words perhaps . . . and she sure hadn't caught them . . . but that wasn't the point. He was trying to start a conversation.

Mary gripped the steering wheel with greater force. She stared straight ahead.

"I brought some food," he said.

"You brought food *where*?"

"Eight pockets." He was lifting his coat as he said this. Sure enough, it had extra pockets. Underwear, or maybe a rag, poked out from one. "You must be hungry."

"For what you've got in there? I don't think so."

"Without even looking? You can't be serious."

But there was no point in looking—a hunch proved correct when her father produced the Yuletide M&Ms. These, she knew from experience, had been purchased on December 26th, right after Walgreens marked them down. Always stocking up—always saying he was saving so that Mary could go to a "real college," have a "real career." What excuse had he been using the past three years, now that she was "real gone"?

"Merry Christmas," she said. "What year are those from?"

"My deepest apologies, but there was a rush on Doomsday candy." He held out a bag and rattled its contents. "I've told you before, expiration dates mean nothing in an arid climate. It's just the corporations' way of tricking you into discarding perfectly good food. Some business major in a four-by-six cubicle came up with the idea." Mary said nothing, knowing better than to ask, "And how big is *your* cubicle, Dad?" She'd sat in it once, on a Take Your Daughter to Work Day. As she remembered it now, the business majors had bigger cubicles.

"You should eat," he said.

"I might get something at the next rest area."

"Didn't we just stop?"

"I need to make a phone call," she said, and while this was true, she also had to pee or die. "Besides," she added, "no one made you come."

"Another phone call? Who are you calling?"

"No one."

"No one?"

"Okay, Dad, I've been phoning the angel Gabriel. To find out what time the UFOs are picking us up." He was quiet after that.

The whole idea of being pregnant confused her, especially now that, with the Cleansing on hold, there would really be a baby—an idea still taking root. Mary pictured an infant. Cooing, drooling, wailing. She wondered if her child-to-be would forfeit its tiny soul for helping to mess up the Dawn of the New Millennium. But then, it wasn't just *her* child. And how could the offspring of God's Chosen One be evil? What if Jesus had fathered a baby by Mary Magdalene? Wouldn't the sin of fornication have been canceled out by the holy lineage? Was it even possible to commit adultery with someone like Jesus or Daniel? Wouldn't marriage be the automatic result? The Teacher had more power than any priest at a wedding, since His power came directly from God. It only stood to reason that a woman who knew Him in a Biblical sense would have to be His bride.

But then, her mind crawled back to that earlier, uglier thought. *I corrupted Daniel. He had no interest in earthly pleasures. Forget the baby, and forget all that auto-bride stuff. I'm the one that's evil.*

Or—her head was really hurting now—maybe she was carrying the *New* Chosen One who would free mankind. The Son of the Son of. Maybe that had been the plan all along, a more subtle Cleansing, redemption delivered in the form of a child. The Teacher would have seen no reason to fill her in on the details. Her knowing wouldn't have mattered. She'd just be the vessel.

It hit her that this baby, whatever the role that awaited, would have the strangest coupling of grandparents ever. God, Creator of the Universe and Knower of All Things. And Scott Chambers, Chief Advertising Copywiter for Heritage Publishing.

CHAPTER SEVEN

B ev didn't open the diner for lunch.
      She didn't, in actual fact, emerge from her living quarters in the rear of the building. The bright green door stayed closed.

Adrian sat at a table for two, the closest one to the wood-burning stove.

He never got warm.

Even his neck stayed cold, and it was wrapped in half a roll of toilet paper, taken from the customers only restroom. The bleeding seemed to have lessened, as had the intensity of his pain, to where it now felt like a bee sting, an ongoing one, delivered by a bee in no hurry to finish its business. Needless to say, this alone would have given Adrian plenty to be riled about, even if he hadn't discovered he'd missed hearing his ringtone while returning on the snowmobile.

"Please, Mary, please," he whispered into a napkin. "Call again."

Since Bev wouldn't come out to prepare any food, he opened packet after packet of saltine crackers, the only appetizers served at her diner. He helped himself to Coke from the fountain.

His neck throbbed whenever he chewed or swallowed.

The sneezing fit had him wanting to cry.

Every few minutes, he played back the message. *"Adrian, this is Mary—" "I'm sorry, ma'am, but this is a collect call—" "Are you there?" "You can't leave a message—" "I'm coming back. I'll need—"*

He was ready to meet her in Fargo or Minneapolis, had gone so far as to make reservations in her name on two dozen flights out of Denver. His truck was full of gas.

In the meantime, he'd go back to his room. He needed to get his author paraphernalia, the recorder especially. And what about Mary's

Colorado number? His caffeine pills? In chasing after Bev, he'd left too quickly that morning.

Taking a last, quick look around the kitchen for something more substantial than crackers, he stopped to examine the eggshell fragments he'd noticed before on an otherwise bare counter. Holding the largest chip between thumb and forefinger, he whispered, "Dried out, broken, and chipped around the edges. I know how you feel."

He really needed to hear Mary's voice.

He knocked three times on the green door.

"You want to talk, Bev?"

He didn't hear a sound.

Leaning over his table a few seconds later, he tore open one last packet of saltines, and discovered they didn't taste half bad with maple syrup.

His hands felt sticky. He wiped them with a napkin. The stickiness remained, and this necessitated another trip to the restroom. Once there, he lingered a few extra minutes, enjoying the splendor of heated water.

After returning to the dining area, he pulled on his cocoon, adding one adaptation, a cell phone squeezed into a mitten where he would feel it vibrate. He then walked back to the green door.

"I'm go-ing to my room at the Val-faard." He spoke loudly and slowly, trying to minimize any ski-mask distortion. "I'll be here la-ter if you need to un-load."

◆

In Room 17, shed of extra insulation and bolstered by two caffeine pills, Adrian pressed auto redial for what had to be the hundredth time that day.

"Please, pick up the phone. Somebody . . . Mary . . . Asshole Dad."

Nobody answered.

Just as he gave up and clicked off his phone, the Newsflash ringtone played.

"Adrian C. Hummel!" he answered.

"Another sunny day today."

"Mama."

"You could try and sound more pleased."

No. He couldn't. "Sorry, Mama. I was in the middle of something."

"Like what? A cold spell?"

"Funny, Mama. Funny."

She asked about the book, and he remembered how it was possible to miss someone as much as he missed his mother, yet be thoroughly annoyed each time he heard her voice.

"It's coming, Mama. It's coming."

She started in on another favorite topic, the climatic differences between northern Minnesota and northern Florida. "Is it really as bad up there as they're saying on the Weather Channel?"

"Better than being sweaty and sunburned in muggy Florida." He missed muggy Florida. "The weather here is invigorating, good for productivity. You'll see that when my book comes out."

"I'm sure I will, dear."

He tilted his head back, and this resulted in an involuntary "Ouch!"

"Are you all right?"

"Nothing, Mama. My neck. I must have slept in a bad position." Refusing to give his mother any satisfaction, he kept his next thought, *Meaning way too far north of the equator*, to himself. "Why'd you call, Mama?"

"Mimi June."

"Mimi June?"

"Your fiancée? Your *ex*-fiancée?"

"I know that, Mama. Is she all right?"

"She's getting married."

Adrian was silent.

"Someone she worked with. Here. I've got the announcement. Not sure why she mailed one to me."

Because she knew you'd call me, Mama.

"This is from the *Starke (Florida) Badger*," she said, "where you used to work." Adrian held the phone out in front of his face so that he could properly glare at it. This didn't prevent him from hearing the name of Benmont duBlanc . . . or "*The Third*" . . . or "*former Travel, Entertainment,* and *World News Editor recently promoted to Owner and Publisher."*

Mama was back in his ear now: *"The ceremony will be held at the Starke Golf and Country Club, where three hundred guests will help the joyous new Life Mates celebrate their eternal love flame."*

Foolish Mimi June. There was no way that small-thinking hack loved her.

"Adrian, this should be your wedding."

"I am shocked," he said. "Who would've thought Starke had a country club?"

"Your *wedding.*"

"Hey, Mama, I'd love to keep chatting but I'm waiting for an important call right now."

"And what does that make this call?"

"Love you, Mama," he said as he pressed End Call.

Once again, he was grateful his mother did not have some magic spy phone that allowed her to see him here in the motel. He was grateful, too, for the Weather Channel scaring her out of visiting Room 17. He knew what she'd say: "This is a far cry from that house you gave away. The one that would've been yours after the *wedding."* His pillowcases stank of bleach. His heater was loud and bipolar. On most days, like this one, the thermometer near his bed showed nothing more than a speck of mercury, but during the heater's manic phases, an unbroken stripe of silver topped out at eighty-five.

On those rare mornings when he'd been able to sleep, Adrian woke to see a man in what looked to be military fatigues fishing for trout. The man stood in a painting, about the same width as the room's twin bed, bolted to the wall above the headboard. Adrian saw the painting when he opened his eyes because it was duplicated in reverse by a mirror on the opposite wall. (The mirror, too, was fastened in place with bolts he hadn't been able to loosen.) The harsh, solid greens and blues reminded him of being in high-school art class. Make that junior-high art class.

He had to brave the bathroom's arctic tile floor to appreciate the lone piece of décor that had come here with him. *The past is like a shoe that won't stay tied,* read the wooden plaque that, along with his anchorman hair and 1989 Ford F-250 pickup, made up Adrian's inheritance from the old man. *It keeps tripping you up.*

He liked this better than the words his father used to pull out to motivate Adrian. "Do anything you got a mind to." Days before Adrian got the advance for his book, a heart attack sideswiped the old man, leaving Pa to die in the arms (and legs) of someone who wasn't Ma. As the creed took on new meaning, Adrian questioned everything about the father he'd been trying to impress. Why, for example, had the old man specialized in furnace repair? Tallahassee's average winter temperature was a bearable fifty-four degrees Fahrenheit, meaning that a native Floridian who truly wanted the best for his son would have stenciled the words THE AIR CONDITIONING EXPERTS beneath PANHANDLE PLUMBING AND FURNACE REPAIR on the side of his pickup.

Adrian heard a crash outside his door, followed by what he once would have mistaken for shattering glass. All too familiar to him now, icicles produced a slightly higher pitch after breaking free from gutters and crashing to the ground.

He closed his eyes and imagined himself several climates removed from this place where weather reports routinely started with wind chill. He was sunburned. He was sweaty. He was sitting on wet sand, watching waves come in off Apalachee Bay.

A young woman who had recently emigrated from Guatemala brought him a colorful drink. A sailboat glided left to right, then vanished from sight as another icicle hit the pavement outside.

◆

Adrian had not always been so cold, or bitter, though he'd begun to forget what it was like to be otherwise.

"God Boy, why couldn't you have been right?" he whispered, taking a seat on the edge of his mattress. Solid, unbending, it felt like a park bench. He stared at his image in the dead TV, focusing on the sweatshirt. Hard to believe he'd once worn nice clothes, expensive clothes, nothing but. When he lived in Starke, he enjoyed driving his Jaguar all the way to Tampa—and even Miami—to find the best shopping. Now (because driving an old Ford pickup to Minneapolis didn't sound even remotely enjoyable) he shopped at a department store named Kohl's, in Canterbury, a town of eight thousand, twenty miles south of Trappers Point on 71. He didn't go there often. Most of the items in his current wardrobe, excluding his sweats, fit snugly or not at all.

Adrian sneezed, and on the small, round table near the front window, which again needed scraping, his laptop's screen came out of hibernation to display a classic, near-mint Jaguar XK8 Roadster convertible. He got up from his bed, walked to the table, and took a seat. With a click of his mouse, a title appeared, left from the night before. *ABOUT THE AUTHOR.* He couldn't recall how many pages he'd typed this time. (His record was nine.) He did know he'd meant to delete it, sticking to his usual practice.

A native of Tallahassee, Adrian C. Hummel grew up unafraid of life, unintimidated by its agenda. As a teen, Hummel was confident, even a bit cocky. The French Club president called him a bully. (Everyone knew this was an exaggeration, the product of envy.) Hummel made him take it back, in English and French, before a packed lunchroom.

He racked up a 4.0 GPA. The first member of his family to make it to college, he got into North Florida on a partial scholarship. Student loans covered the balance. He applied for his first credit cards and learned he could live comfortably through debt. The other kids had roommates. Hummel shared his dorm room with a Sony WEGA 62" HD-Ready widescreen TV and a massage chair purchased at Sharper Image. He bought his first car, a three-year-old Jaguar XK8 Roadster convertible that looked brand new.

"Idiot," he whispered to himself, "why are you reading this?" His index finger lingered above the Delete key. "Press it." But he didn't touch the key.

Hummel put in two months as a field reporter for the Starke (Florida) Badger *before getting promoted. Now he was Fashion, Sports, and Local Affairs Editor. The owner's daughter, Mimi June, agreed to go out with him. The owner needed an oxygen tank to breathe; the future looked good.*

Adrian C. Hummel, Publisher, Owner. He dined at the old man's house, helped light the old man's cigarettes.

Adrian burped, releasing the aftertaste of saltines and syrup. Then, stretching his arms, he noticed he felt better. He'd arrived at his favorite time of day, when he'd successfully attained a balance between caffeine pills, sleeplessness, stress, and self-pity. It was a shame life couldn't stay this way, a shame the next pills he downed would upset this fragile compromise.

He wished he could think of an activity, something fun or even exciting, to better exploit this valued state. But as on previous days, nothing came to mind. He unplugged his laptop and carried it to the bed.

By the time he turned twenty-six, Adrian C. Hummel didn't even care that he'd said something insensitive at a drive-in movie and was no longer engaged to the Badger's oh-so-sensitive heir. New York wanted his insider's view of life in a cult—in paperback and cloth. Once again, something good had come without effort.

Hummel quit his post at the Starke (Florida) Badger *without giving notice, instead waving his $10,000 advance check in the air and telling his should've-been-dead-by-then boss that Mimi June was "unmarryable."*

The book idea had been a gift of sorts. From the first day he'd landed in Starke, Hummel had been looking for one that would place him "inside" some phenomenon (preferably while generating a spouse-free income more in line with his expenses). Toward this end, he had contemplated hurricanes (plentiful near Starke but too short in duration) and the Florida State Prison (just down the road but way too scary). Then came the night he worked late to make up for a long (two martini) lunch with the owner. Benmont duBlanc (the small-minded opportunist) came in just before seven, holding a cigarette in one hand, and a real newspaper, the New York Times, *in the other.*

"Have you been reading this shit about Dan Hawker?" duBlanc asked his colleague. "Started a cult in the middle of nowhere. Thinks he's God, and he's not alone."

"I think I saw him on the news," Hummel replied, though it might have been Inside Edition.

"I've got something," duBlanc said next. "Years ago, this same Dan Hawker worked at Walt Disney World. Doing magic tricks for the turistas. My source has it he got transferred to Disneyland, out in L.A., because he said or did something improper." The Travel, Entertainment, and World News Editor lowered his voice to a whisper, odd since there was no one else in the two-room office. "I don't think it's been reported anywhere. I'm thinking there's a book here. I'm half-tempted to write a proposal to my agent."

In actual fact, as Hummel knew from previous conversations, Benmont duBlanc had only corresponded with said agent. He wasn't that skilled a writer, and nothing he'd submitted had ever been taken.

"I don't know," Hummel replied. "It's kind of interesting. But a book?"

Over the next few weeks, Hummel affected a polite smile each time he asked DuBlanc, "Do anything with that book proposal?" And he was always relieved to hear a "No," since Hummel was fairly far along on his own. "I am willing and ready to infiltrate the cult," he wrote in his cover letter. "This shouldn't be too difficult. I have a brother in the cult." Having fibbed once, he added, "I am a serious journalist. My articles have appeared in Newsweek and Rolling Stone. I can give you inside access."

Here the text ended, no more ABOUT THE AUTHOR. This, apparently, was where he'd lost interest (or realized he was being too honest) the night before.

He recalled one more thing from the day he ended his newspaper career. This was the face of Benmont duBlanc III, turned cold and impenetrable as frost on a window. "Well then," duBlanc had said. "I wish you all the luck you deserve."

♦

His neck itched, and so he peeled away the last dressing of toilet paper. Thank God, the bleeding had stopped.

Adrian typed, It was true. Everything came easily to Adrian C. Hummel. Until . . .

He sneezed, reached for the Kleenex box on his nightstand.

The pain raged again.

Strike the until. In actual fact, things still came easily. Only one detail had changed. They were no longer good things.

A soiled ball of tissue hit the pile beneath his sink, the one concealing his wastebasket. He wondered when the maid had last been in.

Consider, for example, forty-one pounds and a five-digit credit-card debt that could no longer be described as "in the low five digits." Add to that the outstanding student loans and misspent advance, and, well . . . Adrian C. Hummel wished he'd never pulled those A's in math.

What hadn't come his way was a best-selling book that wiped out his debt. He didn't even have a book that would sell just enough to patch the gaps on his résumé. A few good reviews to make up for the lack of (favorable) references.

"Should've kept quiet," he said in a whisper as he finally deleted his document. "Should've . . ."

Who would have thought he'd be nostalgic at twenty-eight? But at that weary moment in that dreary room, the job in Starke looked good to him, as did the house he would have inherited from Mimi June's father.

He recalled one of the awful country songs his old man used to love. It wasn't that Adrian held any particular bias against country. He didn't like music, any music. This corresponded to a broader opinion of artistic expression. It had no point. At the urging of a college girlfriend, he'd once signed up for a music appreciation class. He gained another A, along with what his professor lauded as "an insightful grasp" of how music was assembled. "Ever think of changing majors?" It was the last time he'd listened to any at his own instigation.

If you're gonna burn a bridge, the song his old man loved had advised, *get off the damn thing first.*

CHAPTER EIGHT

Mary looked back at her dad and took pleasure in watching him squirm—he was always so impatient. She was using the pay phone next to a "You Are Here" map of Colorado's highways, mounted behind glass like a valuable piece of art. He was in the bus in the rest area's parking lot, pretending not to spy on her.

She dialed Adrian's number. Off to her left an elderly man was trying to walk his elderly cat, but the gray-and-white tabby showed no interest in cooperating. Seated on the dry brown grass, claiming the sunshine for its own, the pet rocked gently on its frame like an old jazz musician. If only it knew how lucky it was to have the grass and sun this day.

The operator told her the line was busy. "Would you like to try another number?"

Mary said yes. This time, her call was answered on the third ring.

When she climbed back into the VW bus, Dad handed her the keys and asked, "Who did you call?"

"No one."

"The same no one you called last time?"

"One and the same." The engine started and she jerked the stick into reverse. "So are you going to take my keys whenever we stop?" she asked.

"I don't want to see you pulling away."

"You never get out of the stupid car."

They were clear of the parking space, but two other cars were backing out ahead of them. She wondered if he was suspicious about her condition—he sure seemed to be goading her—then wondered why she cared.

He asked, "What happened to being in a hurry? If we keep stopping like this—"

"I am in a hurry. You're just—" She adjusted the rearview mirror. "—in the way." Another crunch, and they were moving forward, building momentum with all the urgency of water being coaxed to a boil. "We're picking someone up," she said. "That's who I called."

"We're stopping for passengers?"

"No more questions, Dad. I need to think."

"But—"

"This car is noisy enough without your help."

"Dammit, Mary, this is your father you're talking to. You seem to have forgotten that."

"You won't let me forget it, *Dad*. Can't you just . . . be . . . quiet."

"I don't believe this," he sputtered.

"Believe it," she said, feeling a tightness in her throat and stomach. Couldn't he tell he was forcing these reactions? Why couldn't he just thank her for putting up with him this far and letting him play with the keys whenever they stopped? Why was he always like this?

An awful question came out of nowhere. Or maybe not so out of nowhere. *Why hadn't he ever hugged her?*

Mary stepped on the gas, more anxious than before to get somewhere, but the speedometer indicated only sixty. What a piece of garbage; the engine sounded like it was ready to burn up.

"I am your father," he whispered.

If she'd been pressing any harder, the pedal would have gone through the floor.

◆

Scott could tell there was an accident ahead. There had to be—traffic moved too slowly to accommodate any other explanation, bad weather and construction zones included. A wide gray sign welcomed them to Nebraska. He glanced at the speedometer. They were moving at four miles per hour . . . when they were moving.

Orange safety cones funneled the convoy into one slow-moving drip of a lane. "Good Lord," Scott whispered as he took in the smoldering, compacted remains of a white SUV, turned upside down, its twisted, burnt wheels bubbling up blackened like marshmallows that had fallen into a campfire. Coming up on their left, a state trooper questioned a UPS driver—identifiable by the brown uniform—whose double-trailer rig had sledded to a stop on the median, while twisting into a tight U-shape. The cab faced west, the first trailer north, the second east. But all three units were right side up and untouched by flame. "Apparently," Scott said, "the SUV is not at the top of the motor-vehicle food chain."

"That's not funny, Dad. There could've been children in there."

"I thought everyone was supposed to be dead today." He knew he was being insensitive, of course—it was hard work under these conditions. But he was seeking a response. "Destruction and carnage. I could have sworn you said these were good things."

"Dad!"

"You're not going to tell me to shut up again?"

"So that's what this is about."

The silver-gray Lexus ahead of them sauntered to the right to avoid crushing a piece of chrome, and Scott recognized the outline of a Christian fish emblem, presumably knocked free from the back of the SUV. It glinted briefly in the sun, but his daughter must not have seen it. There was a small crunching sound as they moved forward.

"You know, Mary, when you talk like that you—" He didn't finish the sentence, didn't get out the words, *remind me of your mom.*

As true as this was, Mary hardly needed to speak to stir memories of Liz. This was something she'd been doing all morning, with each shake of her head or roll of her eyes. Occasionally, Scott caught himself shaking his own head in response. He winced fairly often as well, because revisiting Liz was, for the most part, like watching an accident. Like the one he'd just seen, between mismatched vehicles.

When Liz moved out she left a note—if "notes" by definition are allowed to exceed two pages in length. Neatly written and efficiently constructed, her "reasons for leaving" did not skimp on detail or substance. He counted no fewer than twelve of these reasons, although further scrutiny revealed that several were variations on the theme, "goal disoriented." Number nine: "Dickens produced more than a page a year."

The note concluded, "It's over. I must go. Mary comes with me."

That Liz counted the four-year-old Mary as one of her possessions had been a source of surprise, if not bafflement. Had Liz ever once slept on a bedroom floor, her mattress a doubled-over sleeping bag, waiting for Mary's fever to break? Or transported her daughter to a doctor's waiting room without first protesting to Scott, "You should be the one taking off work—my job's important"? Here, he'd always defended himself, pointing out that he did take Mary to most of her appointments and that his job was important too, although he knew the latter wasn't true. (Reason number six: "No Ambition.") But none of this mattered. They—Liz *and* Mary—had gone. They had gone to a place where the price of lawyers ensured he couldn't follow.

He was hurt most by her second reason for leaving. "Parenting Skills Need Work and You Refuse to Work on Them." It wasn't that the charge came up short on legitimacy—the truth of her words was what gave them the power to wound. For as long as young Mary had been making friends, Scott had tended to criticize these friends in adult terms, causing him to say things like, "That Billy Hathaway is an arrogant, irresponsible sociopath. He thinks the world revolves around him." He recalled Liz's reaction to that one. After rolling her eyes and sighing, she'd said, "Jesus, Scott. Billy Hathaway is three."

The note ended on a favorite topic: the choices Scott made by avoiding choices. "You write for a living. You supervise writers. You'll never have another job. Yet you hate writing as much as you hate writers."

He found the note shortly after The Christmas That Would Not Die or Go Away, when Liz's mother, father, brothers-in-law, sisters-in-duplicate, and screaming infant niece had driven to Aurora in a single overcrowded van to see the new split-level house on Turnbolt Drive and to celebrate Liz's latest promotion. The sisters, Susan and Rebecca, also wanted to "see Colorado, buy some Coors to take back, and try skiing."

Despite the airs of worldliness they shared with Liz, sisters Oozin' and Upchucka had never before traveled west from Omaha. There was one more peculiarity. The two women walked and talked like they were the offspring of parents who bore much more resemblance to the Rockefellers than to the middle-class van owners seated at his kitchen table playing Double Solitaire. Yet, the sisters had not even briefly considered flying, renting cars, or paying for motel rooms.

Regarding his private nicknames for Susan and Rebecca, Scott knew these were hardly worthy of a professional copywriter, and ideally, he would have borrowed his epithets from literary sources, like *Hamlet* or *I, Claudius*, perhaps the Brothers Grimm. *Were evil stepsisters even given names?* But nothing came easily to mind, and he decided it wasn't worth his effort. His nineteenth-century novels and English lit textbooks remained in their boxes in the one-car garage.

His marriage might have survived the visit had the Omahaians stayed only a few days, had there been enough beds, had there been enough bedrooms, had the sisters stepped outside to smoke, had the baby stopped screaming, and had Scott and his asshole brother-in-law Michael been able to disarm a tornado-siren-strength burglar alarm. Or . . . maybe not. Susan and Rebecca seemed to have made total core meltdown their goal from the start, and unlike Scott, the poorly nicknamed sisters did not lose sight of their goals. Rather, they hunted them down with a ruthless carnivore logic.

And so it was that the Ford Econoline's engine had barely cooled from the trip out when Susan said to Scott, "It's nice. For a starter home."

"What do you mean, starter home?"

"You know, a starter home. The kind people buy with a starter job."

The burglar alarm was next door and it was very loud. It went off on Christmas Eve because Scott had offered to feed the neighbor's cat and had failed to memorize the burglar-alarm code—or remember where he'd placed the sheet with that six-digit combination. Liz's explosive reaction—she called him "an overqualified moron"—made her sisters seem pleasant. Three neighbors phoned the police, who ended up searching the Shepherd house for more than an hour looking for an override key or a phone number, while Max, the unfed cat, shot off never to be seen again.

"That's why I don't believe in burglar alarms," Scott reminded his fuming Liz while their four-year-old watched in silence. "Boethius was right. If you own nothing, there is nothing to steal." She, in turn, suggested he save his Boethius for the Shepherds, who were returning early from their vacation that afternoon on account of the missing pet. "I'm sure they'd enjoy it." The exchange might have taken place over breakfast the next morning—Liz really hadn't been much of a morning person. *Yes,* now he was sure of it, *it had been the next morning.* Her relatives were sleeping in. Susan was snoring on the foldout bed Scott had rented.

The cat-free neighbors hissed and bared their claws for as long as they shared a chain-link fence with Scott, which ended when the Shepherds unloaded their starter home. But the feud was unilateral; Scott never returned their rage. The Shepherds, after all, had done him a favor. As he quickly learned, with an ex-wife came ex-in-laws. He never saw the sisters again, and spoke with Susan only once. That took place some five years later, within days of Liz's death, when Susan threatened to fight him for custody of Mary. "My sister told everyone she knew she'd never let Mary return to that house," Susan said on the phone. "I have witnesses, even if Liz didn't write down her wishes."

Scott told Susan to stay in hell and leave him alone. "You have no business up here on the surface."

◆

They passed a Ford Taurus. A dull plum red except for one gray door, it couldn't have been going more than fifty miles per hour. It had a Nebraska plate and a bumper sticker that argued, IT'S A BABY NOT A CHOICE. An elderly woman clutched the wheel, which seemed to be holding her up just high enough to see out the windshield. She was traveling alone.

Scott felt his own right foot pushing against the floorboard, as if he could help by pressing an imaginary pedal. He timed the effort. Two minutes and thirty-eight seconds, with a Greyhound bus growing larger the whole time in his rearview mirror. He took a deep breath when the maneuver was finished and the bus blurred past. "Nice work," he said at last. "Anyone else want to mess with us?" But he knew the Taurus had been an anomaly; they weren't likely to pass many cars on their journey.

The radio in the bus was pure static now, and so he turned it off. Mary didn't respond. It was ten past noon. The Greyhound bus was a dot in the distance.

He looked over at his daughter, now visibly lost in her own landscape of thoughts, and was tempted to tell her, "I'm sorry. For everything." These were the words he'd almost said to Liz one morning in the Heritage lot, a few months after the divorce—and after one more evening had gone on too long, giving him time to wonder what life would be like if he tried a little harder. Liz caught him off guard that morning, by smiling as she climbed out of her Audi in the parking lot's reserved section. "I don't suppose you've come to congratulate me," she said before he had a chance to speak. "What? Haven't you heard? They're making me vice president."

Liz perished trying to cut her company's printng budget, circling the globe in pursuit of low-cost suppliers. Her departure was swift and exotic. Her plane couldn't have crashed over the continental United States, say, Wisconsin or Ohio; it had to be Sri Lanka.

More than that, her death was unforgivable. Typical, selfish Liz. Scott knew she had triumphed the moment he first heard the news from a Senior VP. Liz would shine forever as the perfect, sainted parent, the one who couldn't be criticized.

By then, Mary was nine and shy around others her age, and Scott, still in that house on Turnbolt Drive, was surprised at how single he'd become. He was no longer dating, having tired of seeing how quickly each new coed copywriter would tire of him and his copywriting skills. He did not frequent bars and he belonged to no organizations, taking special care to avoid those like the Metro Denver Ad Club that actively sought his participation. For the most part, however, he had adjusted well to being alone. He never talked to himself, even on the most endless of weekends, although he wasn't above lecturing his inanimate objects. The toaster ("I'm already late for work, let's go!"), the ice maker in the freezer ("What is your fucking problem today?"), the bar of soap crashing to the shower floor ("Oh *come on.*").

It was only after Mary returned to live with him that he realized how much he had missed her. "You broke my heart," he whispered into her room one night when he knew she was sleeping. "I tried not to notice." And if he had not yet stumbled upon an ideal set of parenting skills, he made up for it with a new eagerness to drive her to school, help her with homework, and prepare her lunch each night before bedtime.

Though it would puzzle him in hindsight, Mary made things easy by never asking questions about Liz, as if her dead mother had never been part of the story. Scott took this to mean that Mary was well-adjusted. On the day she turned ten, he gave her a handsomely bound collector's edition of the *Lord of the Rings* trilogy. *The Hobbit* was included in a special commemorative box. Hugging her, he said, "Your dad will always be proud of you."

CHAPTER NINE

"**I**'d like to know what they think they're thinking," the clock radio weighed in. It was tuned to KNMN, *Classic Talk*.

"I mean, who do they think they are?"

Adrian needed news, however unreliable the source. On other days, he would have doubled-clicked on AOL. But the laptop was bundled up, ready for its trip to the diner.

"I don't know about the rest of you, but I'm tired of working for the Jew."

Adrian glanced over at the space once occupied by his Sony WEGA HD-Ready wide-screen TV and had trouble believing he'd gone eight months without it. He found it even harder to believe that something so beautiful had caused him such anguish (and reflux). But that it had, and he'd been wary ever since of driving to Canterbury and using one of his thirteen credit cards to procure a new set. (He may even have become a tad superstitious, taking into account what had happened with the WEGA.)

At first, Adrian's mother had balked on shipping the TV and massage chair, saying, "You might as well buy new ones for what they'll charge you." She could never take in the logic of his argument, "MasterCard can afford it." This left it for Adrian to haul his prized possessions north in the back of the twenty-year-old pickup inherited from Pa. Once the wide-screen was in Room 17, Adrian promptly subscribed to a satellite service, getting a free dish as part of the offer. But when the Valfaard's owner saw the apparatus, he wanted three hundred dollars in exchange for permission to secure it to the motel's roof. "Or, seeing's how it's already in place, you can pay me four hundred for damage to my roof—after you take it down."

The area's sole "dish technician" also helped himself to Adrian's shrinking cash supply each time he drove up from Canterbury to repair the rat-bastard thing. "We don't take plastic. It's in our ad." This happened three times, once for each of the blizzards that knocked out Adrian's service. After he was no longer able to make the minimum monthly payments on his cards, he put flyers on the wall of Bev's diner and the Gas 'N' Pass convenience store. GREAT DEAL ON A SONY WEGA 62" HD-READY WIDESCREEN TV AND FAUX SUEDE iJOY TURBO 2 ROBOTIC MASSAGE CHAIR. Three weeks later, he found a buyer. Bev knew she was robbing him. She should have paid four times as much, but Adrian took comfort in assuming he could watch the widescreen whenever he ate at the diner.

It ended up in her private quarters, out of his sight, as did the chair.

"I think we should line 'em all up, give 'em a head start." The radio saved him from these recollections. "Not much o' one, though. After that, it's hunting season on liberals."

Radio here meant *AM* radio, and that translated further into tinny church music broken up by sermons every bit as wacky as the ones Hawker delivered—or talk radio of the variety Adrian was putting up with that morning.

For the next eight minutes, callers complained about gays (there were none anywhere near here), blacks (there were none anywhere near here), and "Hitleristic smoking bans" (there were none anywhere near here). "What right has anyone got to tell me what I can or can't put in my mouth?"

Adrian laughed for the first time that day, noting how fully this declaration contradicted the homophobic rants he'd endured only minutes before.

"America was founded on tobacco. That and the Bible."

Guns, Adrian thought. *You forgot guns.*

Which was funny because Adrian believed in the Second Amendment . . . and smoking in restaurants . . . and ridding our universities of quotas. He didn't exactly approve of gay marriage and had voted Republican the one time he voted. These heavily armed paranoiacs had a knack for bringing out the devil's advocate in him.

The host asked the caller to hold his thoughts.

"A teaspoon should do," Adrian said, giving voice to his own.

The caller was silent, as was the host, a testament to the white man's exceptional self-discipline.

"Off you go," Adrian whispered, bending toward the clock radio. "I need to get back to Bev's diner."

But before he could press the button, he heard the host say, "News coming in from Hallelujah City."

Adrian turned up the volume.

"Feds clamping down?" asked the caller, who had obviously concluded that if the host didn't have to be silent, neither did he. "Tanks on the roll?"

As on previous visits to their planet, the fringe never disappointed. And here they were again, siding with Hawker, believing that anyone who irritated the government had to be doing something right. On these airwaves there was no "Hawker's compound," only Hallelujah City. The caller now asked, "Are we gonna sit by while the storm troopers march in and burn Hallelujah City? Are we—"

"We're getting word," said the host, "that Daniel Hawker has destroyed his neighbor's livestock."

This new detail must have confounded the fringe, because it turned Hawker into an outsider capable of violating their sovereign property rights. This was another recurring gripe. God-fearing Minnesotans didn't like outsiders messing with their stuff.

"Before we judge too quickly," the host continued, "I'm learning that the original source for this story is the Bureau of Alcohol, Tobacco, and Firearms. They're claiming to have witnessed the trespass from one of their choppers."

"Black helicopters," the caller perked up. "I knew it. You can't trust the feds an inch."

"We're getting more information." The host waited four beats, and Adrian suspected him of simply watching Fox News as he spoke. "The livestock's owner has confirmed the story."

"The livestock's owner?"

"Appears to be so. Lost his whole herd. I'd say the government needs to get off its butt and do something."

"Damn right," said the caller.

Two more icicles crashed to the pavement outside. Adrian looked toward the front window and saw that it was frosting back up.

Staring at the brilliant rime, he no longer felt nostalgic, and cringed to think of his sniveling only minutes before. Call it a temporary weakness. Adrian C. Hummel didn't want his old life back. Only his dream.

This was significant. He'd only recently come to regard himself as a dreamer, a serious step down from being the guy with the grades and brains, the guy who set goals and reached them. However absurd it may have seemed now, Adrian really had planned on becoming a best-selling journalistic author. A reasonable ambition—he still believed this—not all that lofty, hardly fantastic. Why couldn't he have it?

Dreamers, he knew from observation, did worse than crash and burn. They smoldered on the ground long after impact. Like Mary Chambers and everyone else ever cursed with innocence, they watched their worlds end, only to discover they still had time, likely thousands of days' worth, all of it punishing. Waking and working and mourning the loss of something they never actually had. All for the crime of over-reaching.

Adrian recalled a line he'd used in the introduction he'd roughed out for his book, the only chapter completed to date: "History is shaped by people who should have stayed home." Was it all just luck? he asked himself now. And if so, where the heck had his gone?

There was a knock on the door. The maid had returned after her latest three-week hiatus. He waited to hear her call, "Cleaning, Mr. Hummer."

But what he heard was, "Adrian, are you in there?"

Bev.

He hurried to open the door. "This is unusual. Did something happen to Gunt? Did I forget to pay you?"

Looking past him she said, "So this . . . is where you live."

He nodded.

"Your neck? Better?"

He nodded again.

"Would I like to come in?" she said. "Why, sure. Thank you, Adrian."

He took a step back and motioned her inside.

"They're saying he killed the cows on his neighbor's farm," she said. "How does somebody do that? Why?"

"He's trying to provoke a reaction."

"A showdown?"

After turning off the radio, he offered Bev a seat at his table. She kept her coat and gloves on. He took the other seat and used his forearm to push a small stack of cassette tapes off to one side.

"My poor, poor Gunt." She paused to clear her throat. "But I guess this cow thing's no worse than what I saw."

"And what was that?" he asked.

"Well . . ."

He picked up his voice-activated digital recorder and whispered, "Is this okay?"

Bev sat up straight and ran a hand through her hair. She must have thought he owned an extremely compact video camera. "Let's just say the crazies have taken over from the crazies," she said. "And that those guards I left you with were the nice ones. The bullies inside were stealing things, looting, like you see on TV, but in the weirdest way. They were fighting over things, and moving their loot into separate piles. But it didn't seem to be going anywhere after that. No one seemed in too big a hurry to get out of there."

"You were inside the Inner Sanctum?"

"If you ask me, I didn't see anything worth stealing."

Not true, thought Adrian. *There was one thing—and it belongs to me.*

Bev was still speaking. "The furniture must have come with the house, a package deal. All those farms were foreclosed, don't you know, resold at auction. Nothing looked very nice or new."

"And you were inside?"

"There was every kind of lewdness, and it didn't all look consensual.

There was this one girl covered in paint. Like maybe they were going to sacrifice her or something."

"What about Gunt? Is he all right?"

"I never found him. Not in his trailer—and not in the inner septic or whatever you called it. I didn't see Daniel Hawker neither."

Bev looked up from the recorder and said, "Maybe the government needs to do something."

"I think they're holding back," he said. "To avoid repeating past mistakes."

"This isn't like that Waco thing, that's what they're saying on TV. Koresh, they wanted in jail. Here, they've got nothing. 'Course that was before the cows. Seems they're going to have to do something."

"What else did you see?"

"Candles," she said. "All over the floor, on every kind of holder. They caught my attention because of the old shag carpet. It didn't have much shag left, but I bet it's still got plenty of burn."

The recorder slipped from his hand (caffeine in the ascendancy), sliding off the table and hitting the floor, where it ejected three AAA batteries. It took him a minute to round these up, longer still to reinsert them in the proper positions. "Sorry," he muttered as he got back up to reclaim his seat.

"So. Adrian. You were one of them."

"I—" He did something that made him feel dense afterward, holding up his hands to form air quotation marks. "—was never *one of them*. I'm writing a book, remember? I *infiltrated* the cult."

He was, in actual fact, surprised that Bev seemed interested now, seeing that she'd already let two years pass without once asking a question like this. But he quickly realized she was looking for small talk, for a distraction from her son's predicament.

Whatever her motive, he welcomed the interest and company. It beat waiting for his phone to ring.

"How?" she asked.

"How'd I get in?" He turned off the recorder. "I still had confidence then. In myself, in my plan. I paid for my room two months in advance, thinking I'd just use it to store my clothes and equipment. Until I had my story."

He thought back to the second morning he woke in the Valfaard, a motel shunned by journalists on expense accounts, even though it was close to Hawker's compound. He'd slept well, and why not? He owned a nice car. He had three thousand in hundred-dollar bills hidden in a pair of hiking boots.

"You probably don't remember the first time I ate in your diner. Pancakes, at least one stack too many. Don't be offended but I thought you were just a waitress."

"Offended? My goodness, Adrian. There's worse things to be."

"I left a good tip."

"That must have been the morning I retired and moved to Hawaii."

"Then it was off to find God."

"Or," Bev surprised him by adding, "a generic substitute."

"Given the absence of heat that day, the sun seemed out of place when I turned right onto CC." Three miles north of town on Highway 71, County Road CC offered the only direct route into Hawker's compound. He could picture the sign that announced CC, white, rectangular, relatively small—and perforated by bullet holes. Welcome to hunting country. "I still had my car. My gold Roadster convertible. Jaguar.

"You probably remember, there were hardly any reporters then. Just a couple of tents."

"Hard to picture now," said Bev, "the way they took over that spot."

Too true, thought Adrian. After God Boy delivered his doomsday announcement, the press made that area their beachhead, with dozens of tents, as white and bright as the SUVs parked between them, rising from the banks of the gravel road's mouth.

"I saw two men out for a smoke," he continued. "Magnificently bored, they looked like soldiers in a lull between battles. Neither of them so much as glanced at me. 'Go ahead,' I whispered to myself. 'Ignore me while you can.' I knew I could trump them if I just pulled off the next step of my plan, which happened to be the only step of my plan.

"For the next quarter mile or so, I hardly had to steer. There were two deep ruts, hard as rock, guiding me like rails beneath a train. The pen on my dash rattled and I had to keep grabbing at it to keep it from falling. It was the ballpoint used by Studs Terkel to edit *Working*. I got it on eBay. There were a couple sharp turns. I saw this big old school bus. Painted blue and parked sideways, it marked the compound's entrance. Blocked it, too. Forget the sign that warned, Private Road Beyond This Point. That just seemed redundant." That sign, too, had been brutalized by bullets. He'd counted fourteen holes.

"I've seen the bus," Bev said. "When I tried using CC. Blue like the sky."

"You could tell the paint job went back a few years. The blue had faded to white in places, creating the effect of hazy clouds."

"It just looked like a big wall to me. Something you couldn't get around."

The heater came on in Room 17 of the Valfaard Inn, grumbling and rumbling and grinding with an anger that suggested it wanted to break free of its enclosure. The temperature stayed constant.

"Sounds like a train going by," said Bev.

"It only produces noise," Adrian said. "I think it's designed to take your mind off the fact you're freezing."

"With nothing to show for all that commotion?"

He imagined his mother in the room, saying, "Sounds like someone we know."

Adrian shuddered, and returned to his story. "Looking through the trees, I picked out the corner of a doublewide trailer and knew I was close. I saw two eagles circling high to my left. They seemed other-worldly; I thought of Native Americans.

"Staying in formation, the pair descended. An invisible corkscrew pattern. I followed their movement till my eyes lighted on a woman in a field, standing alone, scattering seeds. The woman saw me too. Dipping her hand into a wide, white apron, she started walking toward me."

He saw no need to share the next detail, of how the woman in the field had reminded him of the waitress who'd just served him pancakes in the diner, more notable for her width than height.

"She came over to welcome me," he told Bev instead, "just as something caught my eye from above. The eagles were flying east, their altitude reclaimed.

"The woman stopped on the ditch's north side and asked what I wanted. She had a friendly gap-toothed smile and was older than I'd been expecting from what I knew about the cult's demographics." He borrowed a sentence he'd been saving for his book: "She was older indeed than the middle-aged fisher of men known for baiting girls not out of their teens."

"Sorry?"

"Hawker," Adrian said. "She was older than Hawker."

Bev nodded.

"I told her I believed in the Teacher. And that I wanted to enlist. She started with a 'Sugar,' something I'd never been mistaken for before. 'You've come to the right place,' she said. And though I never got a name, she turned out to be pleasant . . . and talkative, full of *honeys* and *sweeties*. I felt like I knew her after five minutes.

"I asked her what I needed to do to join. 'Sugar,' she said without losing the smile. 'Why don't you pop by same time mañana?'"

Bev pushed the black ashtray, one of three in the non-smoking room, and now overflowing with thoroughly used Kleenex, to the table's far side. "And just like that you were in the cult?" she asked.

"I got there a good hour early the next morning—and waited three times that long. It was their way of letting me know just who held the cards. Finally, someone new came out to greet me, a girl maybe twenty. Like the older woman the day before, she walked to the edge of the field to my left, stopping just across the ditch. She had coal-dark hair, scouring eyes, and features just as hard. She didn't smile and said only one thing. She couldn't help me."

"That was it?"

"That was it. When the girl turned away, I declared, 'I live to serve the Teacher!' But she kept walking.

"'Hey!' I heard myself shout. Just before I added something I hadn't intended. 'I'm a professional journalist! I'm here to help get his word out!'

"The girl stopped . . . 'I shouldn't' . . . and turned back to face me. She asked if I had something with my number. In case the Teacher came up with a use for my talents.

"She moved toward me as I pulled out a pen and obliterated the old Florida address on my business card. She crossed the ditch. I circled the number for my cell phone and leaned forward. While taking the card (snatching it, really), the girl glanced around, toward the field and the trees. Like a spy in a movie, afraid she's being watched."

Once again, he kept the next part from Bev. This was where he'd introduced himself by name. "Hmm," the girl had said in response, and he detected more interest. She seemed to like him . . . right up until she asked, "Anyone ever tell you you smell like soap?" He, of course, was taken aback. "You'd be the first," he replied. "Must be my shower at the motel. I'm already starting to miss hot water." But her question had been rhetorical. The girl was gone, moving briskly toward the trees. She couldn't have heard his response.

"Later in Room 17," he told Bev now, "I heard my cell phone's ring-tone. It was ten fifty-nine." He didn't mention that he'd been sniffing at his underarms to gauge the level of soap-smell at the time. "When I picked up, I heard the voice of the second woman, the younger woman. The Teacher had called me, she said. They expected me back there at five a.m."

As if to help illustrate the story, the cell phone sitting on his table produced the shrill dots and dashes of the Morse code ringtone. "Sorry," he said as he grabbed it.

"Adrian C. Hummel!" he answered.

Bev got up and, smiling weakly, backed out the door.

"No, Mama," Adrian said in response to his mother's new questions, "I wasn't upset. There's just a lot going on here today."

He stared at the door, and reminded himself that, no matter how anxious he was to hear Mary's voice, he needed to check Caller ID before grabbing the phone.

CHAPTER TEN

"You're famous, hon." Semolina Bath was seated directly behind Mary in the middle seat of the Volkswagen bus. Her wide face was a chafed winter red, her gap-toothed smile briefly visible each time she spoke. The cigarette in her right hand was unlit, unlike the one that preceded it. "They're looking for you, Mary."

They had stopped in Ogallala, at a gas station just off the interstate, to pick up the passenger Mary had warned Scott about. There, he'd been surprised to meet Ms. Bath, having expected to see another woman close to Mary in age—and not someone older than he was.

"Who?" Mary asked now. "Who's looking for me?"

"Well, CNN for one," Semolina replied.

Scott could no longer keep quiet. "CNN is looking for my daughter?"

"Daniel talked with them by phone. Just over an hour ago. He mentioned Mary's name, said he wants her back."

"The Teacher mentioned my name?"

"I believe that's what I said," Semolina replied. "He told them something big was going to happen. Tonight."

Scott's daughter sighed almost imperceptibly. "He mentioned my name."

"He said something else. He said you *carried the answer.*"

Mary said nothing. What Scott would have given to know what she was thinking.

"So?" the new passenger pressed.

"It's definitely curious," Scott added.

"I don't know what He meant," Mary said sharply. "I just know He wants me by His side in Hallelujah City. No one here seems to believe it, but the Teacher is loving and caring. At least to those who love and care."

"C'mon, sugar," Bath said with a cackle. "Don't get all schoolgirly. Hawker's a fraud. Part your eyelids. How else do you explain that we're still here?"

Scott was intrigued by his daughter's reply: "What if God had reason to call it off? What if someone corrupted Daniel?"

Semolina didn't waste a second. "Corrupted him, my ass." The smile was back, and Scott saw the expression for what it was, the corporal equivalent of an exclamation point, a device Bath would have used excessively had she been one of his copywriters. "How could anyone corrupt Daniel Hawker?" she asked, her free hand patting the pack of Marlboro Lights on the seat to her left. "That man's got all the restraint of a mosquito."

◆

Sturdy of build and outspoken by nature, Semolina had married three times and had buried as many husbands. The first, Robert Bath, held on the longest; their matrimony was in its third decade when the Ogallala City Alderman found himself golfing with God after ignoring the roar of approaching thunder. She kept the Bath name in recognition of his staying power, something Two and Three found themselves short on. By the time Semolina hit fifty-one, she was an expert on life insurance policies and the companies that issue them. "You hear all the time how they discriminate against people in high-risk groups. Believe me, sugar, they discriminate against widows too."

Scott wasn't exactly buying this, but he was thinking he had met a potentially useful ally in the older woman. He didn't even mind the burning in his neck and shoulders, compliments of a pinched nerve that stung like a wasp when flaring up, caused by turning his head to give Semolina the attention she deserved. "I lost my wife, too," he stated now with due solemnity, forgetting to mention it been a two-part process, with divorce preceding death.

"Bone-picking bureaucrats," Bath continued as if he hadn't spoken. "Suspicious deaths, that's what they said. Since when is it suspicious for men to have heart attacks in their forties?" Scott was assured he could safely bet his ass on the fact that she had loved Red and Garrick as much as one could love second and third husbands—screw New York Life. "And I wouldn't've loved them no less if they'd been uninsured. But that's one lesson I learned from Robert. A good marriage is only worth the value of your Whole Life policies.

"Problem is," the older woman said, "I gave the money to Hawker."

The smile was mischievous now. "You might say Danny and I have one thing in common. We both took a bath."

There was something else on the middle seat, resting next to the Marlboro pack. A flat silver flask with intricate engraving that could have been a prop in an old Western. "I never go anywhere without Jack," Semolina said when she caught him looking. "Daniels, of course."

Scott chided himself for thinking of Bath as an "older woman," realizing that she couldn't have been more than six or seven years his senior. It was easy to forget that time was so out of control. Only two more birthdays and he too would be in his fifties.

She found a book of matches in the bulky purse that complemented her figure-less figure. And if Scott didn't automatically offer to ignite the bobbing cancer agent, he refrained from sharing his opinion of slow-motion suicide. It was an opinion formed long before Philip-Morris conceded he was right, an opinion held ever since Oozin' and Upchucka had filled his new house with throat-scratching toxins.

"Thanks for picking me up, dears," Semolina was saying. "I really needed to get out of Dodge, what with the world still here and all." The smoke burned Scott's eyes. "Around here folks still know me as the wife of Robert Bath. How many times do I have to remarry, for heaven's sake?"

"The wife of Bath," Scott said. "You must get a lot of jokes."

"About what, sugar?"

♦

This wasn't the plan, thought Mary. Not even close. Semolina Bath was supposed to be concerned for the Teacher, was supposed to be eager to return to Hallelujah City and stand behind Him, all the while offering up joyful acclamations and affirmations of His greatness. Her father, meanwhile, was supposed to listen and fidget, finding himself outnumbered two to one.

But now he had an accomplice, someone to encourage, and it didn't take much in the way of encouragement for Semolina Bath to blabber and curse and lie and blaspheme. She'd been riding with them for just over an hour—an hour without a single redeeming minute. Mary was almost glad the accident had slowed them down after she first phoned the old woman, making Semolina wait just that much longer for them in the convenience store by the Ogallala off-ramp. She probably drove the clerk there crazy.

"I don't think we'll find Danny, hon," she was saying now, "whatever he said to CNN."

"Then why did he say he wanted me there?" Mary asked, but the widow didn't seem to hear.

"Time we get there he'll have barbecued paradise and flown to safety, out of the flames. Like some bird named after a place in Arizona . . . Tucson or Flagstaff . . . that's what they're saying on the news. Danny Boy gets clean away. With everything he wanted."

"And what do you think the Teacher wanted?" Mary said without looking back.

"Well, he took every quarter I earned from my insurance. So he must've liked money. And he's probably sick of sex by now, much as he was—to put it your way—corrupted. From what I saw through these baby blues, old Skeeter Peter got corrupted by every disciple less than half his age."

Another cackle. "Guess it's true what they taught us as children. God loves everyone . . . or tries to."

No, this wasn't the plan. This wasn't the plan because Semolina Bath was not the same person Mary had known at Hallelujah City. During the year they'd spent in neighboring Stations, Mary had not heard word one

about life-insurance payouts, generous bequests, or husbands dropping like gnats in a cold spell. Quite often, Disciple Bath had seemed
like a den mother, an older friend helping the others through trials
of conscience, ready to lift their spirits at the slightest flagging. Sure,
she'd been loquacious, a regular talkaholic as Cher put it. Bath seemed
to fear silence and the introspection it invited, but she was a good follower, and she'd been every bit as enthusiastic as the others about the
End of the World and all that it meant. This had been true right up
to the moment Mary dropped her off on the drive west, only—and
impossibly, four days before. Bath's parting words had been, "See you
on the other side, sweetie."

Now, Mary could see the obvious—that the high spirits she'd witnessed at Hallelujah City had come out of that same silver flask. "All
I can say is Hawker missed a damn good thing on account of his age
discrimination," Semolina Bath continued. "Youth may have a lock on
beauty, but there's nothing beautiful about inexperience. If Hawker
wanted to see God, he was looking up the wrong legs—"

A car horn blared from behind them. Mary, her concentration tinted
by red, red rage, had strayed into the passing lane.

"I'm not going to deny I can be physically demanding," the old
woman added, refusing to be interrupted by something so trivial as the
prospect of a high-speed collision. "Just ask my last two husbands."

Mary pulled back into the slow lane. "Soulless doubters," she whispered as the gold BMW shot past, the peroxide-blond infidel in the passenger seat staring back from behind dark glasses. "You're not supposed
to exist today."

After that, Mary tried harder at shutting out the serpents. She
imagined herself in a race with the coal train to their left, a wheat
field's width away. The train was favored to win. She counted the
slim green markers dotting the freeway's right shoulder, knowing
that each one put her a tenth of a mile closer to the Grand Island
exits, where she knew she'd find gas and phones. "You know," she heard
Semolina say, "Danny Boy never told me who I was supposed to rescue. Whoever it was, we didn't meet up. Guess I could've used more

detailed instructions." Mary bit her lower lip and tightened her grip on the wheel.

What if Semolina was right? she worried. What if Daniel *was* planning to destroy Hallelujah City, and He'd sent her away to keep her and the baby out of danger? Was there any chance she'd get back in time?

Daniel, I'm coming. Don't leave me on the outside.

"Garrick and I had a deal." The widow offered up another non sequitur. "Anything happened to either of us, there'd be no life support."

Don't leave me here with this.

"Nada, none."

Were the city to vanish, what would it mean?

Is this child the Redeemer?

The clock moved slowly; she was glancing too often. Like everything else in the Volkswagen bus, it had an odd, antiquated look. Round and black with only four numbers, it reminded her of the timer in her dad's electric oven. The other dashboard gauges offered even less in the way of distraction: one measured engine heat; another the pressure of oil. The odometer owned up to a scant twelve thousand miles, but only because it lacked a sixth digit to tally the missing hundreds of thousands. Her coal train pulled ahead. She checked the mirror outside her window; two semis were gaining on them. The mirror had seen its share of violence: a jagged chunk of glass had been whopped from the upper right corner, while the remaining reflection was rent into halves by a San Andreas fault of a crack that ripped through sky and fields. Clouds were bisected, blue moving vans too, then placed back together out of alignment, the tops and bottoms resisting each other like magnets with mismatched polarities.

"Remember the sheep?" Bath asked out of nowhere, exactly as Mary had been dreading she would.

Of course, she remembered the sheep. How could anyone who was there that day have forgotten? "I doubt my father is interested."

Bath didn't seem to hear. "The sky sure let loose that morning," the widow said. "But it wasn't all bad. It cooled off the trailer and called off work. No outdoor chores, no pulling up weeds or putting down seeds.

The word came down we'd use our time for prayer and Life Review. I knew that meant *indoor* chores."

Mary, too, had welcomed the rain. It was her second summer in Hallelujah City, her first as a disciple. July had been surprisingly uncomfortable, with humidity clinging the whole day through like a damp bathrobe. Mary and her Station mates—minus Cher Balser who, the whispers suggested, had received an assignment to pick up supplies in town—were folding towels when they heard a knock.

Mary opened the door to find the Teacher, framed by granite-gray drizzle and a few dozen sisters wearing black hooded raincoats. The Teacher's raincoat was yellow. He looked like a very tall grade school student, a patrol boy who'd flunked at least ten grades. She smiled when she saw the black rubber boots.

The other three disciples in Mary's Life Ark Station pressed up against her, making sure they were visible to their caller. Mary, in turn, stiffened her arms and upper body—she thought of a robin, puffing up its feathers—to secure the center position.

"Teacher?"

He said, "Today you see how my Father works."

"So it was on with the rain gear, goodbye to the grind," Bath continued her take on that day. "I got to admit I was excited . . . and more than a little curious. I thought we were going to see something nice and uplifting."

Then they were walking to the Field of the Eastern Star. In one low spot where water had pooled, Mary's boots became suction cups, trying to hold her in place. The hood of her raincoat—the Teacher called them Macs—gave her a set of blinders, eclipsing peripheral vision. Above and before her, a charcoal sky drooped to where it almost touched the trees. "It's . . . to pour," said Cassie from Missouri. Painfully shy, far worse than Mary had ever been, the seventeen-year-old spoke in her usual muffled tone, itself a sort of drizzle. It was the kind of voice that left it to listeners to fill in spaces. "Lucky . . . coats."

"We kept slogging through tall, wet grass," the widow said now. "I remember how when we got to the edge of Danny's property, he lifted the bottom of a barbed-wire fence to create an opening. 'It's okay,' he said. 'My Father owns all things.'"

Bath took a swig from her flask and coughed.

"I guess God owned a wooded area, because we found ourselves in one. All oak and elm, with the leaves growed together to make one big umbrella. Couldn't see the sky, though it still leaked plenty. We stepped on patches of dirt turning to mud, on what used to be a path. Danny kept moving at a pretty good clip. He'd been there before."

All-Knowing Father, Mary prayed silently. *Get her to stop. We don't need to hear this story now.*

"That's when old Danny started in on the preaching," Bath continued, affirming once more that God had no ear for Mary's requests. "'The mountains don't need tending. Neither do the deep places of the Earth. My Father's hands formed all things, the Gobi Desert, a kitten's whisker.' We'd just crossed into a meadow lived in by sheep that didn't seem to care for the rain."

Mary recalled the tickling sensation that ran up her arms. Apprehension mixed with anticipation, probably more of the latter.

"A handful of trees broke up the terrain. The sheep cowered under, in groups of five and six."

She glared at Bath in the rearview mirror. *For once in your life be quiet. My father doesn't need to hear the rest.*

"There was thunder in the distance," Bath said. "I looked up and saw high-voltage lines. They seemed out of place in the middle of nowhere. 'Course you might say the same about me."

Mary could picture the great iron towers, black and cold in the artificial twilight. She'd felt as if she'd entered Mordor.

Bath kept yakking. "The rain picked up even harder. Daniel told us to stand in a circle. Then we were supposed to turn round till we all faced out. Talk about tension. You could see it in the air, thick as the rain. 'Behold the flock in need of a shepherd!' Old Danny, too, was pouring it on. 'Behold the bloody family of man!'

"Well, dears, I tried my best to behold these things, but what I really beheld was the lightning's flash. I swear it x-rayed everything—

the utility poles, the trees, and the sheep. They all got jittery and skeletal."

Mary aimed for a pothole, and when that didn't work tried pumping the brakes. Bath couldn't be disrupted.

"The next one was brighter and ten times as loud. The dozen or so sheep in my line of sight quivered. Like having minor seizures, that's how it looked. But before I got through taking it in, the sheep toppled over, one right after the other. Going, going, gone."

"The sheep died?" her father asked.

"Just like Danny knew they would. I looked over at him and wanted to shout, What in blazes is going on here? But nothing came out of my mouth."

The others, Mary recalled, made up for this rare lapse. The sisters were screaming. The sisters were crying. "Jesus, don't let me die here!" shouted Cassie from Missouri. Mary screamed too, even after she realized she wasn't about to join the sheep. She wiped her eyes with the raincoat's rubber sleeve, an effort that didn't do much, and turned her head to verify what she already knew to be true. Dead sheep circled the trunk of each tree, like petals fallen from huge white roses.

A sulfur smell tainted the air, followed by that of what had to be burnt wool. She still heard sobbing from her sister believers, though it was much more subdued than before.

It took her a few minutes to grasp that they were alive not so much by the grace of God as by the insulating quality of rubber boots. It took even longer for her to notice the sputtering power line at the meadow's far end and see what had killed the sheep.

"But how could Hawker know that lightning would strike?" her father asked now.

"It wasn't the lightning," Bath replied. "It was the rain."

"The rain?"

"One of the power lines had come down," Bath said. "But not while we stood there. The strikes weren't that close. So you've got to presume the power line had already snapped. It'd been touching the ground all along, just waiting for the right combination of sheep and water."

"Meaning . . . he orchestrated the whole thing?"

"There's no way," Mary finally had to speak. "The Teacher didn't sever that power line."

"Although this clearly occurred to you at the time?" Dad said smugly.

"There's just no way."

"That smell, the insanity," said the widow, leaning forward. "The crazy part was, why did we stick around afterward? Why didn't we all just scram? There's the real madness."

Leave it to Bath to exhume these questions—and leave it to Dad to add an obvious "How could you stay? How could any of you have stayed? I don't understand."

No, of course you don't. You weren't there. And even if you had been— So what if Mary had been repulsed by the dying sheep? So what if she'd been frightened and confused? When she turned to the Teacher for an explanation, lightning again swapped white for black and turned human flesh to marble that's been loved by a sculptor's hand. In that instant Mary saw something Scott Chambers and Semolina Bath could never see under any circumstance, owing to the blindness they so proudly shared.

Mary beheld the face of God.

It wasn't just that the Teacher looked like a movie star cast in the role of Savior; He always looked like that. Standing in that field, in that dark, killing rain, Mary's eyesight played only a small, small part. What she took in she took in with her entire being—and it was magnificent. Power, grace, *certainty.* Like she had never known. Like others could never imagine.

There it was, the light that shone from within and without, the fire that singed every eye lucky enough to come too close. And before the sky had a chance to roar "I am," Mary was transformed, either that or she realized how much she had changed since coming to Hallelujah City. Her nascent, shifting faith had been replaced by something solid and whole. It had become the rock that stands firm in the flood's swelling rage. "I am!"

The hair on her arms still tingled, and would continue to do so for days. While savoring Daniel's Sermons by the Lake—and lingering in the weightless well-being of Illuminary Essence—Mary wondered if the change had been physical as well as psychological, if the surge hadn't penetrated her boots and altered her atomic makeup. She thought about electricity and how it moved everything, how it was pretty much everywhere. She recalled the high-school science teachers who once numbed her with trivia. They seemed to know what electricity did, but none had come close to explaining what it was.

Now, Mary knew.

"Makes you wonder what else he's capable of," Bath said, once more interrupting her thoughts.

"Sheep die every day," Mary said. "Just like your husbands. Wouldn't you prefer to know there's someone in control? That there's something behind all this seeming disorder?"

"You're not saying you stayed—"

"Yes, Dad. *Because* of what I saw. Not *in spite* of."

After that day, they didn't see rain for weeks. Mary felt certain the sheep had been transported to another world, that their souls were all right. God was not cruel. Come nightfall, during the Sermons by the Lake, fireflies jumped from star to star. When Daniel reached the call-and-response portion—"Who will live and die for glory?"—Mary responded so loudly she couldn't hear the others. "I will live and die for you! I will live and die for you!"

◆

Bath lit cigarette number five, ending the drama. She'd only given her dad six and a half minutes to step in and show his gallantry. Good thing he didn't have any. Mary felt a burning in her nose and eyes, the first exhalation having gone right for her head. She rolled down her window, surprised at the force required to get it started.

Scott and the widow had been quiet for several minutes. Mary's last comments had seen to that. The peace, of course, couldn't last.

"You need some help with that window, hon?" Semolina asked, without leaning forward to back the offer. "What's holding this thing together anyway? Sounds like it's missing a few bolts." She followed the observation with a prolonged coughing fit. It had to be painful—embarrassing, too. But Dad was laughing at the stupid "bolts" comment. Mary's teeth dug deeper.

"I've never been one for America's car culture," he said, as would anyone who still drove a twelve-year-old Civic. "What is it but marketing—a kind of fashion shopping for men? But still . . . one might expect God to own a nicer car."

Semolina chuckled. "Are you sure this handsome gentleman is really your father?"

"Oh puke," Mary whispered, now glaring at the postmenopausal Lolita in the inside rearview mirror. It was time to unleash the words she'd been holding back, words picked up from a Sermon by the Lake: *Deuterogamy isn't a book in the Bible.*

But Mary was silenced—as was her father—when Semolina revealed that "Danny could probably afford a BMW bus, if there is such a thing." She had given the Teacher almost two million dollars. "One-point-seven to be exact. It's probably in Switzerland. Waiting for Danny. I should've supported the A.S.P.C.A. I don't know—Habitat for Humanity or something."

"How about the F.T.A.D.H.?" Mary's father suggested.

"The F.T. what?"

"Free Thinkers Against Dan Hawker. Scott Chambers, President for Life."

"She's not your type," Mary said to her father. "Stop trying to impress her." She adjusted the mirror until she was looking straight into Semolina's face. "Maybe if you'd kept the insurance checks. Then he might like you. Dad here covets the one thing he's always pretended to hate. He wishes he had money."

"Well, right now, sugar, so do I. And if that lying, lecherous, made-for-TV messiah hasn't had the sense to crawl under a rock and hide, I'm going to get mine back."

Her father grabbed the steering wheel. "Jesus, Mary, watch the road," he said.

◆

The widow was laughing at one of Scott's better one-liners when the Volkswagen's tires banged into the curb, causing the bus to bounce back a few inches before wheezing to a stop in front of the Kwik Fix convenience store. Scott didn't have to ask for the keys. Mary seemed to be aiming for an eye when she threw them at him. Then she was gone, out of the bus, into the building.

"She sure needed to go," Semolina said without looking up. She was rummaging through her purse again. Finding another cigarette pack, she gave it a quick shake, then pushed it back down, inventory complete.

"She needs something all right," he said, not wishing to discuss the root causes of incontinence. Stepping outside, he was caught by surprise—they must have changed seasons as well as time zones. His coat went on for the first time that day, losing a half-empty bag of M&Ms in the process. He opened the side door for his new acquaintance. "She also needed a phone," he said, taking Semolina's hand. "She's still trying to call someone."

Climbing out of the Volkswagen bus took intense concentration on the widow's part. Her high-heeled boot poked tentatively into the air, as if she were preparing to step onto ice. "Maybe she's got the number for Danny's hotline," she said, her leg finally bending at the knee. "There was only one phone as far as I knew." The other leg wasn't so fussy. Its boot caught up quickly to the first, and was nearly on the pavement. Semolina slid forward, gingerly.

"If it's Hawker she's calling," Scott said, "he's not picking up."

That was when Semolina lost her balance, stumbling then leaning then surging forward, a tsunami wave of blue-green blouse, dotted with dozens of tiny white flowers, more vivid than before. Doing his best to remain upright, Scott felt her full weight pressed against his. He stiffened his legs, leaned into the swell and held his breath, expecting to crumble like a sand-bucket sculpture.

He was still standing. *They* were still standing. She sighed in relief; her breath warmed his ear. But she quickly pulled back. "What's this, Scott hon?" Looking both startled and intrigued, she slipped a hand inside his hip pocket, the one that held his secret. "Are you happy to see me, or is this what I think it is?"

He looked around nervously. "Protection," he said. "I . . . have enemies."

She smiled slyly. "You're not thinking of taking revenge on old Danny Boy?"

"I don't know what you mean."

The smile was still there. "Don't worry, doll." She used the fingers of both hands to turn an invisible key in an imaginary padlock. Then, getting her hands mixed up, she pretended to swallow the padlock.

CHAPTER ELEVEN

"This is Adrian C. Hummel. I'm not in right now but—"

"Sorry." He'd picked up his phone. "I was indisposed."

"Adrian!"

"Mary?"

"Will you accept the charges for a collect call from—"

"You bet. Mary, where are you?"

"Try stuck in a steel cage with a pair of infidels. Contestant Number Two's a professional widow." She looked inside the Kwik Fiks store. Her passengers had not yet come out of their respective restrooms. "That secret route you know. Can you help get me in?"

"My pleasure," said Adrian. "But you need to hurry. Something's going on there, something strange."

"How do you know that?"

"I'm an author, remember? You're not my only contact."

Mary didn't respond; she was wondering who his other contacts were.

Adrian continued. "He's trying to provoke the federal agents, à la Waco. You're not going to believe this, but he executed his neighbor's cows."

"Oh no."

"Mary, do you know something? This isn't something that goes on up there, is it? Sacrificing livestock?"

After catching her breath, she said, "Give me credit, Adrian. Give us credit. You don't think they might be making these things up? To give themselves an excuse to go in?"

"I just know there's some weird stuff going on inside. I don't know if Hawker's planning to fight or pull a Jim Jones. I haven't seen any Kool-Aid delivery trucks, but he might have stocked up for a rainy day."

"Careful," said Mary, but she wasn't really bothered by his sacrilege.

It was good to hear Adrian's voice. For nearly two years—really, since their third or fourth meeting—he'd been a comfortable, predictable part of her life. She'd felt bad when he got exiled and never once regretted their meetings at the edge of Hallelujah City. Waiting by the Field of the Eastern Star, he was ready to listen to her smallest concerns—a service no one provided inside. He in turn loved catching up on "palace intrigues," as he referred to conflicts in Hallelujah City, though he promised to "never repeat gossip" in his book. "I'm a professional," he told her once. "A journalist. It's my job to listen, not judge."

Even so, she'd never shared news—the sheep for example—that could be misinterpreted by the doubters.

"I tried calling you before," Mary said now, into the pay phone. "They told me your line was busy."

"Mama," he said. "Tying up the line."

"Did you know the Teacher's been asking for me?"

"He is? I mean, yes, he is. I heard that. All the more reason for me to help. The press get hold of you, you're as dead as a fox with its leg in a trap. They'll use you to hurt Daniel. You know that."

Then he was asking, "How close are you? There might not be much time."

"Grand Island. Nebraska."

"How far is that from Omaha? Can you get to an airport?"

She looked off into the distance, across fallow gray fields. A stand of wind turbines added a second dimension to the horizon, which elsewhere came close to being a perfect straight line. "You don't think there's any chance of Daniel taking off?" she asked.

"Why? What do you know?"

"Nothing," she said. "Just the widow. She's trying to drive me *Girl, Interrupted* by saying He'll be gone."

Through the glass, Mary saw Semolina Bath walk out of the ladies' room—and go straight for the candy aisle. Then Semolina was weighing her choices, assigning a disproportionate gravity to each type of snack. She'd stop, stare, reach without grabbing, then move a few feet to her left or right to consider new sources of nonnutrition. Finally, she did exactly what Mary had been expecting her to do. She failed to make a choice. The insatiable Bath simply went for the works, picking up Cracker Jack, Cheetos, Twizzlers, and three brightly packaged candy bars. But her hands weren't so full as to prevent her from heading to the pour-your-own fountain to score a forty-ounce soft drink. Diet, of course.

When Mary caught sight of her own reflection, guilt struck like a gust of wind. She had never understood her own anger, her petulance . . . her hypocritical need to judge. Since when had she been pleased with her own body? And when over the past three years had she not hungered for chocolate-chip cookie dough and all the other temptations now just beyond the storefront glass? The widow, at least, seemed secure with her own presence. She didn't go on diets, trying to reign herself in. Her desires and passions needed room.

Semolina juggled her rations, moving slowly to the register without spilling a single Snickers bar. Watching this display, Mary was revisited by a familiar thought. What would her mother have been like if she'd lived? Was everyone programmed to age as sloppily as Semolina Bath and her father? Or was there such a thing as graceful atrophy? Daniel, of course, was technically the same age as her dad, but He didn't count. He was of two worlds—the physical and the spiritual. He was simultaneously forty-eight and ageless. Somehow, this made Him look like He was in His mid-thirties. God, apparently, went easy on His direct descendants as they advanced through middle age.

She could feel Daniel watching her, could feel the warmth of His blue, blue eyes, as if He were right there in the Kwik Fiks lot.

"Mary?" Adrian C. Hummel was close to shouting. "Are you there?"

"Daniel?"

"Yes, I told you. He's still here."

Semolina came out the glass front door, pushing with a backside that doubled as a public-service billboard showing the more visible side effects of gluttony. *Hypocrite, hypocrite.* She placed her candy on the Volkswagen's roof. The ridiculous paper cup stayed in her hands as she surveyed the parking lot and adjoining fast-food restaurants—a

McDonald's and Taco Bell—but she didn't take a sip. Turning in Mary's direction, she asked, "Whose ear you chewing, hon?"

Mary gave her a look that said, *Can't you see I'm on the phone?* and turned her back to the widow. "I really need to lose these two," she whispered into the mouthpiece.

"So do it, get rid of the baggage. Then call me from an airport."

"Dad's got the keys," she said just as Semolina figured out that phone calls were ordinarily limited to two participants and moved a few feet away. "Won't leave me alone with them."

"Say, Mary. Why does your friend think Hawker might bolt?"

"She's just nuts," Mary said, lowering her voice. "She thinks Daniel was always in it for the money."

"Money?"

"She's the one who gave it to Him. Almost two million."

"That's money." Once again, she heard excitement in Adrian's voice. "Enough to buy a new life, someplace warm. Maybe slip out while the compound burns."

"Tell me you're not buying this."

"No, no, of course not," he said with considerably less enthusiasm. "Just trying to make sense of your friend's goofy theory."

"She's not my friend. And another thing—"

"Yeah?"

"Don't call it a compound."

"You need to get up here fast," he said. "Drive to the nearest airport and call me from there. But try to be invisible. Don't say your name too loud."

◆

Scott had waited four minutes for the stall in the men's room, time enough one might have thought for the previous occupant to pollute each last molecule of breathable air *and* flush his waste. Scott pushed the lever the three-hundred-pound man had apparently found immovable and tried holding his breath, a feat he nearly pulled off. Then, his fingers trembled as he tucked his gun into a sweat sock to give it more padding and make it less conspicuous. The barrel snagged; he worried about it discharging.

"Self protection," Scott whispered to himself. "We all need to be protected from our selves."

He was thinking now of Semolina Bath and the threat she represented. Scott rarely liked people the first time he met them, or for that matter, the second and third times. Yet, he liked Semolina. He simply wished that he could trust her.

CHAPTER TWELVE

"**D**ear God." Adrian C. Hummel was praying. "Watch over Mary on her flight out of Omaha. Keep her safe and punctual." Adrian had always considered himself a believer (of the real God, he would have been quick to add, the one who didn't live on a rundown farm in northern Minnesota). But before leaving Florida, he'd never felt a need for prayer, primarily because he'd never needed anything from God. In Trappers Point, he prayed often. Today, he finished with something new: "Thank you."

Adrian was back at the Trappers Point Diner, though he had yet to see Bev this visit. The sign on the door still read Closed, but he'd found the door itself unlocked. His neck was aching again; he considered applying some ice. From time to time, he thought he heard the hum of a massage chair coming from behind the green door to Bev's private quarters.

Adrian sat at his usual table in his corner of the diner, his cell phone, digital recorder, legal pad, and bottle of caffeine pills arranged left to right, in that order, on the blue-and-white checkered tablecloth that matched the window curtains behind him. His laptop was up and glowing. Every other time he'd come here, he'd switched off the cell phone to prevent the risk of speaking with representatives of Citibank and Interlink. Today, he felt ready to face that danger.

A cheesy thrift-store light fixture meant to look like a cheesy thrift-store candelabra had been mounted, crookedly, on the wall to his left, a foot above his head. One of two bulbs had burned out before Adrian first ate in the diner, and there were two more empty sockets. But the one working bulb more than compensated for this pattern of neglect. It burned, it blazed—and basically provided way too much illumination for glasses and plates that were cleaner when dark. Adrian, however, had been drawn to its light from day one. The table seemed perfect for writing. It looked like a writer's table.

It was where he'd typed his Introduction, many months before.

Using the 800 numbers scribbled on the back of a business card, he made three more reservations for Mary Chambers out of Omaha's Eppley Airfield, two to Minneapolis, one to Fargo. Now all he had to do was wait and let everything fall neatly in place. He looked at his Hooters (Sarasota) bottle opener/key ring lying next to the phone. *Where it's always Spring Break.* Everything in place; Adrian was ready.

He smiled, a rarity in itself these days. And he whispered, sincerely, "Thank you, Mary."

The green door opened. "Are you hungry?" Bev asked as she emerged. "I could fix us something to eat."

A few minutes later they were dining on reheated meatloaf. It marked the first time he'd seen Bev use a microwave. She had joined him at his table. The food tasted great.

"So where were we?" she asked.

He shoveled a decent-sized chunk into his mouth and chewed rapidly. After swallowing, again too hurriedly, and taking a drink from his Coke, he said, "It was my fourth day in Trappers Point. Just as I'd been told to, I showed up at Hawker's compound at five in the morning. The air was icy, the school bus dark. I parked my car a few hundred feet shy of the blocked-off entrance. I pulled it as far as I could off the side of the road, where the ditch wasn't that deep. I hid my keys in a shrub nearby. I didn't want anyone to touch them once I was inside."

Bev laughed. "You left a new Jaguar on a dirt road?"

"This isn't Miami. I didn't think you had car thieves here."

"What about drunks who think they're hunters? They've got a thing for still targets, don't you know. Worse if they see something shiny, like a headlight or mirror."

He had to admit he hadn't considered the possibility of bullet damage at the time. But he had seen leaving his car on County Road CC as a calculated risk, which translated further into, there were no good choices. When Adrian worked in Starke, the First Union Bank had sent at least one repo man to steal his car. He'd assumed they hadn't forgotten him—and that repo men were available for hire in Minnesota.

Instead of explaining this rationale, Adrian told Bev, "I tried to make it as inconspicuous as possible. Parked way off to the side."

"I get it," she said, though the incredulous smile made him think she didn't. "What happened next?"

"I waited six glacial hours."

"Glacial?"

"Slow moving and cold. It was time enough to realize they were testing my sincerity. I was close to giving up, in actual fact, when I saw the young woman from the day before. 'I'm Disciple Cher,' she said as she approached on foot. 'Welcome to Hallelujah City.'

"She led me to a doublewide trailer, the kind poor people live in. 'Hurricane bait,' my pa used to call them, and he was hardly rich. Cher told me this would be my Life Ark Station. 'Last stop before home.' She didn't mention it would also be Life Ark Station to five other men and a child. The kid was still in diapers, and he had to be four. His father ignored him completely. During my stay, I saw no other small children in the compound."

Bev interjected, "I read somewhere Hawker don't like kids."

"That would make sense, the way he kept husbands separated from their wives. What better way to keep children from occurring?" He looked at Bev's plate. She'd barely touched her food. "Over the next few days, Hawker kept testing my sincerity. How? By treating a professional journalist like any other enlistee. Denied an audience with the messiah, I couldn't even get close during the sermons that ran for nearly an hour each evening. I stood at the back."

Adrian didn't tell Bev how he'd drawn comfort from the fact that the rabble was almost entirely female and young.

"The sermons themselves ranged from hard-on-the-ears to mesmerizing. There were times I could see why a smart young man like your Gunt would be sucked in. But even when things got weird in there, I remained optimistic. And why not? Less than two weeks had passed since I'd landed the advance for my book." He sneezed and reached for a napkin. "When Mary Chambers befriended me, I assumed it was at Hawker's bidding. She came out of nowhere. God Boy had to be feeling me out. Play my cards right, and I'd become the insider I was under contract to become."

"This Mary?" Bev said. "She's someone important?"

Wiping his upper lip with a second napkin, Adrian nodded. He said, "Though reluctant at first, Mary seemed glad to make a new friend. She also seemed nice, a trait that didn't do much for me. From all I've ever observed, nice just makes you a bad judge of character. It makes you join cults, makes you trust shysters like Daniel Hawker. But as resources went, the girl was golden. Hawker, I could see, had singled her out.

"Over time, I acquired a more complex view of the girl. What I'd first seen as sweetness revealed itself as guardedness. Mary Chambers needed approval. She kept opinions to herself to avoid disappointment."

"Disappointment?"

"In not getting that approval. At home. I blame it on her father." Though Adrian could have talked for hours on the topic of screwed-up fathers, he knew better than to start. "Let me read you something from my book," he said, while pulling his laptop closer. He spoke out loud as he clicked the built-in mouse pad. "*Folder—Last Days. File—*Here we go, *Introduction.*"

He felt pride as he began reading, "*If the girl from Colorado seemed too smart to voluntarily commit herself to this madhouse, it's not like we're dealing with some run-of-the-mill cult leader. As smart as he is slick, Daniel Hawker boasts charisma enough for five false prophets. The author personally witnessed the charm and experienced the charisma (if only from a distance). He also heard the taped original music, listened to it, in actual fact, with pure objectivity.*" Turning to Bev and winking, Adrian added, "Sometimes it helps to dislike music."

He read again from the screen, "*Hawker, for all it's worth, is a talented composer and player. Complex and diverse, his music incorporates a variety of classical elements.*"

The author smiled, recalling how his girlfriend at North Florida (the one who'd pushed him into the music appreciation class) would melt whenever he talked like this. Tam could never fully believe he didin't care for music.

"*One only needs to hear past the New Age veneer,*" he resumed. "*That simply comes from Hawker's reliance on synthesized keyboards. The foundation itself supports more melody than most jazz, and far more sophistication than blues or early rock. Which isn't to say Hawker is above tossing in a few pentatonic or heptatonic melodies. The composer uses anything and everything, shifting tempo and scale (major, minor, chromatic, you name it) even more often than he employs modulation. The dynamics (the rises and falls, sighs and explosions) could come straight from the one composer Hummel identifies with, the one who didn't have to listen to his own compositions.*"

Adrian added an aside for Bev's sake, "I never bought into that *inner ear* crap. Though no one else seems to understand this, once Beethoven lost his hearing, he saw music exactly the way I do, as math, as language, as markings on paper that affect smart people in stupid ways. God Boy sure sees it that way." He returned his gaze to the screen.

"*Because just like history's favorite deaf composer, Hawker knows how and when to manipulate reactions: You're weak, you're small, and now, thanks to me, you have joined the greater whole. Like closing with a battle hymn or national anthem. Get on your feet. Go, team, go.*"

Adrian looked up at Bev and realized he was losing his audience. Her eyes had that faraway look, much like the mounted stag head that watched over her dining area from the back wall. With two clicks from the mouse, he closed his file and folder.

"I'd been there three weeks," he said, "getting closer every day. Then I got busted. It was late afternoon. The men were wrapping up chores, sorting the mushrooms the women had gathered. I slipped off for a bathroom break. The Inner Sanctum looked deserted. I changed directions. Moments later, I was standing in the shadow of Hawker's modest ranch house. Light was coming from a basement window, its curtain barely parted. Interpreting this as good fortune, I lowered myself into the window well."

"What did you see?"

"An evasive cult leader, sitting at a desk, just off to my left, where he appeared to be sorting a stack of sheet music. I couldn't make out the titles or credits on the paper. The pages looked old and congested with notes.

"That's when I felt a hand on my shoulder, a massive hand, a boulder with grip. One of the sentries had snuck up behind me. I heard the word, spy, maybe five or six times, as he yanked me from the well and dragged me round the house.

"'I didn't see anything,' I protested as I was thrown to the gravel in front of the Inner Sanctum. When I told him the Teacher would have his ass, I felt a boot heel grinding in between my shoulder blades."

"Hawker stood over me, scowling. 'Precisely whose ass am I going to have?' he asked. My back hurt like hell. The goofy plastic keys seemed larger from my angle.

"Looking past him to the extent I could, I saw how the gravel filled out a large circle, a turnaround that doubled as junkyard. God Boy didn't take care of his toys. A black El Camino crouched on flat tires. A lime-green Toronado reminded me of a high-school buddy, a poor one who lived in a trailer court. And as far as the Corvair and Plymouth Horizon went, who paid money to keep junkers like those running?

"There was one more car, in actual fact, invisible beneath a protective tarp. But I recognized the shape. My Jaguar XK8 Roadster. Hawker had taken it, worthless cockbite. Sorry, Bev."

"So what did you do?" Bev asked.

"I told them I'd seen an injured bird in the window well. I felt more than a little defiant, after seeing my car. 'I had to help,' I said. 'Like Jesus would have.'

"The sentry behind me snarled, telling Hawker he'd seen no bird. The heel dug deeper.

"'And *I* didn't see anything,' I maintained with the breath I had left, '*while I was down there saving the bird.*'

"It didn't seem to help that, apart from the bit about the injured bird, I believed my own defense. I hadn't seen anything odd or deserving of suspicion. Had I?

"Hawker finally spoke, the voice of God, definitive, final. There was no bird.

"'How could you know?' I asked, and he told me he knew all things.

"I immediately regretted my response: 'Then why all the questions? Why don't you just tell me what I saw?'

"The boot moved to the back of my head, pressing my face deep into the gravel. Hawker asked the questions now, and these had to do with *why* I'd been spying. My body quaked—with anger, not fear. I was sure I'd have new dimples in my cheeks and chin.

"They had me believing I *had* stumbled onto something. If only I could figure out what that something had been.

"'I told you,' I spat through gritted teeth and gravel, 'I was trying to rescue a bird.'

"A second guard joined the brutality. He kneeled on my back, like some kid trying to squeeze the last air from his inflatable pool toy. I repeated my alibi. He pushed down harder. 'We could stay here forever,' I heard one of them say. 'Or until you get tired of lying and hurting.'"

Taking a break to finish the last few bites on his plate, Adrian enjoyed Bev's impatience more than the meatloaf. No doubt about it, he'd won back his listener.

He washed the food down with Coke and resumed. "The pain was almost unbearable."

"And you couldn't move?"

"'I'll tell you what I saw,' I said at last, and the boot on my skull relaxed its hold. Then, while trying my best to look up at the so-called Teacher, I made my confession. 'I saw sheet music, that's all, proof that you're a musician.'

"I swear Hawker seemed disappointed. It was something in his eyes. Lamenting, 'I had plans for you, Novice Adrian,' he quietly slipped away. As for me, I was hoisted to my feet. Within seconds, a beat-up old Datsun pulled onto the circle. Two additional felons sat in the small red car, more than filling the front seats. My guard popped open the right rear door and stuffed me inside. 'Wait,' I demanded. 'Where are you taking me? *I didn't see anything.*' The giant squeezed in beside me, and we moved, if just barely. We couldn't have been going five miles an hour. And even then, the car bottomed out a few times. When we came to a stop, a few minutes later, I knew where we were. A school bus blocked the road. Without warning or farewell, the guards shoved me back out. For the second time that day, I fell face forward to the gravel, a kid going down at recess.

"The driver said something that made no sense: I'd have to toss his salad if I ever came back. His cohorts joined in, shouting nonsense like 'prison buffet' and 'all you can eat.'

"I rose to my feet and brushed off my pants, trying to regain some dignity. 'What about my car?' I shouted.

The Datsun pulled away, still bottoming out on the more pronounced bumps. As soon as they were gone from sight, I limped my way to where I'd parked the Jaguar. A few more labored steps and I found my keys. Right where I left them. One of Hawker's thugs must have hotwired the car."

"They really stole your car?" Bev asked.

"And I still owed more than Blue Book. Believe me, whenever the banks call about that one, I tell them, 'Be my guest. I'll give your repo man directions to where I keep it parked.'"

"I guess I'm not surprised," she said. "Not after what I saw this morning. They didn't seem too big on their *Thou shalt not's*."

"It all made for one long, hard walk back to the highway." Adrian continued his story. "Some of the gravel had dug in pretty deep."

"You walked to the Valfaard?"

"I got a reporter to give me a lift. I let him believe I had the goods on Hawker."

"The goods?"

"By the time we got to the motel, he couldn't wait to let me out. Probably the bleeding. I wasn't the neatest passenger."

Bev got up to clear the plates, carrying them to the diner's recessed kitchen. When Adrian heard the sound of water running, he welcomed the timing, because the next part of his story seemed better left private. *Take your time, Bev. Make sure you get that ketchup off.*

◆

The morning after his expulsion from the compound, Adrian paid the Valfaard's desk clerk fifty dollars to drive him into Canterbury. They got lost a few times, relying on his cell phone to regain bearings. Finally, they found the Greyhound station (which was better described as an elderly woman sitting at an old wooden desk near the back of a convenience store, just outside the restrooms). Six hours and twenty-three minutes later, he began the journey to Tallahassee. Without including transfers in Chicago and Atlanta, he counted sixteen stops. His mother was watching his wide-screen TV from her place in the massage chair when he walked in and surprised her. "I believe Dad left me the pickup truck," he said. "I'll need it to take my belongings to Minnesota. Things are moving fast. I've already met the leader, one on one, just as I had planned."

Mama wore a breezy (translucent) bathrobe, a moonlight white. She held a glass of wine, purple in color. Her long, bluish hair had not been brushed yet that day, and the tan on her face and arms made her look sixty-five, a twelve-year increase. He knew the effect she was after, this borderline alcoholic widow of an adulterous furnace repairman. Evelyn Charlize Hummel saw herself as the faded southern belle.

"The TV and chair?" she drawled sweetly, and he knew this wasn't her first glass of wine. "I could ship them, you know. How much could it possibly cost?"

"They're going with me in the truck," he said. "First thing tomorrow."

Unable to sleep, he set off just after midnight on what turned out to be the most ass-numbing trip of all. His last remaining prized possessions rode in the back, tied down, covered up, and making it impossible for him to leave the truck unguarded for more than a speedy bathroom stop. When he arrived back at the Valfaard Inn twenty-eight hours later, he prayed for the first time since he was a child. "Dear God, you can stop testing me any time now. I could use a break."

◆

Returning to Adrian's table, but without reclaiming her seat, Bev asked, "So what's the story with this Mary? How'd you hook up with her?"

"It started after you got your brother to let me cross his property," Adrian said. "On my third trip to the compound's southern border, I spotted Mary Chambers, out for a walk. She recognized me, asked where I'd gone. She sympathized when I told her I'd been expelled for trying to save an injured bird."

"Nice," Bev said.

"We agreed to meet there every few weeks. It became more regular when you started taking packages to Gunt."

"What about your other contact? Wasn't there a girl you met in town?"

"That one didn't work out so well." He took another sip from his Coke, while Bev reached down to pull at the edge of the plastic table-cloth, trying, he guessed, to remove a crease.

"And that's how you did it?" she said.

He laughed into his half-empty glass. "Which? Infiltrated the compound? Screwed up my big chance? Got a headache that lasted for weeks?"

This time when Bev got up, she headed for the green door. "You're welcome to stay out here, don't you know," she said before vanishing.

◆

Now that Bev was in her private quarters, Adrian was grateful she hadn't asked *why* his arrangement with the "other contact" hadn't worked out.

When Cher Balser first called Adrian in May of last year, he looked for significance in her timing. Since his expulsion, eleven months had passed, none of them gracefully. The summer had come and gone with its sportsmen and bugs. Fall became winter, and winter spring, though most of the changes were imperceptible to Adrian's senses. It got cold. It stayed cold.

As for the world inside Room 17 of the Valfaard Inn, Adrian no longer owned a wide-screen TV and massage chair. His reserve fund had dwindled, and the credit-card companies no longer sent cash advance paper checks. He'd gained seventeen pounds from eating at Bev's diner, and he didn't need a book on interpreting dreams to figure out the nightmare he'd been having, the one that made it impossible to fall back asleep. On more nights than not, he ran down the hard clay bed of an empty irrigation ditch, its banks collapsing behind him.

He'd done what he could to keep *The Last Days* breathing, mostly by repeating the same weary Internet searches. But he found few details to fill out the outline that was God Boy's pre-messianic life. Predictably, no hits were scored on DANIEL + HAWKER + FLORIDA + SCANDAL. Less predictably, he'd uncovered no specifics on Hawker's stint as a session musician. This left Adrian with questions and theories. Had Hawker worked under a different name? Had he only backed singers and songwriters whose CDs were released directly into oblivion? Or had he been difficult to work with, resulting in his parts being scrubbed and redone by other musicians?

The Internet had established Hawker's presence at Disneyland, if not its sister theme park in Florida. Scrolling through a site called disneyfan.com, a webshrine devoted to *Walt Disney and his lasting imprint on modern culture*, Adrian came across a *high-resolution scan of a vintage nineteen-year-old flyer recently auctioned by Sotheby's online (image exclusive to disneyfan.com)*. And as easy as it would have been to miss a small item buried in its text, his eyes went straight to *Mind Reading! Sleight of Hand! Balloon Animals! Marvel at the magic of Dan Hawker! Every afternoon outside the Kodak store.* Unfortunately, subsequent Yahoo! and Google searches for other performers mentioned in the promotional piece (excluding Mickey, Donald, and Goofy) turned up nothing. This left it to Adrian to phone hundreds of Californians who shared names with the performers, using numbers he'd saved from the Yahoo! White Pages for the Greater Los Angeles Metropolitan Area. After being chewed out by thirty-two Mike Connelly's and eighty-six Bob Carr's, Adrian came up empty again. *Help me, Jesus. You know what I'd give for a firsthand account of the miracle worker's apprenticeship.*

Apart from that find and the few details provided by Mary, Adrian had squat on Hawker's life before Minnesota, not even a birthplace. All he knew was that Hawker had briefly resided in England, on a street named Portobello, where he supposedly picked up an accent. (Adrian couldn't recall hearing a British accent during his one less-than-satisfactory encounter with God Boy.) Mary also reported that Hawker's mother was dead, a fact that resonated with the girl from Colorado. (Mary had also lost her mother.)

As for Hawker's alleged time in Florida, Adrian had not been able to confirm this. If only he'd thought to pump his former colleague for information at the appropriate time, specifically, *before* he stabbed Benmont duBlanc in the back. *What exactly is the rumor about Hawker and Disney World? What got him in trouble? Where did you hear it?*

By the time Cher Balser contacted Adrian, Hawker had already announced his schedule for Armageddon (effectively, Adrian's deadline for getting his insider's account). "Four seasons and one," God Boy had apparently preached.

By the time Cher contacted Adrian, in actual fact, nearly two of those seasons had passed. Still, the call that originated from the pay phone outside the Gas 'N' Pass convenience store gave him hope. It also gave him plenty to think about. In addition to the *Why now?* there was also, *Why me?* And more to the point, *Why Cher?* Apart from showing him to his trailer that very first day, Cher had not talked with Adrian once inside the compound.

God Boy must have set up the contact. But toward what end? Was he trying to repair damage? Would Adrian get his exclusive access?

The first meeting with Cher clocked in at less than two minutes. "I need to talk," she said. "There's a lot I have to tell you."

"So tell me."

"No time." Then, with audible pride, she revealed, "There'll be other chances. I'm the only believer entrusted to come into town for supplies." He knew better than to ask if her sense of power wasn't tempered somewhat by making the trip behind the wheel of an ancient lime-green Toronado.

Through May and June, he saw her every other Friday on the north side of Gas 'N' Pass. Cher, Adrian learned, had come to Minnesota with Mary, same day, same sky-blue school bus. The two had been good friends, in actual fact. "Past tense," his new source emphasized. "She's got Daniel fooled. He can't see through her like the rest of us." Cher believed that the relationship between Hawker and Mary had turned sexual. But despite Cher's stewing resentment, the affair sounded tame to Adrian's ears.

Sometimes, after meeting with Cher, Adrian felt like his younger self, oozing with self-assurance, ready to take on every sniveling French Club President in America. And why not? Hawker was opening doors for him, even if Cher wasn't telling him much he didn't already know about the compound. If Adrian could just exercise a modicum of patience this time, he'd be sitting with God Boy, one on one, his recorder faintly purring.

So why was he sleeping less and less? Why wouldn't the nightmare leave him alone . . . and why had some raccoon decided to scratch at his door every third or fourth night, like a cat wanting inside? Twice, Adrian had been brave enough (and fast enough) to yank open that door. But the critter was faster. Twice, he saw nothing.

On the first Friday in July, Cher greeted Adrian by saying, "I'm not sure this is safe."

"But I . . . Hawker didn't sanction these meetings?"

"You're kidding, right?"

Adrian suggested they relocate to the alley behind his motel. "No one will see us there."

"Next time," she said, already turning to go.

"If you're not doing this for him, why are you here?"

"Because." She waited a few seconds before resuming. "You're writing the book. I seem to be the only one in Hallelujah City who appreciates this and how it could help. I don't want it to be Mary's story." This left Adrian to wonder if Cher knew about his meetings with the Chambers girl. "I want it to be Daniel's story." *Yeah, and maybe a little bit Cher's story*, he thought.

By that time, Adrian understood the schism between Mary and

Cher. The former wanted power, wanted to be the second most important member of God Boy's cult. Mary, on the other hand, had fallen for her Teacher in more ways than one.

Adrian asked Cher, "Why didn't you contact me earlier?"

"The press used to follow me into town. It took them forever to lose interest in me. They learned they couldn't break me, that I was too loyal."

The meetings continued for thirteen more weeks, with the last rendezvous taking place inside Room 17 of the Valfaard Inn. That was when he learned how much Cher liked Mogan David blackberry wine.

Freed by the contents of that bottle he'd picked up for eight dollars at Gas 'N' Pass—and, Adrian surmised, by a growing sense of betrayal—Cher finally opened up. She spoke of her upbringing in Aurora, Colorado, of losing her virginity at fourteen, of wanting to be an actress. As she rambled, Cher drummed on the edge of Adrian's table with her fingers. This was one of her nervous habits. He'd witnessed it before, outside the convenience store, when she tapped unconsciously on the dumpster's lid.

Cher boasted about her status in the compound. "Daniel anointed me one of The Seven."

"You talked about The Original Seven," Adrian said. "In our earlier meetings."

"Three of them deserted."

"So he dropped the *Original*?"

She tapped in the affirmative.

"And added three new members?"

"Just me so far. I think he'd like to keep The Seven smaller from now on . . . What? You think that's funny?"

Things got interesting when Cher gave him a peek at Hawker's sexual proclivities (of which, apparently, there were many). Threesomes, foursomes, and occasionally moresomes, Hawker indulged an insatiable appetite for all things sensual. Cher spoke proudly of being among the most dedicated of followers at sating that appetite.

Mary didn't appear in these stories, and Cher left out few details. If anything, Adrian could see, Mary's (alleged) affair with Hawker would have seemed tame in a chapter devoted to God Boy's carnality.

"Forgive my ignorance," Adrian said at last, "but a holy man . . . a holy place. What about morality?"

"God's children aren't bound by the rules of man."

"The Bible?"

"Man's Bible. Didn't men criticize Jesus for taking an interest in Mary Magdalene?"

"Thou shall not—"

"You have to be married to commit adultery."

"I don't follow."

"Marriage *is* sacred," she said. "No question there. But in Hallelujah City, we're married only to God."

He kept his reaction to himself, but he must have looked critical.

"Daniel teaches that God gave us flesh so we could enjoy its gifts."

Adrian was sorry he'd spoken up because his questions killed the momentum, sending Cher back to her previous favorite topic. "That mousy hypocrite with a halo. What kind of spell does Mary have over Daniel?" It was jealousy in its purest form, proof that best friends made better enemies. Cher believed she was losing Daniel to Mary, despite Cher's assertion, "There's no envy in Hallelujah City." Adrian found it hard to believe they had come there together.

"Is that the last of the wine?" Cher got up and walked over to the dead TV. Kneeling on one knee, she pressed every button on the set's front panel. The set, of course, stayed dead. "Got any music?"

He tried to regain control of the situation. "Has Daniel Hawker ever talked about Florida? California? Did you know he worked as a theme-park magician?"

He couldn't regain control.

"Have you ever witnessed a miracle, Cher?"

"I thought you said you had a wide-screen TV."

The visit ended badly, badly enough to sever the Cher connection. If only Adrian had tried to resist the wet, sloppy kisses (and with them the risk of picking up every sexually transmitted disease incubated inside the compound). At least the intimacy had shut her up, because he'd felt uncomfortable after she started posing the questions. "Why do you want to be a writer? I don't see any books here. You'd think a writer would read."

Helping him pull off his shirt, she'd whispered, "You do smell like soap, you know," words that still bothered but no longer surprised him. He'd heard them from others in town.

When Cher said, "Could we turn out the lights? *All* of them?" he practically flew to the switch. Whatever he was feeling, it wasn't physical attraction. To put it most forgivingly, Cher had looks that were perfect for the stage, for a play or ballet, meaning she didn't look bad at a distance. Up close, however, everything seemed exaggerated—her naturally full lips, her blocky nose and wide brown eyes, the latter almost as dark as her mudslide of hair. Not that Adrian claimed to be any sort of physical prize after months of eating at the diner. It wasn't just that he'd gained twenty-two pounds. His flesh had the consistency and color of dough, unkneaded by even the mildest exercise. As such, she needn't have worried about the lights staying on. He didn't brave sex in lighted rooms, except when he was alone.

To Adrian's relief, Cher didn't stick around to say, "Good morning." To his astonishment, he'd slept nine hours. He immediately checked to make sure the tape recorder was where he'd last seen it, off to the left of the dead TV.

Further relief: the cassette was still inside. Cher hadn't known she was being recorded. But he figured that if she ever found out, she'd be grateful to learn he had not preserved the audio portion of their sexual act. This didn't mean that some deeply buried set of ethics had been exhumed at the last possible moment, however. Rather, Adrian's machine had run out of tape minutes before she started to find him attractive (there had been one very loud clicking sound from the recorder to indicate this) and he'd been too buzzed to devise a covert way to insert a new cassette.

He listened to it for the first time that morning and was impressed by the effect it had. CHER BALSER-SEX WITH THE SAVIOR proved much better company than the flesh-and-blood Cher. In bed, she was just about as lively as a passed-out drunk. (He felt 90 percent sure she had not lost consciousness until after he'd finished.) But on tape, Cher smoldered. On subsequent nights when Adrian felt lonely, he cued up the tape and reclined on the bed. *The bodies were coated with sweat, every part imaginable. I'd stick out my tongue, never knowing what I'd taste.* All he had to do was add the visuals, though sometimes his imagination had trouble keeping up. When God Boy screwed around, he didn't screw around.

The tape was golden, the best thing by far to show for his time in Minnesota. His appreciation of its value didn't stop him, however, from going online and ordering a state-of-the-art digital recorder. (*Save up to nine hours of conversation without changing media*, the description promised.) He couldn't afford to be switching cassettes in the presence of God Boy.

Adrian had listened to the tape on Doomsday Eve, in actual fact, seeing it as a fittingly irreverent soundtrack to the Apocalypse—and, of course, because he was horny. *The Teacher commanded me, Turn around where I can better see you. No . . . not your face.*

Briefly now, sitting at his table in Bev's diner, he wondered what the other girl from Colorado would be like in his lumpy twin bed smelling of bleach. She'd have to perform better than Cher had, of course. How could she help but excel when it came to being appreciative or encouraging? "Are you sure you've got an erection?" Cher had asked flatly. "I can hardly feel a thing."

Mary's voice had been fragile and soft the last time he'd seen her. The white sky was shedding crystals of ice as he looked at her from just across the barbed-wire fence—the closest he'd ever gotten to her. "I have done wrong, and with sin comes consequence," she confided, words tailor-made to seize his attention. "There's more, Adrian. I've got an enemy. Used to be my friend. But now she wants me out." Mary didn't have to provide a name for him to know who the enemy was.

"Take my card," he said, "in case you need help."

"There won't be any phone service in the New Millennium."

"If he sends you away—"

"The Teacher will stand by me," she protested, but she sounded uncertain, a suspicion confirmed when she took the card and slipped it into a pocket.

◆

Adrian heard noise coming from Bev's private quarters. She was watching TV. His TV. He refilled his Coke, downed a few more caffeine pills, and looked for the remote that controlled the compact set Bev shared with her diners, the 20" Sanyo supported from the ceiling by black metal brackets. He couldn't find the device, not on Bev's counters, not in Bev's cabinets. Finally, he stood on tiptoes to turn on the set. A hockey game filled the screen (which didn't take much filling). The dish was tuned to ESPN, the preferred channel of vacationing hunters who came here to get away from their jobs, wives, kids, and neighbors, but not their TVs.

He found a button that in theory changed channels. But nothing happened when he pushed it, and nothing happened when he pushed it repeatedly. Where the hell did Bev keep the remote?

A commercial interrupted the contest on ice. "Best price. Best picture. Find the wide-screen HDTV you've been looking for at our factory-direct sale . . ."

After stretching once more to turn off the set, Adrian drew a long, slow breath through his nostrils and vowed to remain calm. Why should he care if his Sony WEGA was producing a glorious 62" picture only feet from where he was standing, on the other side of Bev's green door? Good things were coming his way. He'd concentrate on that.

With Mary's phone call, everything had changed. At last he'd have access to God Boy. And Hawker would finally be convinced that Adrian represented his last, best hope of gaining public acceptance and the immortality that went with it. Adrian would hold out his recorder, Hawker would rant, and the book that hadn't been happening would basically happen by itself.

In the meantime, he just had to wait—and hold on to these thoughts.

The phone rang and he grabbed it, sure that Mary had news.

"Mr. Hummel? The patient folks at MasterCard would like to know—"

Adrian made a clicking noise with his tongue. "Sorry, call waiting. This could be important." He wasn't going to let them bring him down. Not this time.

He sat back down and placed a finger on the laptop's mouse pad. But as the monitor bounced back to life, Bev's TV behaved strangely in the distance. Adrian saw fire on the screen, and with it came sound, that of people screaming in panic. He jumped up, intending to get a closer look, only to watch as the set reverted to its lifeless state.

Sleep deficit, he thought. That and a serious caffeine surplus. Time to pull back. Yet, the image had seemed real, as had the shrieking.

Maybe he'd only imagined shutting off the set.

The roar of Chevy Suburbans steered his attention to the diner's front windows. Black and in a hurry to get somewhere, these vehicles resembled the others he'd seen the past few days. They belonged to the United States government, FBI or ATF.

He thought of something he'd meant to do, and that was to put away the cassettes he'd left on his table in Room 17. With handwritten titles like CHER BALSER-EARLY MEETINGS, CHER BALSER-MIRACLE WITH THE DOG, and of course, CHER BALSER-SEX WITH THE SAVIOR on their labels, these tapes didn't need to be seen by Mary. He'd have to make sure they linked up here, at the diner.

Feeling the beginnings of a sneeze, he grabbed a napkin.

Lord God almighty, his neck hurt again.

"There will be a book," he whispered to himself.

Soon Mary would call from Eppley Airfield, giving him her flight number and asking him to meet her when she landed. He applauded himself for being prepared, for filling his tank the afternoon before at Gas 'N' Pass. He could be on his way to Fargo or Minneapolis in the time it took to start a truck.

"There will be a book."

CHAPTER THIRTEEN

She awoke in a black, black forest, the eyes of wolves upon her. Hungry, unblinking, advancing as one. "I tell you what, sugar," the lead wolf was growling, "a sixteen-ounce steak would sure taste good right now." Mary shook herself further awake, and the predators' eyes became the headlights of oncoming cars.

"Baked potato on the side," the wolf turned widow said. "That's one good thing about living in Nebraska. Folks aren't afraid of a little red meat."

Her father was holding the wheel. "Mary? Were you sleeping?"

She must have dozed off—not the smartest thing to do behind the wheel on an interstate highway, however briefly. Making it worse, she'd experienced one of her night terrors, getting stuck in a place between wakefulness and sleep. This had been happening a lot lately, if not when she was driving. After years without recurrence, here they were, snakes oozing from carpets, great white spiders suspended in air, and the one she'd been hit with two nights before leaving Hallelujah City, the Grim Reaper, sickle in hand, standing so close she could touch him. The visit had seemed real, as real as Disciples Heather and Brooke sleeping across from her in the bunk bed that matched her own, as real as Cher's empty cot. When Mary was sixteen, she'd been sent to a specialist on sleep disorders. Night terrors, it was subsequently explained, were simply dreams that kept going after Mary woke up.

"It feels like they're coming from somewhere outside me," she'd told the therapist.

"In olden times," had come the response, "the superstitious mistook the pavor nocturnus for spiritual visitations."

She shuddered now as a memory broke loose, and she recalled the vision that had caused her to scream only hours before, waking that morning in her room in Aurora. Five shrunken heads, circling her father.

She looked at the clock: 4:33. The sky was darker than it should have been, thanks to a new wave of winter clouds. "We need to stop," she said to her passengers. "Maybe one of you can drive the next stretch."

Big surprise, she was wide-awake now. Her father had switched on the overhead light and was studying his atlas. "We're getting close to Lincoln. There's not much more Nebraska after that, maybe an hour, even in this thing." Holding the map away from his eyes, he seemed to be squinting. "There's an exit with amenities just up ahead."

"That's good, hon," Semolina said. "I'm getting low on amenities."

"You really are hungry again?" Mary said.

"Smokes. Last pack."

The dome light went off. "Say, Dad, whatever happened to all your speeches on smoking and certain death? Have you changed your position?"

She heard him start to speak but Semolina got in first: "Your father and I have a secret."

"Then, please, keep it." These words were more reflexive than anything else, and as Mary watched her dad stiffen from the corner of her eye, she was sorry they'd escaped. She wanted to know what the secret was.

◆

However close they were to Lincoln, thought Mary, it wasn't close enough. The widow, impossibly, seemed louder. "I'll give Danny Boy one thing. He played a mean piano. I don't know much about music, but I know what I like, and Danny's music was like nothing I ever listened to before."

After that, she started in on the End Time Announcement: "Four seasons and change. That's what old Danny Boy said."

"Four seasons *and one*," Mary whispered under her breath. "That's what Daniel said. If you weren't always busy thinking of things to say next, you might hear what others are saying." *And so it will be,* He'd preached. *The doubting billions deserve it not. But my father's patience is boundless, and this time shall be theirs. As of this day they have fifteen months. To mock us or repent.*

"I can't deny it was exciting," Semolina said. "Don't ask me why. Thinking back now, the end of the world doesn't sound like all that good a thing."

One of the Original Seven had owned a fireworks store in Nevada before finding salvation, and there was a show above the lake when Daniel revealed His vision of the world's end. Elaborate, professional-looking bursts of color, reflected on metallic ice. Mary hadn't known if these were supposed to be festive or symbolic of the coming destruction, but they were beautiful all the same. Splashes and streamers and super-novas, trailed by ear-pounding echoes of cannon fire from European wars fought to give history teachers questions for pop quizzes. Yet, the disciples saved their biggest cheer for a meteor that flared between explosions, knowing that Daniel had ordained it.

This is it, He proclaimed of the End Time, now officially scheduled for the March after next. *All we've waited for, all we've been working toward.*

"The cold air crackled with new energy for weeks," Semolina said. "Wide-eyed kids showed up every day, seeking to get in on the Rapture's ground floor. We all got along like family."

That was true, Mary recalled. Harmony prevailed. Cher Balser sat next to her at mealtime. Twice.

"None of us was thinking," Semolina continued. "That's what I think now. Those sheep that went down, they was just symbols of what laid in store for everyone on the outside. We'd be the ones with the rubber boots on."

"It does seem a bit harsh," Mary's father joined in, "toppling a few billion nonbelievers onto their sides."

Mary could have pointed out that, in prophesying the Cleansing, Daniel had not only offered the strayed a chance, but all He'd ever threat-ened to take from them was their existence—to take *back* that which

He'd so generously loaned them. In His Sermons by the Lake, the Teacher said nothing about eternal damnation or suffering of any sort. The worst He could offer was, *Imagine their surprise, the looks in their eyes, when they realize that He who gave them breath—the very One who gives the sun permission to rise each morning—doesn't care much for ingratitude.*

Semolina said, "It was crazy, mass hypnosis. I see that now."

"You see only with your eyes," Mary spoke up again. "Like Dad here."

"Better than letting someone else do my seeing for me," he said.

"You want to know one of your problems, Dad?" Mary kept her eyes on the road as she spoke. "You need words. Some things have no words, no explanations. Some things just are."

"I don't know," Semolina said. "Danny Boy never got lost for words."

Mary was grateful for one thing. She possessed memories that Semolina didn't share, memories the shallow widow couldn't break into and corrupt. Like the time last spring when Daniel surprised her by standing in her path as she returned to her Station after a sermon.

Mary pretty much froze in place, unsure of what to do or say. A good six feet remained between her and the Savior.

"Your spiritual development is a joy to observe," He said in an even, quiet tone.

Her "Thank you, Teacher" was barely audible.

"You were skeptical at first."

It was hard to find words, let alone the right ones. "I was the seed in your parable, Teacher, the one used to sand and clay. I wasn't ready for the rich black soil." She cleared her throat and shyly added, "Sorry."

He moved closer. "But what a beautiful flower you became. Too many follow for the sake of following. It's not the same as wanting *to be led.*"

The Teacher sniffled, and Mary knew it was true what she'd heard of his allergies.

"My Father's given us another beautiful night," the Teacher said next, letting Mary catch a trace of His faint British accent, which was nowhere as strong as when she first met Him. Dismissed by the doubters outside as pretentious, these shifts in pronunciation had thrown Mary at first, too. But she came to accept a more innocent explanation. The accent's occasional reemergence betrayed a simple nervousness, a stage fright of sorts. That's why it seemed to parody itself whenever he met with reporters. The Teacher possessed human frailty. His accent, like the allergies, showed just how much God loved us. In wanting to save us from ourselves, God needed first to understand us. And this required being like us.

"Walk with me," He said to her next.

A ballad of a breeze came off the lake, turning the scene into a dream. They stopped beside the water and heard a chorus of croaking frogs. He asked, "If you were given a choice between being a genius and having everyone think you were a genius, what would it be?" She recalled the look of surprise on His face when she gave her reply: "I guess genius would be okay."

A dragonfly hovered close to the ground, a foot or so in front of Daniel, as if stopping to hear what came next. "Really?" He said. "That's how everyone answers, but everyone else has been lying."

"Hmm," she responded. "What's this got to do with saving souls?"

He took hold of her hands for the longest time. "My precious lamb," He said quietly, "I trust you more than the others." He looked into her eyes—Mary's eyes, not Heather's eyes, not Cher Balser's eyes—and He smiled. Like a child. Like an innocent, golden child. "You are very special, Mary." Shyly, she lowered her gaze. But she wanted to say, "I do feel special. And needed. And happy." She wanted to say this because she'd never come close to knowing these feelings before. Finally, she whispered, "I owe you everything, my Savior."

They strolled to the small wooden platform He sometimes made His pulpit. Flanked by a pair of stately oaks, it offered clear views of both the lake and trailers. And looking toward the blackness she knew to be water, she noticed that lightning bugs and bats had taken the place of dragonflies.

"Everyone here is so warm," Mary said, though even as she made the remark she thought of exceptions. "Always ready with a hug when I've done good. It threw me at first. There wasn't a lot of touching in our house."

"You deserve to be hugged," He said at last.

"Tell that to my father."

Daniel was quiet again, and Mary worried that she'd told him too much. But then He said something that really surprised her: "Your mother is an extraordinary being."

"My mother," Mary faltered, "is dead. She died when I was nine."

"Your mother is an extraordinary being and she loves you greatly."

"Now? My mother loves me now?"

"She's pleased you're here. Come the Day of Judgment, both the living and dead will be held accountable. I have it on good authority that your mother soars through with flying colors. You'll be with her in the Palace of Light."

She'd wanted to ask if her mother had watched her grow up, but there was something more pressing: a desire, an urge, an unallowable urge. Daniel must have sensed this.

"Mary Chambers," He whispered, "you are a sweet, delicate flower. But flowers wither in darkness. It's time you got some sleep."

When He stopped outside her Station to wish her "Dreams of glory," she felt like the second most important individual on Earth. *Everything, my Savior.*

It was nearly midnight. There was no moon.

◆

By the time they pulled into the Bulldog Truck Stop, six miles west of Lincoln, Mary was thinking it could snow. The clouds had that look. Semolina was still blabbing. "I haven't lost faith in something greater. There's something out there. We just don't have the brains to understand what it is."

"It's a nice thought," her dad said. "But wanting something to be true doesn't make it true."

Mary almost felt as if Daniel was speaking through her when she said, "Yes, but wanting something to be true hardly precludes it from being true." It sure sounded like the answer He'd give. But she knew it was more a case of paying attention in class. She'd learned so much from her Teacher.

"We all miss the days when we believed in fairy tales," her dad countered as they pulled up under the automobiles canopy.

The next thought came from her own mind and nowhere else. *Then, how about this? I want to believe Daniel is a thousand times smarter than my pathetic, earthly father and, guess what, He is.*

"My last two husbands weren't religious," Semolina predictably resumed. "Garrick was a Baptist. But he couldn't help it." When they came to a stop, the widow seemed surprised, as if she hadn't been present when they pulled off the highway, waited for a red light, and made two hard lefts.

"I'll just be a minute," Semolina said. "You two go on." Once again, she was digging around inside her purse.

Mary was facing the gas pump when her father grabbed the keys and headed for the building. "You're welcome," she said, ramming his Visa card into the slot. He didn't seem to hear. "R-E-M-O-V-E Q-U-I-C-K-L-Y," urged the red square letters scrolling by on the LCD panel. "B-E-G-I-N F-I-L-L-I-N-G." The cap came off, the nozzle went in; she wished she'd put her gloves on. Her breath emerged as pockets of steam, but this was nothing compared to the ghost-white geyser erupting from a grate near the building. No wonder her dad had moved so fast; just wait till he got to Minnesota. The idling semis looked like factories, their pipes turned into billowing smokestacks.

The side door opened . . . slowly. The widow lowered her bulk the last twelve inches to the pavement. As the gas pump clanked noisily off, Semolina declared, "I don't need to pee."

Though Mary wanted to say, "*No, who would after drinking a Coke the size of her head?*" she told Semolina, "I need to get something to eat. Why don't we all meet up in the restaurant?" Mary rubbed her hands together for warmth and screwed the gas cap back into place, deliberately taking her time. She peeked over her shoulder to make sure the widow was moving toward the restaurant.

◆

No sooner was Scott in the bus than Mary reached over to snatch the keys. "Where's Semolina?" he asked as the engine started. "What could be taking her so long?"

He felt the VW move forward. "What are you doing?"

"Rescuing our eardrums," she said.

"What do you mean? From Semolina?"

The bus was gaining speed. His daughter's eyes were as fixed on the exit before them as were their headlights. "She's a blasphemer and a liar. I won't have her in Daniel's car."

"Her flask," he said. "She left it on the seat."

"Yeah, along with all her candy wrappers. If you want her to have it, you'd better grab it and toss it out."

He disappointed himself by doing as his daughter ordered. In his outside rearview mirror, he saw the metal container spark as it bounced along the pavement. "This isn't right," he said.

"I suppose I could turn back, if that's what you really want. She never did let me in on that secret of yours."

Scott didn't speak. His daughter could still see through him, a talent he never cared for.

"Half these trucks are headed west. Your girlfriend'll find a horny old trucker to take her back to Ogallala. They'll probably be married by the time they get there."

"Mary—"

She surprised him again by placing her hand on his leg, just above his knee, and squeezing it in a way that suggested anything but warmth or affection. He yanked his body away, jabbing himself hard with the window lever. Perhaps this was what she wanted—to see him puncture his appendix.

"Just you and me, Dad," she said.

CHAPTER FOURTEEN

There was a time when she'd been proud of him. Her father the writer. It had a way of impressing her junior-high English teachers.

Together they listened to NPR over breakfast, shared the morning comics. He helped her with homework, told jokes on her level. She was allowed to read his books and go through his modest collection of albums. Though she liked the Pretenders and U2 okay, her favorite composers stood side by side in a Time-Life series of boxed sets that he had picked up used. Bach, Beethoven, Mozart, Tchaikovsky. Each of these guys had his own brightly colored box with his name embossed in bold silver lettering on the spine, shared only with the series' title, *Great Masters of Music*. The albums inside these boxes were better than CDs because they demanded total concentration, an opinion picked up from her dad. She couldn't press a button and skip blithely ahead to the next track, as all her friends were able to do.

But somewhere, somehow, something changed. Something beyond the usual onset of tension between a single dad and his teenaged daughter. A cold spell set in, and while she didn't know what had precipitated the change—or when exactly it had taken hold—their relationship was different. Muted. Her father had started it, of this she was pretty sure. But then, she didn't really remember it starting so much as just . . . *being*.

It was as if he'd lost interest in being her father, like he wouldn't have cared if she just disappeared. It didn't seem to matter if she got in trouble or attained a 2.0 GPA entirely with Cs. A flat, predictable lecture was the most he could muster, and he usually ended that by placing the blame on classroom overcrowding, rabid consumerism, and Eddie next door—like she wasn't worth getting mad at.

She made friends on the Internet, smoked bud with Eddie Jones, who took pride in knowing that Mary's old man considered him "a slouching tattoo canvas," and discovered that CDs really did sound better. Bach was pretty much replaced by musicians her dad wouldn't have liked or understood. But then . . . who knew what was going on inside his head? If he was listening to records and reading his books, he was doing it when she wasn't around. His La-Z-Boy reclining chair no longer faced the stereo speakers, its back to a window that once provided light for the words of John Irving and E. L. Doctorow. Now, it faced the television. A different kind of light.

He'd shown up backstage after the last performance of Aurora High's *Stop the World—I Want to Get Off,* that was true, but he would have done better to stay home in his chair. Mary had been an assistant set designer, a role volunteered for at the insistence of classmate Cher Balser, who'd taken one small step toward her dream of becoming a movie star by landing the role of understudy. The play had gone well, with the background designs upstaging the actors in more than one scene. But when the other parents hugged their glowing starlets and orchestra members and junior AV technicians, her father took a few steps back and stood rigid as a tree, awkward as an exclamation point. Certain the others were watching them, Mary grabbed hold of the initiative. She moved forward and wrapped her arms around her tree of a dad, now shifting its weight from root to root. His arms stayed at his sides. "Why don't we just go," she said quietly, no longer interested in being part of the cast party.

It wasn't the last time she wanted to kill him. Just before her senior year she caught him staring at her friends sunbathing in their shoebox of a backyard. He looked like he was going to whip his thing out right there and start . . . you know. It was the first time she saw him for what he'd become. An old, lonely creep. There may also have been a little jealousy on her part, as much as she tried to bury the thought. Her friends got all the attention.

When Mary called from the police station hours after Cher and Di had convinced her it was cool to help "test drive" the Camaro convertible that belonged to Di's mom—without first asking permission—her dad stayed firmly in character, showering her with indifference. Cher was grounded for days; Di was limited to viewing only one DVD per night; and Mary barely got a reaction. "You should know better," was all he said on the drive home.

Mary had a boyfriend, briefly and just barely, during the fall semester of her senior year. When her quasi-romance failed to develop a plot, sputtering to an end while still in the prologue, with Mary waiting for a homecoming dance invitation that never came, her dad didn't seem to notice. Not once did he look in her room to see her clutching her one-eyed Raggedy Ann doll for dear life as she tried to sleep, hoping half earnestly she'd never wake back up. That was when she first realized just how much she resented her father, hated him even. She wanted to get as far away as possible, adding physical distance to all the other kinds between them. She would move to Tibet, change her name, burn off her fingerprints.

But . . . there was always a stupid *but*. In many ways she was just like him. She had taken his religion, which was none. She thought sports and the personality cults that went with them were brain-numbing diversions for those whose brains didn't need more numbing—as if all the other stuff her father watched on TV had some hidden merit. She "questioned authority." (He must have been sorry for teaching her that one.) Worst of all by a long, long stretch, she'd adopted his lazy intellectualism. She liked novels, poetry, and more styles of music than her friends knew existed. But she didn't believe in working too hard to suck the last bit of marrow from a couplet or musical phrase. She skipped over most of the tracks on the CDs she owned and mostly read stuff that she'd been assigned.

She lacked passion. Just like him.

Not so fast, she thought now. *Let the defendant speak.* There had been one trait that differentiated old Dad not only from her, but from most living creatures. Her father didn't seem to need anything from others, particularly when it came to affection and acceptance. Mary, conversely, would have died for either while stuck in that house. At night in her bed, she prayed to a god she didn't believe existed, asking for a boyfriend who wasn't killing time until something better came along, and for a dad who'd tell her she made him proud. She asked, too, if she couldn't be more like her friend Cher, dreaming of something she'd never come close to getting. Mary didn't want fame, but during her brief stint as set designer, she'd enjoyed hanging with dreamers who were reaching for something unreachable. Weren't these supposed to be innocent times? That's what everyone said. She wanted to know what that meant.

On some nights she got up from her bed, tiptoed to her desk, and wrote short notes destined to be shredded in morning's light. *"What did I do to disappoint you?"* *"Have you looked around lately? There are two people living in this house."* *"I'm not contagious."*

◆

Mary met Daniel a few weeks after her high-school graduation, in the pizza place she frequented with Cher and Di—admittedly an odd place for the Son of God to drop by on a Friday night. Not that there was anything wrong with the Pizza Paradiso. Quite the opposite. Its owner had taken an unprofitable Pizza Hut restaurant and made it interesting, adding a video jukebox, virtual darts, and an old piano on a corner stage for anyone who felt an urge to play.

Daniel singled her out from the mostly under-twenty crowd and asked if she'd ever heard of him. Her two friends didn't really try to suppress their giggles as he talked of holy missions and his lush new Eden of a spiritual retreat in Minnesota.

"Then what are you doing *here*?" asked Cher.

"A messiah's got to eat too." He smiled, and the warmth emanating from his soft blue eyes could have humbled the huge conveyor ovens running at full capacity in the kitchen behind the service counter. Okay—he was old enough to be one of their teachers, possibly as old as mid-thirties. But Mary was thinking more along the lines of *actor*. He was close to being that handsome—and tanned. "I was passing through." The smile again. "It's as simple as that . . . Mary."

"You know my name?"

"I had a vision of our meeting."

"Cool," said Di. "Were we in it?"

"He's been spying on us," Cher volunteered. "He's no psychic." She was tapping on the table, quietly, *klup klup klup*, a habit the others were used to. She was always tapping on something, building a massive conceptual drum kit from every surface she encountered. A desk at school: *Brack-a brack brack.* Glass of water: *Tenk-tenk-tenk.* Di often told Cher she should take up smoking to keep her hands busy.

"I have visions too," Mary told Daniel, hoping to hush her friend. "They're not a good thing."

"Hey," Cher said, "you've got long hair and everything, but isn't Jesus supposed to have a beard, like in pictures?"

A gentle laugh. "In my family, fashion's pretty low on the priority list. But you do know your history, Cher. You're not thick." Mary noticed the British accent, diluted but appealing. "Yes, my brother had a beard last time he was here. You treated him poorly."

"Wait a minute," said Di. "You're telling us you're Jesus's brother?"

"If thou sayeth."

"*If what what*?" Cher's eyes became hard dark slits. "None of us said shit—"

"I am the Word, the Light, the one way out."

"You mean, the *other* way out?" Di corrected him. "If Jesus is really your brother, I mean. He's a way out, too."

"True enough, Di, but my brother's not on-call right now. I'm the only savior working tonight."

"Anyone can say they're God," Cher was quick to point out.

"And many do. But not many of us can say it truthfully."

"Once when my cousin was high," Di said, "he thought he was Zeus."

"Your cousin should lay off drugs."

Cher did a quick drum roll, closing with a slap to her paper place mat. "But there's so many just like you," she said. "Like that guy in California with the flying saucers, the one who told his stupid followers to cut off their—"

"Infomercial saviors. Tabloid bloody messiahs. What did my brother warn you about? *Beware of false prophets.* Sometimes, Satan appears in drag."

"And what the fuck are those?" Cher asked. "Keys to the asylum?"

Daniel laughed as Mary caught sight of the three toy keys just below the table's edge. Made of plastic, meant for a baby's rattle. "So some would say," he responded. "I prefer to call them the Keys to Heaven."

Cher wouldn't let up: "Since when are the keys to heaven made by Fisher-Price?"

"A child sees the truth," he said. "It's all he's capable of knowing. Unlike the rest of us, he can't intellectualize away the magic and joy of creation."

"So we're supposed to become childlike," Cher said. "Nice sermon. Let me guess. Now you pass the plate."

"How come you talk with an accent?" Di asked. "Not that there's anything wrong with it. British accents are cool. A lot of actors have them."

"I lived there one summer when I was younger. Twelve . . . thirteen years ago."

"Wow. It's amazing you've still got your accent."

"Yes, amazing," said Cher. "That's *exactly* the word I would have chosen."

Over Cher's objections, the young women ended up sharing their ham-and-pineapple pizza with the mysterious smiling stranger. "Anyone want a drink?" he asked, holding his right hand over the pitcher of water, palm down. Di told him they were underage by Colorado law, saying, "Yeah, I know, it really sucks," and Daniel withdrew his hand. "Then I won't bother changing your water to wine." The jukebox was playing an old song by Fastball, the one about the couple that vanished while driving to a family reunion. "This is what I'm talking about," he said. "Getting on that road paved with gold."

The waitress brought another round of root beers, and Mary asked Daniel, "You like this song?"

"I was working as a professional musician when I discovered the truth of creation."

"The truth of creation?" said Di.

"That God created life so we could perform for Him. My Father loves good music."

"What about acting?" Cher asked. "And painting and everything?"

"When the last band broke up, I was standing on the beach at Ventura at four in the morning. My mother had died while we were on the road. I suppose I was looking for answers—"

"Your mother died?" asked Mary, perhaps too softly for him to have heard.

"The sea was dark—it was longing, and rage—and it was beating against the rocks of indifference, winning the battle but ever so slowly, one grain at a time. There was a full moon just above the horizon, and I saw it not as an object but as a hole in the firmament, a portal to the World of Light. A few wispy clouds stretched out on either side, a chalky, pearl-like silver, made lustrous by their proximity to the hole. 'This is magnificent,' I shouted at the top of my lungs to the roaring sea. 'Nothing made by man can compete with your glory. Not music, not art.' And a voice called to me from within and without, 'Yes, but I once had great hopes for my favorite creation. You must teach them a better song . . . my son.'" Daniel paused, taking a sip of his water. "When I looked again, everything had changed, starting with the time of day. It was morning now, the moonless sky a smooth soft blue. But there was more, much more. New colors were revealed to me. These were the colors of Heaven, what scientists—showing a serious lack of appreciation—refer to as infrared colors. I see them even now in the darkness of this restaurant. I see them in my napkin, in the spectral glow of this candle, in the plastic sheen of the salad bar sneeze guard." Mary and her friends turned their heads to check out the sneeze guard. It looked the same as before. "And I heard joyous music in the songs of the gulls, two octaves above my old range of hearing. Those songs are ever present."

"You hear it now?" Di asked, as Daniel rose from his chair.

"Let me show you something."

He walked to the video jukebox, then bent down to unplug its thick cord, an act that drew groans from the other booths and tables, along with a cry of, "Hey, dickwad, you owe me five bucks." Without acknowledging his critics, Daniel moved to the piano, and soon the restaurant rumbled with low, chunky bass notes. His right hand floated above the higher octaves, like a butterfly looking for the perfect flower, gradually making contact to produce a series of gentle blue-green chords. Throughout the Paradiso, no one ate or talked or threw virtual darts. Cher had stopped tapping. As for Mary, she'd never been more attentive in her life, something that was even more true when the sweet pastoral chords gave way to a riot of angry notes. Often atonal, yet never jarring, the melody lines and clusters swirled around Mary in yellow and red, at once celebrating existence and mourning the loss of something huge but indefinable. When least expected, the music switched time signatures, adding and throwing off rhythm. It modulated wildly in pitch, jumping each time to what had to be the least likely key. Mary had never heard anything like it—and suspected this was true of everyone in the world but Daniel. He closed by recalling the rumbling bass, restoring order to the cosmos, if not without a murmur of discontent. There was applause when he pulled back his hands. No one got up to plug in the jukebox.

The three friends were silent as he rejoined them at the table, his Keys to Heaven fanning out and settling on the table's top. *They seem to be floating,* thought Mary. *Like the petals of a lotus.*

She admired the long, sinewy fingers supporting Daniel's glass of water. Di was the one who finally spoke. "That was really brilliant." Mary didn't understand why, but she wished she'd said it first. All she could do now was nod in agreement.

Cher glared at her friends, then at Daniel. "So you know how to play piano. But why are you here? I mean, really."

"I'm here to free you."

"Free us?" Cher practically spat the words out. "Is that what you said?" Cher wasn't there to be freed; she was there to eat pizza, be seen, and soliloquize on becoming a film star.

Daniel said, "Maybe we do need a little help here." The blue-eyed savior placed his hand back over the pitcher. And this time—though

Mary couldn't completely trust her eyes in the restaurant's miserly light-ing—the water clouded over.

"How'd you do that!" Di blurted out, while Mary sputtered, "Is that . . . purple?" Cher was not so impressed or perplexed. She claimed she couldn't see a difference. "No way," she protested. "You're all full of shit."

Daniel filled their glasses, and Mary took a drink. It still tasted like water at first, or was that really true? . . . She took another sip, held it on her tongue. And sure enough, there it was, that sweet bitterness of dark red wine, even if this wasn't as syrupy as the stuff Eddie Jones used to get, before they sent him away. She took a third, longer drink, and saw something else she wasn't supposed to believe in. Their new acquain-tance had—it took her a second to remember the word—an aura.

So what had just happened at their table in the Pizza Hut? Had Daniel dropped something in the water? Maybe it was just food color, with all the power of any other placebo. Her father sure would have been asking these questions.

"It's all a trick of the mind," Cher volunteered. "I saw a TV show. It's just something you want to believe.

"And besides," she added, pinching three fingers together in front of her mouth as if holding an invisible joint, "Phhhhhhhhhhhhh." She nailed the sound of sucking in smoke. Sometimes, she really was a good actress.

"That was two, three hours ago," Di responded. "I don't know . . . maybe."

But Mary didn't feel stoned. And the aura was there, as real as it was resplendent. Woven of light, of the most delicate strands, it was so much more beautiful than the harshly rendered halos she'd seen in cof-fee-table art books. Those had always looked as if they'd been assembled with glue and bathroom tiles.

The phenomenon was helped, once more, by the luminous smile—and by a further dimming of the dining room lights. Daniel took his cue. "Here is the truth," he said, speaking softer than before, speak-ing mainly to Mary. "Your life is nothing more than staring at a long, unbroken wall. This wall, by your name, is time. You are unable to move your head, so you stare at that narrow fixed portion you know as the present. And though you can't turn your head to be sure, you sense correctly that the wall is unending, extending to opposite infinities on either side of where you stand—of where you happen to be standing by placement of birth. You strain your eyes, peeking to the left, trying to reconstruct the past. You peek to the right, trying to predict the future. But it's all a blur. Peripheral vision.

"Follow me, and I will teach you to look *through* that wall, past time itself. On the other side there are no sides. It is space without space, time without time. Beyond the wall—that's where the action is."

He took a sip from his wine and scratched the side of his head, his fingers poking through the aura. "So what else would you like with your pizza tonight?" he asked. "Redemption? Grace? I'm here to take your order."

"You're a lot more interesting than other preachers," Di said, and Mary nodded, though she had nothing in her personal experience to really compare him to.

"What's wrong with everyone tonight?" Cher asked, attaching the sigh she'd perfected as a high-school thespian. "We're supposed to be enjoying our last summer before college, and here we are listening to some psycho who probably wants to bury us in his backyard. Time is not a wall. Time is time. A wall's a wall." She looked straight at Daniel and declared, "I hate fucking religion."

"God hates religion," he said without hesitation. "Religion is an excuse to stop thinking after you turn twenty, so you can focus on more important things like cars and careers and changing diapers. It's the human way of ensuring that everything in the universe remains fixed while you talk on your cell phones at the mall, saying, 'I just found the most darling dress on sale at the Gap.'"

"I don't believe in cell phones." Mary cringed as the words left her mouth—the quote was her father's. Proof again that if her dad was the old block, dead and unfeeling, then Mary was nothing more than the proverbial chip. But then, how shocked would he have been by her other thoughts that night? Like, *This meeting was meant to happen.* Or *Dad might just be wrong about the purpose of knowledge, the meaning of being, the reason for waking each morning—or basically, everything* but *cell phones.*

"Religion," Daniel was still speaking, "is an excuse to stop fearing uncertainty. To stop fearing death. But my Father doesn't want you to get the idea it's some easy transition . . . that you'll hold onto the stocks in your 401k . . . that you'll still be jogging with your purebred Samoyeds. Death's a big deal, just like life. Some thinking is required. So, Cher, you're not the only one who hates religion. My Father despises it. My brother was killed by it. We place our faith in risk and reunion, in truth, sacrifice, and renewal."

There was silence, followed by more silence. Cher finished the last slice of pizza, while Di tried thinking of something to say. This turned out to be, "I really liked your playing."

When Daniel directed the smile at Di, Mary felt what she knew to be jealousy, something she rarely experienced with these friends. "Yes," she added. "It's beautiful."

"Ugh, vomitorium," said Cher. "Not you too."

Daniel said, "Mary, I care about your soul. Stay. Listen."

Di asked if she could stay too. "Maybe you could play some more." Getting up from her seat, Cher said she was going to find some new friends who weren't committable. This probably meant she'd call Justin the Junior, her sometimes boyfriend. He was Justin the Junior because he'd flunked one year. From the little Mary had observed of the pair, Justin seemed too wasted to notice that the status of his on-again, off-again romance was consistently determined by whether or not Cher needed something from him, whether sex or bud or simple attention.

"See ya," Cher said to Mary and Di.

"One second." Daniel shoved a piece of paper into Cher's hand as if serving a subpoena. "This will make sense to you."

Cher scowled and hurried away, but held onto the paper.

An hour later, Di was ready to move to Minnesota, and Mary was, well, uncommitted. Di leaned over and whispered, "His halo, can't you see it?" Mary agreed to talk more with Daniel. Day after tomorrow. At Cherry Creek Reservoir.

That got a reaction from her father. "Let me get this straight," he said the following afternoon, standing in her bedroom doorway, right after she explained why she wasn't interested in washing his car for a little spending money. "You met Jesus's brother in a Pizza Hut and he wants to reclaim your soul on a dairy farm in Minnesota? This is not what I meant by 'college of your choice.' I will not allow it."

"Di's mom said she could go," Mary lied, though not excessively, since Di's mom was unlikely to withhold permission. Privately, Mary worried that her father would make the decision for her, that he'd say something so stupid she'd end up going to prove him wrong—and not because she was sure. "I might have to see for myself," she said. "That's what Di's planning to do, to see if it's real. I can always leave."

A smart father would have said, "*I think you should meet with them tomorrow and listen critically to what they say. When you're not high. See how much you actually agree with them.*" But no smart fathers were on hand that day. "You don't know much about cults," he said. "There's no thirty-day trial period."

"Dad—"

"You're too smart," he said. "Too analytical." Meaning, *You're too like me.*

◆

The afternoon at Cherry Creek Reservoir turned out to be more pleasant than revelatory. Mary and Di listened as Daniel shared tales about heaven, spring in Minnesota, and looking for a decent cheeseburger in London. He seemed self-assured, if not in the negative way she was used to seeing in her father. Of greater importance, he listened with an equal measure of attentiveness each time Mary or Di added something to the conversation. Their questions were answered respectfully.

Later that evening, her father asked, "What happened at the reservoir?"

He shouldn't have smirked when she said, "Nothing." She could easily have answered, "Everything," because this was true as well. Not that his opinion mattered at this point. She had already promised to return the following day and could think of little else. Mary was falling, though she would have been quick to point out, *but not in love.* This was something better.

Instead of asking what she'd meant, her dad said only, "You couldn't have expected anything else." But the smugness in his expression said much more. He thought he had triumphed through superior logic. As she observed this, Mary knew she was going to a place called Hallelujah City, to at least give it a try.

◆

The Volkswagen bus was vibrating more than usual. They were crossing a bridge over the Platte River, and Scott knew Omaha couldn't be far. The radio was on, reception clear, *All oldies from the Nineties.* Everything has a sell-by date, he thought, our clothing, our music, our cars. It wasn't hard to see how a charlatan like Hawker could make an alternate world sound good. Scott recognized a song. The theme from a TV show that Mary watched when she was ten, it hadn't improved with time.

He saw frontage roads, bustling with sports utility vehicles headed for Sam's Club and Grease Monkey. On the bumps of hills to their left, guarded by too many streetlights, identical houses grew in identical rows like oversized, manicured shrubs. He and his daughter had entered the outskirts of Omaha, outskirts that Scott had not seen before. For some inexplicable reason, the city was thriving.

This was confirmed by a sign marking the official border, which placed the population at 362,000. Scott much preferred the Colorado custom, linking a city (like Denver) to its elevation (5,280). This implied permanency, a measure indifferent to human busts and booms, needing adjustment, at most, every epoch or so. Still, there was no denying that either approach—using population or elevation—was superior to the one he'd come up with in his imagination, the one that resulted in a sign reading, WELCOME TO OMAHA. HOME OF OOZIN' AND UPCHUCKA. There was, in fact, a positive message in posting the latest census results, this being the assurance, "We have 361,998 residents who have not conspired to make your life miserable."

The interstate traffic was much heavier than he remembered it, even when divided, as it was now, into four eastbound lanes. None of these qualified as slow lanes, which meant that the Ford Behemoths and Chevy Halliburtons had to squeeze past them to maintain their eighty-mile-per-hour momentum. He closed his eyes to shut out the darting, colliding shadows created by their headlights, but this was a mistake. In the imperfect darkness, he re-endured scenes from his first visit to the city that began as a railroad and stockyard center—a crossroads where, fittingly, hapless creatures came to be slaughtered.

Memories are a lot like home videos, he thought, *harsh and unflattering.* And while Scott disliked home videos—an opinion he never failed to express when the topic came up at work—they at least could be erased.

"Copyrighter?" had been the first thing besides cigarette smoke to come out of Susan's mouth. "Does that require a law degree?"

"I don't think I'm following—"

"A legal background? To work with copyrights?"

"It must pay well," Rebecca joined in, sniffing blood. "I mean, to give up private practice."

"What about your writing?" Susan asked. "Literacy fiction—is that what Liz called it? How do you find time for hobbies like that? . . ."

His daughter located a classical music station on the radio and turned it up loud. He knew this was to keep him from talking, even though he had not so much as cleared his throat since leaving the truck stop. She could crank it up louder for all he cared. Given the places his mind had been dragging him, he was in no position to grumble.

Scott was unable to identify the piece that was coming to an end; it had been a long time since he last heard it, but he knew the composer. Johann Sebastian Bach. *De-de-de, de-de-de* . . . flutes taking flight, strings floating up to join them . . . so gracefully out of place on this drag strip for anarchists. He remembered the title: "Sheep May Safely Graze."

"We're still following the news coming out of Minnesota," a man's voice cut in over the last fading chord. "Again, according to the Bureau of Alcohol, Tobacco, and Firearms, Daniel Hawker is dead. It's unclear at this point whether his death was part of a mass suicide. We will bring you updates as they become available. But what we're hearing right now is that Daniel Hawker, controversial cult leader, has died."

He heard a low, steady cry coming from somewhere inside his daughter's chest. It stopped when he spoke—something he wouldn't have done if he could have helped it. "Son of a bitch, he beat me to it."

"What are you saying? What . . . were you planning?"

He felt the seatbelt trying to cut him in half as the Volkswagen screeched to a halt, just inside the highway's narrow shoulder.

"Get out of the goddamn car," shouted Mary, her cheeks wet with tears that seemed to show anger as much as sorrow.

"But—"

"Out. Now." A three-trailer semi shot by, the last eight-wheeled segment so close he braced himself for the screams of metal slashing metal. It was the first rule of physics and driving: no two objects can occupy the same space at one time.

"At least take me to the next exit."

"The door—use it."

"I'll freeze."

His daughter was silent, looking away. "Shit," she whispered, and the car stuttered forward. It took her awhile to pull back into traffic.

"Mary," he said, "if Hawker's dead, the point is moot—"

"Don't. Talk."

There was a green sign spanning their lanes. 84TH ST EAST 1 MI 1ST RIGHT. His new destination.

"We have an update on the rumor regarding Daniel Hawker." *The rumor regarding Daniel Hawker?* "Apparently, that report originated with a single ATF agent and is being denied by spokespersons for the agency. All other accounts indicate that Hawker is alive, as are the remaining occupants of the compound."

They were back on the shoulder, stopped.

"Mary . . . I'm your father."

"Out, out, out, out!"

He folded his arms to let her know he wasn't budging.

"What if we found some cops, asked how they felt about murder?" Her right cheek, still wet, caught the light from passing cars.

"We need to talk. There are things I should explain."

"Please," she whispered, her eyes on the wheel, "find your way home."

With his head aching and forearms tingling, he considered just how badly he'd screwed up his plan. Perhaps it was time to do as she asked. But then he thought of Semolina Bath, stuck in a truck stop because he wouldn't act. He thought of the deprogrammer he'd contacted that morning, and wondered how long she had waited for him to answer the door at 1225 Turnbolt Drive.

And he thought about the one person he'd left stranded most often.

"We're going together," he said quietly.

His daughter pounded the wheel with both fists.

"Mary?"

She turned to face him but didn't speak. When he saw her eyes, he knew without question who *she* wanted to murder.

Scott looked away, returning his gaze to the swiftly receding tail-lights. Mary silenced the radio, leaving it to the passing traffic to provide the noise—and make him wish they had pulled over a few more feet to the right. Five minutes passed, or so claimed the clock in the dash. He questioned its accuracy. They had been there much longer.

"There are things you don't understand," he said as a livestock hauler tried sucking them into its wake. "Things you don't know."

◆

Mary responded by pressing the gas pedal. She stared straight ahead, hands locked on the wheel, her body supple as a statue. He didn't even catch her checking the rearview mirrors.

The Volkswagen bus inserted itself back into the onslaught, showing little regard for the two-objects rule. One pickup came so close he was able to read the fine print on the PHIL SEYMOUR DODGE mud flaps. "Mary, can we talk?" She must have known how terrified he was by the rapid succession of near misses. Otherwise, why stop accelerating after reaching only forty miles per hour—about half the speed preferred by the drivers now trying to crush them? Once again, he felt his own right foot pressing against the floorboard.

A few cars broke free of the jam his daughter had created, causing a ripple effect of risk and rage as they cut into the adjacent lanes. The truck that inherited their space promptly closed the gap to inches, delivering a message Mary couldn't possibly misinterpret. She had three choices: speed up, pull over, or die.

"Mary!" he cried at the first loss of momentum, knowing she'd taken her foot off the gas. "This isn't a game."

He looked over to see she had fallen face forward onto the steering wheel, her arms limp and straight, extending below the ridge of her seat. "Mary?" The truck issued a final warning, its horn a hundred trumpets blaring in unison. Scott freed himself from his seatbelt. The Volks-wagen gave up more speed, but he was steering it now, gradually, to the right. The box truck thundered past, letting Scott see the Salvation Army logo, as they came to a stop on the far side of the emergency lane.

His pregnant, distressed daughter had not moved once. "Mary, can you hear me?" He tugged at her arm, only to watch it drop back to that space in front of her seat.

Jumping out of the car, he had no definite plan beyond getting to Mary's door. This didn't mean he wasn't grabbing at options as they raced through his head. What if he took the wheel, setting out for an exit with a hospital sign? Perhaps he could flag down a passing car—there had to be one considerate driver in Omaha—and ask to borrow a cell phone. Or should he carry his daughter's sagging body to the Wal-Mart off to their right? Someone there would have to help them.

He ran around front and, closing his eyes to the swarm of head-lights, reached for the handle. But when he pulled, the door wouldn't give. He opened his eyes to confirm the obvious. The button for the lock was depressed—he saw only the dark plastic tip—and I-80 eastbound was no place to loiter. He tapped on the window, and watched as she came out of her coma. "Mary!" But while immense, his relief was short-lived.

"Mary?"

She reached across the seat he shouldn't have surrendered.

"Wait."

The passenger door slammed shut with the force of stars collapsing. "Please."

The Volkswagen bus rolled forward, brushing against the heavy padding that was his coat. He nearly jumped back to give it more room, an impulse he would have regretted, if only for the last few seconds of his life.

He tried keeping up for twenty or thirty feet, but the headlights came closer. His daughter stared straight ahead, frozen again. She was pulling into traffic; it was time to let go.

"I owe this to you," he called after her as the car pulled away. "I did this because I owe it to you."

CHAPTER FIFTEEN

Having walked across the Wal-Mart lot, Scott waited for an RV the size of a Greyhound bus to slowly relinquish its spot in the fire lane. With a driver too short to see over its dash, Scott didn't dare walk behind or in front of it. *That's good. You have it in Drive. Now give it some gas.* He looked back toward the highway at all the speeding cars full of fathers and daughters enjoying cheerful, heartfelt conversations. It was then he saw a falling star, or briefly thought he saw one. The glint of light came from a much closer source. A solitary snowflake, sure to be followed by others.

The septuagenarian in the bright blue frock was all sunshine and dentures. She took time out from smiling only long enough to sing, "Welcome to Wal-Mart!" Even the apron was smiling, in the form of a round yellow face. Bold white type repeated the greeting, "Welcome to Wal-Mart!"

But her mood turned surly when Scott, instead of taking the cart she had chosen for him, asked if she could break a dollar and loan him a phone book.

"Does this look like a bank to you?" she said. "That's why we keep the phones outside, so people won't be tempted to come in here and beg for money."

"I'll give you a dollar for two quarters."

"I don't take bribes."

"It's hardly a bribe. I frequent your stores in Colorado."

Wearing a similar blue uniform, a woman four decades younger than the first shot out from behind the shopping-cart corral. "I am so so sorry, sir." She was still displaying the corporate smile, though it didn't seem to come without effort. JoLeen, her blue-on-white nametag read, ASSISTANT MANAGER. "You can get change at the customer service desk. We've got phone books, too." Then, without the smile, "Bernice, have you had a break tonight?"

"You know," Assistant Manager JoLeen said, "why don't you just go ahead and use my phone. I'll make sure Bernice leaves you alone. Call's local, right?"

As he thanked the stiff, short woman with hair dyed red to match her nails, he had the feeling she found him attractive. "I was sincere when I told Bernice I frequent your stores," he said.

She turned away quickly, and he knew he needed a handkerchief. His sinuses were thawing. The walk had left him chilled.

"I can trust you, right?" She was already heading toward the check-out lanes.

A basic office chair faced the phone, a little lopsided, missing an arm. Smart policy, he thought, coming up with new uses for defective merchandise—even if he wouldn't have been pleased to see amputee furniture in his own workspace. After finding Rebecca's number in the Greater Omaha white pages he was grateful for this chair and the support it provided; with each ring of the phone he could feel the muscles in his legs turning to powder. *Please be home.*

The ringing stopped, as did his breathing. "You have reached the home of Michael, Rebecca, Ainsley, and Sheena Justman." Rebecca's husband paused on the tape. "We're not in right now, so . . . *why are you calling?*" The beep was preceded by self-satisfied laughter.

"Is anyone home? This is Scott. Chambers." He waited. "Your niece is wrapped up with that Minnesota cult. I need your help." The machine beeped again, more of a whistle this time. This spared him from having to add a "Thanks."

That left Susan. "Starter Home" Susan. Custody-threat Susan. While relieved to find the Carpenter-Smythe household listed, he was more than a little tempted to reach in his pocket, the one that concealed his surprise for Daniel Hawker, and save himself from begging her help through one swift act of irresponsible gun ownership. Ah, merciful death. There was sweat on his forehead. He took off the coat.

"Hello?" The tone of her voice suggested that her favorite television series had been interrupted. But then, Susan had always sounded as if she was being distracted from something much more important.

"Listen," he spoke quickly, "this is Scott/yes, that Scott/I'm in Omaha/stuck in a Wal-Mart without transportation/just off the interstate/Mary needs your help/she is making one very wrong choice/I know you care for your niece/you proved that twelve years ago/I understand that now."

Nothing.

"I need your help," he said. "*Really* need your help."

More silence from Susan. Then, "You told me to go to hell twelve years ago."

"Yes, but that will have to wait now." He laughed to let her know he was joking. It came out more like a cough. "There's been a change of plans."

"I haven't seen Mary since the funeral."

He cleared his throat and forced out the words he'd been saving, the ones he knew Susan would relish hearing: "I screwed up."

There was movement on her end. The evil ex-in-law was doing something. Writing a note, looking for a pen, something. "And you're *where*?"

◆

Bernice the septuagenarian greeter was using her break to spy on Scott from the school supplies aisle, while sharing her concerns with a security guard who'd outgrown his uniform by at least one size. Hanging up the phone, Scott looked at the coat tucked between his own feet. A silver-gray that resembled the dull side of aluminum foil, the generously padded garment had rarely left its hanger during a surprisingly mild Colorado winter and still looked new after four months of ownership. He couldn't remember why he'd first been attracted by the prospect of eight pockets, because it shouldn't have taken hindsight to see that seven of these would turn out to be less-than-useful luxuries. If the pockets had seemed to redeem themselves on the first leg of this journey, he sure wished they were empty now.

Why weren't you thinking? he chastised himself. *They're going to think you're a shoplifter. You should have hid your stuff outside.* Images were important here, and it went without saying that a coat loaded down with prepackaged snacks would give a Wal-Mart security guard, fighting off sleep on the day's last shift, a renewed sense of purpose. A bulging sweat sock in the shape of a handgun would lower Scott's standing even further. Only last Sunday, the *Denver Post* had run a profile on "rent-a-cops." Said to have "very short fuses," these were off-duty policemen working second jobs to pay down five-digit MasterCard debts. Six dollars an hour with only one fringe benefit: the power to put Scott in jail for the night.

Using his feet, he gently pushed his coat under the white pressboard counter where JoLeen did her paperwork. But when he glanced down, he saw the bright red corner of a cracker box, poking out from beneath a crumpled sleeve. It seemed to be snagged on a wire or outlet; it would not give.

"Bernice says you don't like paying for things." The guard was standing over him, towering in fact. It only went to figure that Scott would attract a *large* off-duty cop. He studied the structure of his face. Thick brows, wide nose, a lopsided, sarcastic smile. Features to match the roughness of his voice. "Mind if I check your pockets?"

If the man had an Achilles' Heel, Scott saw it in the double chin. He was overweight, from eating to stay awake while working two jobs, no doubt. But this didn't make the security guard look any less dangerous. It simply made him *bigger.*

"Mind if I call my lawyer?" Scott replied. "I think we should first verify that the Constitution has been annulled." There was, of course, no lawyer.

"I told you he was rude." The voice belonged to Bernice. She was smiling, and much more sincerely than before.

"All right, hold it there, bud." The guard had spotted the box of Townhouse crackers; he was patting the walkie-talkie strapped to his belt as if it were a gun. "What say you grab your coat and walk with me?"

Scott held firm. "I brought this from Denver. Since when is it illegal to transport crackers across state lines?" He needed time to sort his options, and for that he needed options. He heard a small tinny version of Eric Clapton, trapped in speakers better suited for announcing price breaks. The British guitarist was calmly confessing to shooting a sheriff.

"What'd he do?" JoLeen sounded nervous, as if she just now remembered it wasn't Wal-Mart policy to provide complimentary phone service to homeless strangers wearing their net worth on their backs.

"He's got half the store under his coat."

It took JoLeen a moment to respond. "I never saw him leave my area."

The lopsided smile was broader now. "No, but he sure saw you coming."

"But she's right," Scott protested. "I never went into your store."

"Then how do you explain this one small fact? You *are* in my store."

The shoppers nearby had stopped comparing prices on Pringles and loose-leaf notebooks. A baby cried; its mother quickly hushed it.

"What say we take that walk, bud?"

Scott waited until they were alone in a cramped backroom with an exit that probably opened to a loading ramp or employees' lot. The guard instructed him to sit. "There. Where I can watch you."

"We're not done walking," Scott said as forcefully as he could manage.

The rent-a-cop smirked. "Say what?"

Scott's change of underwear dropped to the linoleum floor as he removed his weapon from its snug side pocket.

"You're pulling a sock on me?"

Scott gave him a quick jab.

"Ouch. Think you might be using too much starch?"

"I'm sorry," Scott said, "but you've placed me in an uncomfortable position. I have important things to do and I can't do them here. Could you please open the door?"

CHAPTER SIXTEEN

S itting at his table in the Trappers Point Diner, Adrian was compiling
a list of questions for God Boy.

THE LAST DAYS (AND THEN SOME):
INSIDE THE CULT AND MIND OF DANIEL HAWKER
BY ADRIAN C. HUMMEL
© Adrian C. Hummel
When did you first realize you were the Chosen One?
Why in the world is the world still here?
What's next for a prophet in a post-post-apocalyptic world?

Only minutes before, Mary had called from a McDonald's in south-
west Omaha to report she'd ditched her father and was on her way to
Eppley Airfield.

She'd stopped at the restaurant for directions. "They told me to cross
the Missouri and go north in Council Bluffs, then cut back over to the
airport. It's practically in Iowa." Although Mary didn't elaborate, she
was extremely upset with her father over something.

"I know how fathers can be," Adrian had assured her. "I don't care
how much your ticket costs. When you're at the counter, just get me on
the phone so I can pay."

"I've got money," she'd said.

"You do? Then make sure I've got your flight information."

What a difference that phone call had made. Adrian felt industri-
ous, hopeful. As soon as he had the interview on tape, the rest would be
easier than getting Cher Balser drunk. He'd use the Internet to recruit a
journalism major at the University of Minnesota to work as his intern.
He imagined a slender blond girl of Scandinavian descent, sitting up
late in a much nicer hotel than the Valfaard—a Minneapolis high-rise,
with dozens of pay-per-view channels—transcribing the interview onto

his laptop. She could do most of the editing, too. Who said he wasn't magnanimous? He'd pay for the room with new credit cards, selected from his collection of direct-mail solicitations, each complete with a "pre-approved application." So what if his debts passed the fifty-G mark if he could finish the book New York was waiting for. Insert the salacious material from the Balser tape, and who knew? There was still a chance of making things right. *Adrian C. Hummel, Renowned Author/ Frequent TV Talk-Show Guest/Cured Insomniac.*

Whenever he was stuck for an idea, he checked into that room in his head. It seemed so within reach now. Over the past few hours, it had grown to include a minibar stocked with imported beers, five-star room service, and most recently, a thermostat that functioned properly. A subtle detail, perhaps, this last one, but Adrian had been pleased with himself for thinking of it on his short walk to the diner. Now, he pictured his student intern tugging at her light-blue sweater and noting, "It sure is toasty in here, Mr. Hummel."

The woodstove by the diner's back wall huffed and hissed as it consumed a new log—and yanked him from his daydream. First things first, he told himself now, returning his attention to the questions.

How did slumming as a theme-park magician hone your pulpit skills?

Why did you leave Disney World? Is there truth behind the rumors of inappropriate behavior?

I should tone these down a bit, he thought, as the woodstove drifted back to sleep, leaving the room in near-perfect silence. He was alone, completely alone. Bev was back on her snowmobile, ferrying fresh pastries and correspondence to the compound.

Adrian had urged her to be careful on that last black stretch, specifically by staying close to the frozen lake's shoreline. "I'm paying you an extra eighty, for God's sake."

He'd addressed his correspondence to *Daniel Hawker, Messiah*—a first. Previously, he'd written *Mary Chambers c/o Gunt Larsen* on the envelopes. His note, as always, was short and to the point: *Mary wants you to wait for her. She's almost here and has something important to tell you.*

One prospect brought sweat to his brow: *What if Cher Balser intercepts the note?* If things were as bad inside the compound as Bev had said, Cher had to be in the middle of them. And if Cher saw the message, there was no telling what she would do (apart from her first predictable reaction: tearing it up so that Daniel could never read it). Adrian could see Cher urging Hawker to hightail it for Rio. Cher might even take it upon herself to torch the compound or mix the Cheery Cherry Kool-Aid cyanide. Her temper was nothing to joke about.

The thought of Cher sabotaging everything he'd worked for brought Adrian down faster than listening to a Minnesota weather forecast. He saw his hotel room with the topless student intern slipping further and further from reach. Hurry, Mary. Hurry. Call me from Eppley.

He took refuge in labor.

What musicians have you worked with?

How many record companies passed on your demo tape?

Was "Dan Hawker" originally a stage name? Have you used other names?

The questions helped take his mind off the familiar rattling sensation, the hopped-up, dried-out feeling that came from mixing sleeplessness with caffeine.

What's so special about Mary Chambers? Is it that you both lost your mothers?

The questions also helped him forget the nightmare about Blackie. Why, after all these years, was he thinking about the cat he'd lost when he was thirteen? After Blackie got sick she turned the entire house into her litter box. But she wouldn't die, not when she should have, and her will to resist infuriated the old man. "We're not replacing the carpets all on account of some goddamned cat." In the end, Ma told Adrian that Blackie had run away. But if this was true, Blackie did so with the assistance of Adrian's father, because Adrian had seen his beloved gray-and-black tabby caged in the back of Pa's pickup. On her way, Adrian now could surmise, to some cheapskate version of euthanasia.

What did you do with Semolina Bath's money?

Blackie, I still miss you.

How much did others contribute?

Lights flashed in the corners of his vision. He really was tired.

Why Minnesota? Have you noticed it gets cold here?

Adrian paused, skimmed over his work, and reminded himself he needed to practice saying, "post-post-apocalyptic."

He thought he heard someone out front, but it was only the wind. Maybe he'd head south for the transcription process. After all, the "Why Minnesota?" question would apply to him too once he had his interview. It was nice in Tallahassee this time of year.

The cell phone rang, once.

"Adrian C. Hummel."

"*Will you accept charges—*"

"Yeah, Mary, what is it?"

What it was wasn't good. Mary's car had broken down and Eppley Field was closing early. Snow on the way. There was one more flight to Minneapolis that might get off the ground, but Mary didn't think she could get there in time, even if a taxi were to miraculously appear at that very second outside the Exxon Travelers' Oasis.

"Call a cab, Mary. Now."

"It's too late."

"Try."

She said, "I'll find a way there. I just wish it could be faster."

"Yeah, that's great. Please hang up and call a cab."

Leaving his gloves, ski mask, parka, and liner piled on their chair by the table, Adrian stepped outside for nearly a minute. This allowed him to see how much steam a scream lasting that long would produce.

He knew better than to cry. Way too fucking cold for that. So he followed the scream with a whisper, "Thanks, Pa. Thanks for everything."

CHAPTER SEVENTEEN

On the night everything changed, Mary was thirteen and upstairs in her bed. Scott had been thinking about his ex-sister-in-law Susan and the message on his machine, the one that had been there for more than a month. Willfully menacing in its lack of detail, it was her first attempt at contact since she threatened to fight for custody of Mary, meaning four years had passed without so much as murmur.

"It's Susan. Are you there?"

Scott wasn't sure what had kept him from pressing the erase button.

He had tried returning her call at the time, but her machine picked up and all he could say was, "Yes, I'm here." He had not tried since—telling himself he was not about to beg for the privilege of speaking with her—and she made no second effort. Yet, he knew he'd been stupid. He should have pressed redial until he got through, should have left nine dozen messages, because chewable mint-flavored Maalox tablets were now central to his diet. *What did she want? Permission to send four birthday cards at once—ages ten through thirteen—to make up for the years she boycotted? Or was it something unacceptable, an absurdly impossible favor, like borrowing his daughter for a week of brainwashing? "You know she'd love Omaha in springtime. It would give her a chance to get out of that . . . house."*

As on other nights when his thoughts got the better of him, Scott knew that sleep would come with effort, generally three beers' worth. He had no intention of nurturing a harmful addiction with a thirteen-year-old daughter in the house, but this particular habit was healthful, a survival skill even, and he cultivated it with diligence. Working on his first Budweiser, he generally worried about Mary and how she scared him some mornings, coming downstairs to eat looking more like her mother than she had the day before. The second beer helped Scott relax, let him think all was fine at 1225 Turnbolt Drive, let him stop thinking about Susan and Liz, and let him enjoy music or watch TV, though it didn't do much for his reading skills. The third beer, again, delivered the essential knockout blow.

It was important for fathers to get their sleep.

He had just settled into his La-Z-Boy when Mary screamed in her room. It was early, near ten. She must have awakened from one of her nightmares. He lifted the arm of his turntable—he'd been "Running on Empty" with Jackson Browne—and went upstairs. He took his beer with him, leaving behind the first empty cans.

"Will you sit with me, Daddy?"

He took a seat beside her on the mattress.

Throughout his adult life, especially in the years that followed his divorce, Scott Chambers had been hard on humanity. While acknowledging the capacity for art and invention possessed by his species—witness "Running on Empty"—he knew all claims of greatness were ultimately swallowed whole by a rapacious hunger for power, malice, and unearned gratification. Witness Susan and Rebecca. But like most great La-Z-Boy critics before and since, Scott had secretly granted himself an exemption. He not only wanted to rise above his fellow apes, but also believed he was pulling it off. This would change in Mary's room, through what seemed to be a simple action, involuntary at that.

He patted her shoulder, and she started talking about troubles at school. Janet Blackworth, he learned, was an old-fashioned bully. "She asks if she can borrow a dollar, and if you say you don't have one, she threatens to frisk you. She doesn't have to say she'll hit you if she finds out you're lying. You just know it's coming. Everyone says Janet belongs in high school 'cause she flunked a few grades. She's got lots of friends, but I think they're just scared."

Scott responded, "There are times you can take pleasure in knowing everyone else is wrong."

Mary smiled, and he squeezed her shoulder.

The night-light on the far wall glowed in the shape of a puppy's head, making it the closest thing his daughter would have to the pet she'd wanted for three consecutive Christmases. Its fur shone faintly, a dull, smoky yellow.

Mary talked more about her life at school, about the books she was reading, the Phys Ed classes she disliked. Ms. Herman, the teacher of those classes, thought it would be good if Mary's father picked up a baseball and played catch with her.

"Mr. Gonzales said it was neat I knew who Boethius was. I'm getting an A in history."

The hands on her square white alarm clock were invisible in this light, and Scott promised himself to check the Sunday flyers for digital clock radios. "I understand," he said whenever appropriate, "I was a teenager once." He finished his Bud. "It doesn't sound as if school has changed that much."

He looked at the desk, making out several neat stacks of homework. Ignoring his better judgment, he conjured up his own set of maladjusted Phys Ed teachers. Mr. Rath. Mr. Stonefrost. Time had done nothing to soften their image, so Scott forged a note—*My son is too ill to play dodgeball*—and skipped out of the memory. Soon, he was walking the corridors of Lakewood High, where he encountered his own prison-bound bullies, and looked to relive his youthful conquests. *There must have been some.* Between crisp white anklets and miniskirts that, in upholding the school's fascistic dress code, came very close to covering knees, the girls' legs were seductively tanned. It was late in the spring semester. He saw posters for the graduation party at the new Y, banners that implied his class held more promise than one might have guessed looking at its members. And there around the corner stood Liz, the way she looked when he first met her, seven years after high school. She was smiling—Christ, she was hot.

Scott leaned his head back to relax his neck, heard a soft cracking sound. He turned to his right, compressed his face muscles, and opened his eyes to a poster that was new to Mary's wall. Perhaps three feet across, it was a photo of a girl not much older than his daughter, a singer most likely, produced—both poster and singer—on an assembly line at Disney Global Domination. Far more exposed to the elements than the girls he'd just passed in the halls of Lakewood, she looked cold in the grainy darkness.

"Dad—" Mary said something about needing new shoes for Phys Ed, and he remembered he needed to talk with his staff of two about "stressing the positive." He'd been lectured on that subject by one of the production editors only that afternoon. She had not been happy with the catalog page for *Adventures in Trigonometry*.

His hand slipped from Mary's shoulder—literally slipped. He felt almost certain this had not been deliberate. But he was quite conscious of where it came to rest. He was touching his daughter's breast, which was fairly well-formed for a thirteen-year-old's breast. But *knock me to my fucking knees*, it wasn't a "breast," it wasn't a "developing mammary gland." It was a tit, a warm, soft tit, an object and sensation denied him for years, covered by the thinnest of T-shirts.

With a body-wide shiver, Scott pulled his hand away.

"Daddy?"

Quickly pulled it away—where he knew it would stay from that moment on. Away. He concentrated on getting his breathing back to normal.

"Did you fall asleep?" His daughter's voice came from someplace hollow.

There was no danger of drifting off now. What had just happened? Where had it come from? He played her words back in his mind—as he would continue to do the rest of that night—but heard no scolding or suspicion. Mary seemed completely ignorant of his infraction.

"I'm pretty sleepy myself, Dad. Good night."

He would have blamed alcohol if he thought there was any chance of pulling it off. Still—why take chances with so much at stake?—he knew he had finished his very last beer. Awake in his own bed, he told himself he was overreacting, that his *mind* was overreacting. Irrational thoughts were nothing new, after all; this wasn't the first time he'd become lost in that dark, cluttered place where for every simple action lurks a complex, unequal reaction. He told himself he was no monster, but then, wasn't that what monsters told themselves? *Denial. Compartmentalization.*

These were concepts that cropped up in the textbooks he marketed. There was another concern, a more practical one. Scott P. Chambers was a shitty father. And while he knew there were millions of shitty fathers, perhaps billions, he didn't want to be one. He fell asleep at three, woke around four.

His clock now functioned properly, back up to speed, no more getting stuck on 1:09 or 2:18. Staring at his ceiling, which seemed alive in the darkness, an organism constantly regenerating cells, he calmly reviewed the facts. Yes, he had touched his daughter, but accidentally, and so briefly as to escape detection. Yes, he was through with drinking, even if it meant never relaxing or falling asleep with ease or pulling out his Jackson Browne albums again. He no longer saw logic in dialing Susan's number, was thankful he'd hung up right after she answered her phone in the interminable void between 2:25 and 2:26 before he could say, "Ready a room. Mary needs stability. You win."

The dawn light seeped in and his ceiling reassumed the qualities of inanimateness; and while it looked like every other dawn witnessed from this particular angle on this particular mattress, Scott accepted the truth. Everything had changed; this was not the life he'd come home with from work only hours before. The embryonic sunrise, in trying to fob off its image of peaceful continuity, was simply dicking with him. "Get used to it," Liz would have said. "What's done is done." She was the one who had taught him not to believe in repressed memories. No matter how hard one tried, no matter how much effort went into the attempt, there was no beating the damn things into submission. Only the good ones faded.

He would have to work harder at being a regular dad, whatever exactly that was, while making sure he didn't get too close. He would have to work harder because it would be harder. His daughter's sexuality wasn't about to wither and blow away, quite the opposite. She would keep turning into her mom, keep growing into the Eddie Bauer T-shirt she'd inherited from Liz and now wore to bed. She would make new friends, buy slick magazines, and watch slicker commercials that dared her to dress like the girl in her poster. And while all this transpired,

Scott would get no help from church or family, given the absence of both in his life. He would be thwarted by movies and MTV, even the Aurora public schools. Decades had passed since they—cowardly, stupidly—backed away from sensible dress codes.

He needed to build an invisible wall, through which he could see but not reach.

If your right hand causes you to sin, lop it off. He would have done this without hesitation if he thought it would change a thing.

CHAPTER EIGHTEEN

Seething red, burning red.

Maybe it was best that the Volkswagen bus had given Mary something new to be mad at, and maybe it was good that she was through driving for today. Just minutes before, her anger with her dad had caused her to miss the LEFT LANE EXIT signs for I-29 North, meaning she had to cut across three lanes of traffic at an angle closer to ninety degrees than forty-five, a maneuver made even more difficult by the flashing brights and cussing horns of other cars. *How could Dad have used me like this? How could he think of murdering Daniel?*

I-29 had taken her into Council Bluffs on a four-lane stretch that lost nothing to darkness, since darkness was every bit as scenic as the view she remembered. Generic overpasses, a rail yard to the right. There'd been a loud crunching sound—all consonants, no vowels. *Kkkkrrcrcccc.* The bus jerked to a slower speed, giving up power it never had to begin with. Another angry crunch, and it felt like she'd plowed into an axle-high plateau of mud. The speedometer read 40.

Khmm. Khmm. Khmm. A series of punches to the chassis. Thirty miles per hour . . . red, red rage, the world as seen through heat-sensitive photography.

She drove on the shoulder, her vision focused on a point in the distance where shining, colorful logos floated in darkness. *Exxon. Sinclair.* If only she could make it to the exit. Not that she expected to find mechanics on duty with a genius for resurrecting four-decade-old Volkswagens. She just needed a phone.

◆

A truck driver—the most slovenly one in the Exxon Travelers' Oasis, the one with a faded FUCK IRAQ T-shirt framed by an open coat—smiled at Mary with corn-yellow teeth. He may have been renting a room in back, because he leaned over a booth to retrieve a lumpy golden blanket. This, the blanket, triggered memories of Mary's first trip to Minnesota.

It had started in mid-June, nearly three years ago, on a typically cloudless Colorado morning. She'd been standing at Turnbolt and East Colfax, her dad's suitcase at her feet, when the sky-blue school bus pulled up to the curb. "And you must be Mary Chambers." These words were spoken by an Asian-American woman not much older than Mary. She was at the wheel. "Welcome to your life."

Nineteen or twenty other travelers occupied seats throughout the bus. Some were sleeping, most were young, and nearly all were female. There were only two men besides Daniel, as far as she could make out, and each seemed to be with a partner. Mary couldn't tell who the three-year-old boy exploring the aisle belonged to. He still crawled and wore diapers. Diapers and nothing else.

The air in the bus was stale and warm, reminding her of the locker room at Aurora High. She saw blankets and Kleenex wads and napkins from McDonald's, and realized one thing. God didn't fork out for motel rooms. Four or five candles burned in the aisle, pretty far back on the black rubber mat, dangerously close to baby, blankets, and trash.

Daniel was sitting a third of the way back, on Mary's right. And in the seat directly behind his—*Was Mary really seeing this?*—sat Cher Balser.

Mary could only imagine the expression of surprise on her own face, yet Cher's reaction seemed artificially restrained, hand in the air but just barely, smile correspondingly measured, as if Mary had just walked into the school cafeteria. *Over here. I saved you a place.*

"Mary, my child," said Daniel Hawker. "Your presence enriches us all."

Taking the seat across the aisle from Cher's, Mary asked, "What did he give you to read? It must have been pretty convincing."

Cher said only, "The Teacher can help us."

"You didn't believe that Friday."

Mary would have been much less surprised to see Di, since she had backed out only hours before. "Mom scored me a really cool summer job," Di had said when calling to apologize. "Receptionist for a holistic homeopathic veterinarian. Did you know there are thousands of cats on steroids? Doesn't that scare you? Write me from God's place. I want to know what it's like."

The bus vibrated like an airplane struggling to lift off, and the ubiquitous noise made listening difficult. Mary leaned into the aisle to hear Daniel say, "I see each of you as an empty vessel. Needing light, joy, love." The smile made these words believable. "In our city of light I will fill you."

"This is so cool we're going together," Cher said, and Mary wanted to ask her again, *What was on that paper he gave you?*

Her worries and excitement gradually lost out to the rattle and hum, and by the time they left Colorado Mary felt like she'd been on the bus forever. The few conversations that managed to reach her ears lacked urgency and focus. The baby stopped crying somewhere around Ogallala.

Daniel spoke often, but always with forethought. The resulting pronouncements made Nebraska bearable.

"How can anyone believe this hostile environment is truly our home?" he said near Kearney, waving his left hand toward his window, offering the Great Plains as a visual aid. "Right now you're breathing in poisonous gasses, germs, and disease. There is cancer built into your cells, just waiting for its marching orders. Look at the face of a baby at birth. Scarlet, screaming—it's not happy to be here."

The Teacher fell asleep right after that—as in, *right* after that, there'd been no discernible transition. His head tapped lightly on the window, his aura, invisible by daylight, providing no cushion.

Minutes later, a girl who couldn't have been more than sixteen walked up from the back. She placed a slim, silver boom box on the floor between Mary and Cher.

"The Teacher's modest about his musical genius," she said. "That's why I waited till he was sleeping." Squatting by the portable stereo, the girl pressed Play. "He wrote and recorded this in California."

Once again Mary loved what she heard. Though similar in places to the music Daniel had performed on the Paradiso piano, this was more like a full orchestra touring the Earth from another world.

"The Teacher multitracked all the parts on synthesizer and guitar."

When Daniel shifted in his seat, the girl whispered, "This music is divine by nature. You can never get tired of it. Up at the retreat, we like to say it's got . . . a cult following."

Mary leaned toward the girl and spoke quietly, "That word. Cult. My dad must have repeated it six hundred times. The past few days . . . the readings and walks, they've been kind of fun. Why don't I feel like I'm being pressured?"

"Sister—" The girl's eyes were deep warm pools of caring and love, and Mary wondered if she was older than she appeared. "I was joking when I said that about the music. This isn't a cult. We're more like a family."

That first trip ended with The Miracle, the one that inspired controversy even among disciples, mostly because Cher told it differently than Mary remembered it. When they pulled up to a convenience store in Trappers Point, Mary had no way of knowing how close they were to their destination. Darkness had defined the drive for hours, as had the almost empty two-lane highways. They were stopping at a place called Gas 'N' Pass so the driver could run in and grab a few things from a list dictated to her by Daniel, who now occupied the front right seat.

When the driver, Tatsuya, got out, she closed the four-panel door behind her.

"We need to be watchful." The boom box girl was back in the aisle, kneeling between Mary and Cher. "Some of the townies don't want to be saved. They're not very hospitable. You could get hurt here."

Her prediction seemed perilously close to being fulfilled when, a few minutes later, an old man came out of the store, saw the bus, and sidled up to the door. He tapped on a glass pane. The girl walked to the front. "What do you want?" she asked.

But the man looked past her to say, "You're him, aren't you?"

Daniel didn't answer.

The man was skeleton-thin, his head iced over with shock-white hair that begged to be clipped or combed. His skin looked hard and dry, hard and dry and bristly. Like rope. Like the rope Mary had been forced to climb only weeks before in P.E. class.

"You're him. I seen your picture."

Daniel leaned forward in his seat. "I am He."

"I need your help. Can you wait while I get something? It's important."

Mary wondered if they weren't in danger, if this wasn't a set up.

"I'll wait," Daniel assured the stranger.

Tatsuya was back in the bus and reaching for the lever that closed the door when the old man reappeared holding what looked like a rolled-up blanket. This turned out to be a pale golden dog with a face that reminded Mary of . . . it took her a second to place it . . . the night-light she used to have in her room.

The bus doors stayed open.

Everyone watched as the man came closer, shuffling through a streetlight's beam that guarded the Pay-in-Advance gas pump. The dog was a mutt, half cocker spaniel perhaps, half everything else, and it may have had its owner beat for haggardness. Its hair was matted in places; it was fighting to stay awake. "He's sick," the man said. "Sick and old." His voice was quiet now, but there was a bass rumble welling from some-place deeper than his lungs and throat. Mary recognized the sound at once. Collective pain. The residue of generations.

"Can you help my dog?" the man asked quietly.

In what seemed like an instant, Daniel was outside the bus, standing before the man and his pet. He placed a hand on the nape of the animal's neck, and looked upward while closing his eyes. "*Free him, Father.*" It was a whisper that lingered like smoke from a cigarette, mingling with the air. When it finally faded to absolute silence, all life slipped from the dog. *A limp, empty package,* thought Mary. *Like the rolled-up blanket I thought he was carrying.*

"Why'd you do that?" the man cried. "Why the hell'd you do that?"

Daniel was calm. "This soul has slipped its collar and now runs free in boundless fields. Is there anyone here that truly believes he is not better off?"

"But Jesus . . . Jesus raised the dead."

"My brother was a hard one to figure," Daniel said. "Tell me how raising the dead makes any sense. He drags back this sorry Lazarus who's just getting used to the idea that things have changed—*He brings him back to life.* Big words. Big reaction from the crowd. And as everyone knows, a big hit to this day with preachers who play with snakes. But where's Lazarus now? He died again, they cried again, and too much divine might had been spent on a shoddy stopgap measure. My brother should've let Lazarus lie. Your Ted's no longer confined to that battered broken cage you hold in your arms. No appetite or pain. No wants, no fears—"

"But . . . Teddy . . . How'd you know his name?"

◆

Picking at her potato chips in the booth closest to the pay phones in the Exxon Travelers' Oasis, Mary eavesdropped on the long-haul drivers. "Not a good night for heading north," one said to the yawning high-school senior behind the Subway counter who'd just taken the trucker's order for a Philly steak sandwich. "It was snowing like Cain in Sioux City. You can tell it's gonna break loose here any minute."

She pictured her father in the Wal-Mart cafeteria, sipping coffee or hot chocolate, acknowledging defeat, this first intelligent thought of his day spreading through him like the warmth from his drink. *He doesn't know how lucky he is.*

◆

In the lot in back of the Wal-Mart, night pooled, thick as ink. Security lights protruded above the metal door, but no one had bothered to replace their bulbs after vandals shattered them with rocks or bullets. Scott could hear his blood in motion, the pumping of his heart, accelerated now. Fear—the kind he'd forgotten existed. Two elements worked in his favor, however: the darkness and his comfort with darkness. In the first years that followed his divorce, darkness was where he listened to music. Darkness was where he wandered—without getting up from his chair—and darkness was where he wept. It was like a womb, minus the mess and with better acoustics. He was skilled at finding his way in it.

Pointing at the ground with his gun-shaped sock, he told the guard to stop.

"Shit," came the angry muttered response. "Rule Number Eight. I shoulda took your coat. As evidence."

"Slowly," Scott said, now wearing the garment in question, "place your radio on the pavement. Very good. Now move away. Back toward the dumpster." He picked up the security guard's radio and threw it as hard and far as he could. He heard a thump, distant in the blackness, followed by the crackling of brush. The earth dropped off on the lot's far side, *steeply* as indicated by this crude sonar.

"Fetch!" he shouted to the flustered giant, whose crooked smile had been straightened and stripped of all smugness. "There will be much less embarrassment in reporting this to your superiors if you're in possession of your radio."

"Shit, shit, shit."

"Here's one more thing to keep in mind," Scott told him. "As much as I hate the idea, I will have to shoot you if you give pursuit. So please feel free to take your time." Scott started to walk away, but remembered something. "Wait," he shouted. "I need four quarters. Place them on the ground."

"You know," said the man as he counted out change, "you're inviting boatloads of trouble by holding up a store like this."

"A hold up? You think I traveled cross-country in a Volkswagen bus to rob a Wal-Mart? I'm going to kill God. He knocked up my daughter."

The guard didn't have an answer for that.

Turning the corner to the store's west side, Scott heard a snap and a shout. "Shit! Shit! Shit!" The thumps that came next varied greatly in volume, with some quite loud indeed. Scott would need a good hiding place until Susan arrived. The guard was likely to be angry.

The snow picked up but didn't seem to be falling properly. The flakes bobbed and danced as if suspended by invisible strings. *What's up with gravity tonight?* he wondered, feeling lighter than air himself. *It takes down security guards but can't grab hold of a puny snowflake.* He was dizzy and high in the aftermath of an adrenaline surge, but these weren't the words he would have chosen to best describe his present state. Alive. Scott P. Chambers felt alive. In a good way.

◆

Walking quickly, though not so quickly as to attract attention, Scott set out for the pay phones in front of the building, all the while looking for a place to be invisible. He'd have to hide nearby, of course, so that he could see Susan arrive. But he'd already ruled out unlocked cars, thinking that in the process of locating one he was bound to trigger noisy alarms. His second choice, the store's shopping cart bay, proved much more exposed and well lit than he'd been expecting. As for the businesses that bordered the Wal-Mart—a Toyota dealership and a three-story office building—Susan wouldn't think to look for him in either one's lot. Having no way to call her now that she was en route, he scolded himself for failing to ask if she had a cell phone.

His first two quarters got him Information. The last two bought him "Thank you for choosing Wal-Mart. Our store hours are—" He pressed zero and JoLeen answered, "Customer service."

"This is the guy you helped before your security guard went crazy." He heard typing on a computer keyboard. "My daughter is in danger."

The typing stopped. "Your daughter?"

He gave her the abridged story, editing Mary's involvement with Hawker and her present situation to three well-crafted sentences.

"I'm in danger, too," he added. "Your guard will kill me if he gets the chance."

"Kill you?"

"I've read about these off-duty cops working second jobs. It doesn't take much to set them off."

"Off-duty cops?" Laughter mixed with the name as she said, "Dick?"

"My ride should be here in twenty minutes. I'll need a diversion."

"This is for your daughter, right?"

◆

Before this night, Scott had not paid much attention to the trash receptacles that stood outside the main entrances to Wal-Mart stores. Now, he knew them well, one in particular. Although the container before him appeared to be made of metal and concrete, it was actually plastic, its finish molded to resemble a stone aggregate. Of greater significance, it seemed large enough to hold a man of average size, even if that man was wearing an unnecessarily thick coat. The dome was hinged, enabling him to tilt it to one side.

A shopper wearing a white fur hat glared at Scott as he settled into the cold, squishy refuse. She didn't return his "Good evening." Soon, he was all the way in—and filling every inch. With knees pulled close to his chest, he felt pain in joints he didn't know he had. He assessed his mobility and determined he could rotate his head about 140 degrees. His arms moved too, but not very far and only with great effort.

A few minutes later, JoLeen the Assistant Manager with odd capitalization in her first name appeared inside the store's glass doors. He saw this through the west-facing slot in the dome. Sipping coffee from a cardboard cup, she looked around the parking lot, trying to locate his hiding place.

The weather did nothing to improve life in a trash receptacle. Betraying science by ignoring the fact that it was too damned cold for anything to melt, the snow turned to slush the instant it made contact with the dome's plastic surface. Thin, silvery waterfalls appeared on all sides, and some of the liquid curled inward through the openings, hitting Scott's ears, hair, nose, and eyes. He felt a sneeze coming on, did his best to resist. He no longer felt alive in a good way.

A teenaged girl wearing too thin a jacket raced into the store, and Scott asked himself, *Is this what I was so afraid of?* Love and risk feed off each other, heighten each other—Mary had taught him this when she was very young. But he was only beginning to wonder, in this unlikely setting of a frigid plastic trash repository, if he hadn't deliberately killed one to take out the other.

When nine-year-old Mary came back to live with him, she yanked Scott from a familiar, if hardly cozy, rut. But she did this by plopping him into a new one he fully loved, and this entailed risk. For the next four years Scott P. Chambers looked forward to coming home each evening to a trusting child and willing pupil. He looked forward to their weekend explorations of museums in the city and ghost towns in the foothills. He looked forward, knowing it was dangerous, because in looking forward there is always a beyond. With each day that passed he was that much closer to losing his best friend and solitary fan, and to something as useless as puberty.

Weighing it all now, with water that still retained the qualities of ice trickling down the left side of his nose, he wondered what really happened that night in Mary's bedroom, and later, in the neurological backwoods of his own mind. Had he created an excuse to distance himself from the preordained betrayal, from the judging and expectation that drip like melting snow from the mouths of teenagers—and in his particular hell, a teenager who would remind him more and more of Liz?

There was activity outside his slot with a view. The girl's boyfriend swaggered by, making sure that she and anyone else who cared to look would know without question that he was in no hurry to catch up. He wore a baseball cap that pointed backward and a practiced coolness that disappeared—if only for a second—when the trash receptacle threw his lit cigarette back at him. *And what's your purpose on Earth?* Scott was tempted to shout as the boy hurried inside. *Making it easier for others to get into MENSA?*

JoLeen must have caught sight of the boomeranging butt. She was staring at the ill-mannered receptacle from her place inside the glass doors. When her eyes met Scott's, she shook her head in disappointment.

The security guard was still missing in action. But just as Scott considered the possibility that the hill out back was steeper than he'd guessed, Dick lumbered around the building's far corner. Rubbing his chin with a formidable right paw—an action that seemed to indicate a deepening of thought—he stopped in front of the doors. He stared in the direction of the hiding place, and Scott was reminded of a bear searching for food in a mountain subdivision, a large clumsy animal, aware it's being watched but not especially intimidated by the fact. He'd seen photos of these bears in the *Denver Post*, taken just before they were summarily executed for trying to reclaim their traditional foraging grounds. The guard's dark jacket was torn. A gash of white, burning like a flare in the concentrated brightness, extended from armpit to waist. He gave his chin a last good rub and retreated inside, where he stopped to talk with JoLeen.

In a flash, the pair disappeared. The glare of headlights had rendered the store's glass doors opaque. When the approaching car turned into a parking spot, taking with it the source of light, Scott could see that the two Wal-Mart employees had truly vanished. An effective magic trick, he thought, employing distraction to hide the action. Dick and JoLeen must have taken their conversation inside.

Scott felt a pang of hunger—his stomach turning on itself. He thought of fried shrimp, swimming in grease only yards away on the other side of the building's front wall. It didn't matter that he'd barely noticed the aroma when he was inside using the phone; he sure smelled it now. The warm golden scent exaggerated the entrée's merit, declaring it the plumpest, most luscious shrimp ever frozen and shipped to Omaha. If only Dick had not gotten so bent out of shape, Scott would have been sitting in the Wal-Mart cafeteria at that very moment, feeling tired and full while sipping hot tea and waiting for his ride.

Using his left hand, he located a box of Snackwell's. But the low-fat cookies were lodged in place near the bottom of a waist-level pocket. He made out the textures of neatly folded paper towels, his toothbrush, a coin, and a cold, smooth roll of Lifesavers candy, which would have been either butterscotch or wintergreen. He felt another pang—along with something sticky and wet. He lost his grip on the candy.

Backward Cap was back, but Scott had not seen him in time. "Enjoy the popcorn and Pepsi," the boy snarled while walking away. "Homeless fuck." The girl wasn't with him, may never have been. Scott was shaking the last kernels out of his hair when JoLeen reappeared, wearing a long beige parka and lighting a cigarette.

"Break time?" he asked as she approached.

"I need to know why the guy I'm helping keeps a gun in a sock."

CHAPTER NINETEEN

In the time it took to smoke two cigarettes, JoLeen learned more than anyone needed to know about Daniel Hawker.

Now Scott was saying, "I bought the gun a year ago. After I paid a deprogrammer and he disappeared with my money."

"You bought the gun to do what?"

"I'm not really sure. I didn't know what I was thinking."

"And now you do?"

Dick hobbled back out, nodding to JoLeen as he moved toward the lot. Scott watched him slog past the long stretch of handicapped spaces, his head constantly turning, like a frightened young child looking both ways, again and again, before crossing a street.

JoLeen asked Scott, "And you really think shooting this guy will make your daughter love you again?"

"No."

"Then—"

"It might make her know I love her."

Dick was shining a flashlight into customers' cars.

"Sounds pretty extreme," she said.

"It's all I have left."

A film of snow had settled on everything, including JoLeen's hood and shoulders. "Dick said I shouldn't never have trusted you, but then . . . Dick's just a dick. I take a lot of crap here for being gay. He's got to be the worst offender."

Scott felt strangely disheartened, and knew better than to ask, *You don't find me attractive?*

"Going out in a blaze of incompetence. That's our Dick." She pulled a pack of Virginia Slims from a pocket in her coat. "You really think you'll go through with—"

"Talking to ghosts, Jo?"

"Christ in Heaven! Dick!"

"Is there anything else you forgot to tell me?" Dick, for his part, was short of breath. Scott couldn't see him; he'd come up on JoLeen's other side. "You know, about the scrote who held me . . . *tried* to hold me up. Anything he said? Identifying marks? Or do men all look the same to you?"

Her sigh was exaggerated. "Now that you say that, Dick, he asked where we hid our safe."

"And that didn't ring any bells?"

"I'm hardly a trained security professional like you," she said.

"Well, that's true, but . . . why didn't you tell me?"

"I tried. When I called your number, they told me you'd gone for a walk or something. It was Kendall I talked to. I'm trying to recall her words. That's right, she said you were out being a Dick."

"Tell Ken*doll* she'd best stick with being a lesbian. 'Cause she sure ain't no comedian."

"Kendall's not gay. You know that."

"And I'm not a dick. I mean, I am, you know, but not with a small *d*."

"Believe me, Dick, as far as I'm concerned it's capital *D* all the way with you."

"I should have called the police when I said I was going to."

"Yeah, and I still say you'll look better if you catch this jerk first. Seeing that you'll have to tell them how easily he overpowered you."

"He didn't overpower me."

A white Land Rover passed beneath a streetlight in the lot's center, coming their way at a fairly good clip.

"I need to get back to work," JoLeen told the guard, who seemed transfixed by the two-ton status symbol pulling up to the curb. Scott now saw that the car was silver.

"Sorry, ma'am," Dick called out to the older version of Susan Carpenter-Smythe who sat behind its wheel. "You're not allowed to park there."

Scott couldn't hear Susan's response, if indeed there was one. Dick's walkie-talkie chose that moment to show it had survived its ordeal by producing a loud, distorted version of JoLeen shouting, "Suspect spotted! He's hiding in Women's Underwear!"

Though Scott couldn't see his pursuer's face, he assumed the lopsided smile was back in place as Dick hurried into the store.

This was Scott's cue. He popped open the dome lid and pushed down with his feet and arms, lifting his body maybe an inch—and causing the entire receptacle to crash onto its side. To his surprise, the tumble didn't hurt. But instead of being pleased with his padding for absorbing the impact, he felt anger toward the coat—first, for starting this whole mess with the security guard, and now for getting him stuck in a garbage can. With a quick twist he was on his back and pushing even harder—without budging the container. "It can't end this way," he whispered to himself, just as he saw the older version of his ex-sister-in-law, up close now, pulling at the base, while a gaggle of shoppers gawked in the background. He struggled free as she said, "I don't believe I'm doing this."

"You?"

Once he was able to stand—on legs that had fallen asleep—kernels of popcorn and other refuse dropped from his sticky-in-places coat. He lumbered to the car. Susan was already inside, her hands on the wheel.

"Let's go," he said, pulling his door closed. "Turn off your lights in case anyone wants to read your plate."

He wrestled his way out of the coat, shedding more popcorn, crumpled receipts, and cigarette butts onto the leather seat of a Land Rover that smelled so new it could have been purchased that afternoon.

Susan grimaced. "I see your manners haven't improved." She turned down the CD player, which wasn't that loud to begin with. A woman was singing about wide-open spaces. Facing the highest stakes.

"What do you mean?" he asked.

"You could've saved some for me." It was then he saw the golden fried shrimp tails that had fallen onto the Land Rover logo at the center of an otherwise spotless floor mat.

"Sorry," he said, bending forward to pick up what he could of the debris. "I know this is hard for you."

"She's my blood too."

He opened his window, creating an icy squall as he scattered the shrimp tails. Susan didn't wait for him to roll it back up, having already pressed the control on her side. He held his hands close to a heating vent, and told her he needed to rent a car.

"And where do I come in?"

"She has my cards. We'll have to put it in your name."

"And this helps Mary *how*?"

Susan seemed to be thinking, and Scott felt hopeful. Perhaps she was relieved to learn he didn't want to borrow *her* car. But "We'll see" was all she said in response.

CHAPTER TWENTY

When she returned to the diner, Bev seemed even more flustered than before. The plump welcoming face that showed she enjoyed her own cooking as much as everyone else in Trappers Point had lost all trace of color—and this after steering a snowmobile through subzero darkness. Her small brown eyes seemed far away; her chubby fingers trembled. "They're crazy," she muttered. "All crazy."

Adrian got up from his chair. "What happened? You find your son?"

"My poor, poor Gunt."

"I can help, Bev."

Adrian watched Bev as she looked toward the back wall of the dining room, to the pair of photo portraits in matching wood frames painted gold. Her dead husband and wayward son looked remarkably similar with their narrow, fat-free faces, reddish-blond hair, and squinty blue eyes. More than twenty years before, as the tale had been passed to Adrian by the locals, Bev lost Gunt's father to an East Coast hunter a little too anxious to shoot something. Len had been thirty-two, Gunt's age now.

"I pleaded with him," she told Adrian. "Got down on my knees and clutched his legs. 'Think of the diner,' I said. That's when the goons dragged me out of there." She looked away from the photos and sniffled, rubbing her eyes. "Dragged me out like *I* was the problem."

Bev walked to the north wall, pausing by the green door that led to her living quarters. "Things have gotten out of control, don't you know. The stuff I saw. It was worse than before." She took hold of the door-knob, but waited a few seconds longer. "Adrian, you're shivering. Seems plenty warm in here to me. You're not coming down with something?"

◆

The front and rear wipers moved in silence, methodically slicing broad black V's from the whiteness that, just as calmly and predictably, moved in to reclaim the space in dispute. Scott was trying to place the aroma of Susan's perfume. It was delicate, alluring—a sweet envelope of ironic contradiction, given who was wearing it. He was reminded of the lilac bushes that once marked his property line, but this scent had to be more exotic and expensive than lilac blossoms. It had to be made in Paris, sold exclusively in malls with valet parking, and packaged in dark blue bottles with the facsimile of a celebrity's signature raised in gold.

"It sounds like Mary's in deep." Susan's voice tore through the quiet; it was so much louder than the music and wipers and warm gentle currents of a Land Rover's heating vents. "But we'll figure something out."

They passed a sign that read, COUNCIL BLUFFS 2. "Are the rates better in Iowa?" he asked.

"The snow's picking up. You're going to need something more substantial than a hippie van."

"And they don't have those in Nebraska? We are going to stop soon?"

"Soon enough," she said.

"That's good." Scratching an itch on the back of his neck, he found a kernel of popcorn lodged in his collar. "Because there is some urgency here."

"That's the part I'm not quite clear on. Wouldn't it make sense to wait until morning? Let the snowplows and sun do their work?"

"You never had children, did you?" he said.

She answered the question by stepping on the gas, which caused the front tires to briefly lose their grip.

His muscles tensed; he glanced at the speedometer. "If you had," he continued, "you'd understand."

"Look, Oprah," she said. "I never had kids because I never stayed married long enough." She was digging in her purse again. "Does that make you happy?"

Now he was the one without a response.

"Rebecca assures me they're difficult," she said. "I guess Mary showed you that."

But when he told her about the wrapper for the home pregnancy test, Susan backed off, saying, "Oh shit. I'm sorry."

"He's my age."

"This God guy?" She pulled a tiny plastic box from her purse. "I'll kill the bastard."

Scott considered her reaction, then surprised himself by taking another risk: "Don't ask me why I'm telling you, but I plan to do exactly that."

She took her eyes off the road to study him, making him nervous, and not only because he pictured her crossing the median and ramming the blade of an oncoming snowplow. Was he about to be ditched a second time? He hadn't seen any Wal-Marts on this stretch of highway.

"Does Mary know what you're planning?" she asked.

"Loose lips," he said, pointing to his own. "It's why I nearly ended up walking to Minnesota."

Susan's eyes were back where they belonged, focusing on travel conditions. She was quiet for some time, which corresponded to the duration of a song about letting something unspecified rip.

"I like this new Scott," she said at last. "You want a tic tac?"

◆

Something in the Land Rover was making noise, not much of a noise, but noise nonetheless. It was the turn signal, and it was clicking. Susan didn't wait for him to ask. "I just need to pick something up," she said.

"Does it have four wheels and an engine?"

Susan only smiled, prompting him to ask, "What are you up to?" He glanced at his wrist, where his watch should have been.

"Lose something?" she asked.

"Nothing much," he said. "Time."

"Join the club."

The exit ramp led to an intersection with traffic lights, which now turned from yellow to red.

"Wait a minute," he said as they came to a stop. "If you didn't stay married, why is your last name still the same?"

She fidgeted with the tic tac dispenser, displaying the nerves of an ex-smoker. "Clark and I were divorced twelve years ago. I remarried once, took my second husband's name. For all of eight months. By the time Guy dumped me, Clark had been transferred overseas to an office in Malaysia." The light changed. She accelerated gently on the packed-down snow, taking a left across the overpass. "I always liked the Carpenter-Smythe. And in my book, a ten-thousand-mile transfer made Clark the perfect husband."

They were pulling into an Exxon station.

"You were the one who teased me about the hyphenated name," she continued. "You asked what kind of names our grandchildren would end up with. Carpenter-Smythe-Nash-Young? Remember?"

"You're crazy, I never teased you. You were always digging at me."

"We all have our selective memories," she said.

Scott saw something that startled him. Next to the FREE WITH 10-GALLON FILL-UP car wash, the snow had created a rough, featureless sculpture of a Volkswagen bus. But his surprise was nothing compared to Mary's when, half a minute later, he and Susan walked into the convenience store.

"Aunt Rebecca?" she shouted for the benefit of everyone paying for gas, eating fast food, or looking for snacks in the chip aisle. "What's he doing here?"

"I'm your Aunt *Susan*, Mary."

"Then where's Aunt Rebecca?" The volume had not diminished by so much as a decibel. "That's who I talked to."

"And she talked to me." Scott watched Susan move closer to her niece as she said, "Rebecca and I decided you two needed to talk."

Mary groaned. "What he needs is to accept that my life has nothing to do with him. What I need is to get to my Savior."

"We're going to my house to sort things out and get some sleep."

"You go where you want," Mary responded. "I'm going to Minnesota."

Scott was impressed when Susan replied, "Yes, but I've got the car and it's going to my house."

Mary didn't seem so impressed. "Fine," she snapped. "I'll find my own way."

Scott felt his chest tighten as his daughter approached a pair of gawking truckers. "I need a ride north," she told them. "Tonight. I have cash. But I'll give you whatever you want."

"Don't need your cash," one replied.

"I'll do anything."

"Hell, babe," said the other. "I'll give you a ride all the way to the North Pole." Scott saw the yellow teeth and the FUCK IRAQ T-shirt.

He stepped forward, ready to intervene—and be permanently disfigured by two burly truckers.

Susan moved faster. "Forget it, perverts," she said. "My niece doesn't need your help."

"Don't listen to her. She's not my aunt."

"Enough," Susan declared. "You win. We'll sort things out in Minnesota."

He saw tears building in Mary's eyes. "Dad can't go." Then she was shouting, "He can't, he can't."

"Calm down," Scott said. "You sound like a four-year-old."

"He wants to kill Daniel. Did he tell you that?"

Others took notice: a truckers' tribunal. One young driver holding a foot-long Subway sandwich still in its wrapper glowered at Scott with eyes as hard as gears being stripped. He had an American flag patch sewn onto his coat sleeve.

"Sorry, kids," Susan spoke up, placing a hand on Mary's shoulder to hurry her along, "last plane out."

◆

"Post-post-apocalyptic," Adrian whispered, waiting for the recorded voice that represented United Airlines. "Post-post-apocalyptic."

"Sorry for the wait, valued customer. All flights from Omaha have been grounded until morning."

His heart pumped faster: heart attack zone. He hated Midwestern weather like a terminal patient hates the seasons, knowing the next one will come. He hated the weather for what it represented—a world of indifference. This world.

Time is a wall—that's what Cher Balser told him. *Since we can't move our heads, we stare at the present.* This, she said, was one of God Boy's musings. It would almost be worth getting that interview with Hawker for a chance to point out the obvious: Time is time, a wall's a wall. The first you run *out of*, the other you run *into*.

Paying no heed to Main Street's four-block-long speed-limit zone, a semi roared past, rattling the light fixture with its one working bulb. He was tempted to open the green door and trespass into Bev's private quarters. He'd grab the woman by her soft, broad shoulders before her drug of choice, Tylenol PM, fully kicked in, and he would ask, "What's going on at the compound? 'The stuff I saw.' What did you mean?"

He didn't have to. Bev reemerged, wearing a rose-pattern bathrobe so bulky it could have been a down comforter for a double bed. It was held in place by one narrow belt with a matching floral design. "You should turn on CNN," she said.

"The remote?"

"Where it always is," she said, bending down to retrieve it from a cabinet he was certain he'd looked in before.

She turned on the set and found the right channel. "They're shooting fireworks at the compound," she said. "*Fireworks.*"

"One of Hawker's buddies had a franchise," he said. "The real stuff, like you see at county fairs."

Bev shook her head. "All crazy." She walked to the kitchen and poured herself a glass of water. "Good night, Adrian." The green door closed; he heard it lock.

Wait, Bev. What did you see at the compound?

The wind picked up outside the diner.

◆

The fireworks were impressive. Adrian enjoyed them.

But after reporting that Hawker's devotees had tipped a school bus onto its side, effectively sealing off the main road into the compound, the *NewsNight* team moved on to other topics.

There were car bombs in Israel, earthquakes in China—developments that meant nothing to Adrian. When the show's host introduced a best-selling author promoting his "inside look" at a pedophile superstar's most recent legal battles, Adrian turned off the set. Half an hour had passed since Bev disappeared. He knew this from checking the clock on his phone. He felt lightheaded. He swatted away a fly, then shook his head and smiled wearily. There were no flies in March, of course. He was yawning again.

A new fear took hold. Mary would get to the diner just after his months of quasi-insomnia caught up with him. He'd be like Snow White, unable to wake. And Mary wouldn't risk kissing him.

Feeling the effects of caffeine dehydration, Adrian swallowed, a deep, dry gulp. He promised himself he'd get up from his chair and help himself to some water from Bev's kitchen. In just a few minutes.

This time, there was someone outside. Making noises the wind couldn't be making. Had Bev gone to check on her Ski-Doo 250 and locked herself out? What about Gunt? Maybe Bev's pleading had finally sunk in. Adrian made sure his recorder was ready. The Larsen boy would be a useful asset, he knew, however brain dead he'd become at the compound.

The front door opened, releasing a flood wave of cold that reminded Adrian why none of the locals believed in global warming. But he saw nothing, nothing at all. "Diner's closed," he informed the frigid void. "Mrs. Larsen's catching some overdue Z's."

He heard footsteps, loud footsteps, but again saw nothing. Each was measured, deliberate, and he knew what it was to be stalked—like most of the wildlife that came to be shot here in upstate Minnesota. "I don't believe in ghosts," he said. "Apart from the ones in my head."

That was when the room exploded with brightness. At first he couldn't see. The light had somehow made everything darker. He blinked a few times. Nothing.

"Adrian C. Hummel!"

This was like nothing he'd heard before, awake or in dreams. It was the rage of a mob, distilled and condensed. It was the voice of fire, the voice of ice.

It was not a reassuring voice.

"On your knees!"

The room was awash in sunlike brilliance, with most of it concentrated directly before him.

This is no time for a nervous breakdown, Adrian nearly said aloud as he dropped to his knees. But he chuckled at his next thought: *If not now, when?*

His sight improved, and in the dense core of light he saw something more. This was the face of . . . it was still hard to be sure, no matter how much he squinted . . . a baby.

"You know why I'm here."

"Lack of sleep," Adrian responded. "Stress. Caffeine. You're just an hallucination."

"You know why I'm here!"

Adrian covered his ears with his palms, but could still hear the voice. It came from both outside and inside his head. It came from every atom in the air and his body.

"Are you . . . Jesus? A guardian angel?"

"You know who I am! You know why I'm here!"

"I know nothing," Adrian muttered at last.

The face seemed satisfied with his answer.

"I'm so tired. I—" Adrian felt weightless, then felt as if he weighed two tons and would collapse into himself like a telescope. In an immeasurable fraction of time, he saw everything he'd ever done wrong in his life. A lot of information, he thought, to be so thoroughly capsulized.

The face disappeared and the light broke into fragments. Billions of tiny stars now spun around Adrian's head.

"You know what you must do," said the voice. "You know."

The light reassembled. The face reappeared. "You will write your book."

"I will?"

"Millions will read it."

He could feel his lips stretching to accommodate a smile. If this was crazy, he wanted more.

"But you must understand one thing—"

"Adrian?"

Bev had reentered the room—and the spirit had bolted. Gone, vanished. The diner grew dark once more. He couldn't see Bev. He could only hear her voice: "Adrian, Adrian, what are we going to do with you? It's freezing in here, don't you know."

CHAPTER TWENTY-ONE

"After this I'm going someplace warm," Semolina Bath was saying. "I'm about ready for a week on the sun."

"Beats the Midwest," Tank Matthews, long-haul driver for Harrod Freight, said.

She studied the driver's profile in the waves of soft blue light flowing out from an instrument panel that belonged in the cockpit of a jet. He was handsome, in a rugged George C. Scott kind of way. He had a modest double chin, and his cheeks had fallen a bit, but who had room to talk? What was that old saying—*Time and gravity wait for no one*? He was close to her in age, maybe two or three years older. But he probably looked better than George C. did these days, assuming the actor was still alive. And she was pretty sure he owned his own tractor. Tank Matthews . . . sometimes nicknames really fit their owners. Solid, wide, and—if it turned out he wasn't invincible, he might well be impenetrable.

She met him in the restaurant of the Bulldog Truck Stop, where she'd been sitting for more than two hours. He was the one who finally came over and asked, "Everything all right, ma'am?"

They shared a booth till eight. "If you can get me as far as Omaha," she said as he paid for her dinner—chicken-fried steak just a tad overcooked—with a crisp new twenty, "I'll catch a bus north. Must be something stops in Trappers Point. I could at least get to Canterbury. It's a bit bigger than Trappers Point, and only twenty minutes away."

He told her she might as well ride to Sioux Falls, his "port for the night," since it was right on her way and would save him from having to drive into Omaha proper.

"Put you an hour closer."

By the time they crossed the Missouri River into Iowa, on the north 680-bypass, the wife of Bath had completed her tale: three husbands buried, the Holy Land traversed, unfeeling insurance investigators vanquished. Tank had seemed sympathetic. He smiled in the right places. These were good signs. "Have you got family?" she asked.

"Seven kids, and they all turned out okay. Girl's the only one ain't built like me, thank God. Around our house was like feeding a pack of wolves. Fast as I put food on the table, they took it back off. If someone said thanks after dinner I knew one of the kids had a friend over."

"Your wife must be a lucky woman."

"Gone five years now. Ellie was my high-school sweetheart. Married thirty-three years."

"I'm sorry."

"No, that would be me. Ellie's not dead, you see, just our marriage. It was one of those curveballs life throws you. You sure you wanna hear this?"

"Why, sugar? Have I got something better to do?"

"Then consider yourself warned." Tank ran a hand through thinning hair, scratched the back of his head. "Telemarketing wrecked my marriage—that's the long and short of it. I'd been home for all of three days, and the bast . . . bullmongers were hanging up on me every time I answered the phone."

Semolina liked the way he deleted his own expletives. Tank was a gentleman.

"They just hung up?"

"They get their computers dialing three, four numbers at once. Whoever picks up first wins the prize of their attention."

"I didn't know that."

"Finally, one time, I grab the phone and, what do you know, there's someone on the other end. Now that's he's got his foot in the door, the sonofabrick is off and running. Seems I need a good retirement plan, and that means I need a good retirement planner, someone I can trust, and pay, with money I could be saving for to retire with. But fast as this joker's talking, he's in no hurry to tell me who he works for. They try to keep that from you till you're hooked, so's you can't call up and complain. 'Who are you calling for?' I ask for the tenth time.

'Mr. Mark Matthews,' he says. 'No, *who* are *you* calling for—what company do you represent?' He won't say. So I let loose with a few choice words I picked up in my travels. 'Do you use that mouth to pray?' he asks. 'What I'm gonna use this mouth for is to have you fired,' I say. 'Your supervisor around?'

"Funny, but what comes out of his mouth next is hardly what I'd call praying. Maggot knows more words than I do. But that ain't the worst. Before he hangs up, he kind of half-whispers, 'You are a dead man.'"

"Chills," said Semolina, hugging herself. "What did you do?"

"I got him fired. From the State of Nebraska. *The correctional system.* Where all those calls come from."

"From Nebraska?" she asked.

"Close," he said. "Prison. That's who companies hire to do their telemarketing. Get a contract with the state, give the inmates everyone's phone number and private information."

"You're joking?"

"It gets better. Turns out that threatening the life of a law-abiding citizen isn't considered bad behavior by the folks what run the Nebraska prisons. My friend is out two years later. How do I know? We start getting calls at all hours. And by that I mean Ellie starts getting calls—'cause I'm on the road scratching out a living. He's calling to make sure I haven't forgotten I'm supposed to be dead. So she hears all kinds of gory details about the steps I'm taking to get there."

"Just because you stood up to him."

"I'm thinking it was more because he was a violent psycho who all of a sudden had too much time on his hands. I was just cheap entertainment."

Semolina was also impressed with Tank for holding his own in conversation. She had always prided herself on her speaking skills, and took "loquacious"—a word used to describe her at the compound—as a well-deserved compliment (after looking it up, of course). People were much too content to listen these days, and they didn't even listen to those around them, but to pleasing faces on the tubus de boobus. Semolina couldn't understand why it was okay for some actor famous for reading things written by others to share his views on global warming, but not for the rest of us. Her views on the weather were every bit as important as Matt Damon's or Reese Witherspoon's. And she delivered her own opinions with grace and aplomb, qualities that once meant something.

Tank was still talking. "These threats, finally, bother the cops, and Prayer Mouth's back doing time. But now Ellie tells me she feels more alone than ever before with the kids all grown and me gone five quarters of the time. 'Why don't you come ride with me?' I say. 'You know I can't work at Taco Hell. I got two TVs, you can still watch *Judge Judy.*'" He reached up to the right of his visor, pushed a button on a silver box that reminded Semolina of her missing flask. She heard radiolike static. A tiny red light blinked twice. "Too late, Tank. Turns out Ellie'd been getting solace from my brother. From when she first got the calls. Jake was there. I wasn't. Makes it kind of hard for me to go back now. When I do, I stay with my girl."

"And where's back?"

"Storm Lake. Iowa." He checked his left-side mirror before changing lanes. "Mostly I live on the road. She never gave me no grief, and the way they keep cutting our pay, you got no choice but to rack up hours."

"Your truck's really something." She looked about the spacious cab, making sure Tank could see how impressed she was by the DVD player that shared a screen with his computer. "All these lights," she said. "You've got everything you could possibly need right here. Well, *almost* everything."

"I'm not so sure about that," he said. "But I do know one thing. The prison workforce can't find me here." He told her that the TV in back had a full 25" screen. "There's a refrigerator, too."

A two-trailer truck plowed past them. "Man, I hate those things," he said. "After all the . . . muck they drug us through, now they find the nerve to double our loads."

"It's those three-trailer ones frighten me," the widow said.

"They scare me, too, but for different reasons."

Heading north on I-29, with the snow picking up, she told him about Daniel Hawker. "You didn't have to be an idiot to believe this holy grifter, but it helped. I'm proof enough of that, I suppose."

She reached for her purse on the plush mat carpet that felt so good against the bare skin of her feet, giving Tank time to say, "I'd hardly call you an idiot, Mrs. Bath."

"Sweetie, I told you before, my friends don't call me Missus. It's Semolina or nothing."

A self-effacing smirk turned him into a child, into a child whose mom had just caught him flushing her best nylons down the toilet. "So I got a question. What was it like in that compound of yours?"

"It got pretty crazy. There was this one girl, Cher Balser. She believed Danny was the reincarnation of Jesus . . . *and* David Koresh. You know, the wacko from Waco. I set her straight. 'But, sugar,' I said, 'he died in ninety-three. Danny was born way before that.'"

"Meaning you can't be in two bodies at one time?"

"You got it, sweetie." She now had a cigarette. Tank popped out his lighter and did the honors. "This Cher wanted to be an actress, and I guess it made sense since she was always putting on a show. Danny sucked her in by making her think some big producer wanted to make a movie about his mission, with the disciples playing themselves. All it took was an article from some Podunk paper."

She told Tank about the last days in Hallelujah City. "There was a paranoid theory round every corner. Dears, I said, who cares what the FBI's planning if God's about to take the world off life support?" She told him how The Seven, or what was left of them, bickered over the most trivial matters. "They couldn't decide if they should pay their bills for the whole month, or just up to Doomsday."

He chuckled, the way husband Garrick once did. Gently. Soothingly.

"But Jesus H. Charisma kept things from exploding. Right up to the moment he sent me home. I'm sure he did that to be alone with my money."

"I don't mean to be disrespectful," Tank said, "but . . . you went home thinking the world would end, and since that didn't happen, you want a refund?" He adjusted a dial on the Full Cab Comfort thermostat, and added, "Why hand it to this joker in the first place?"

"There were lots of reasons made sense at the time."

"Try me," he said. "I'll settle for one."

"How about . . . the way of the world, the way it is now? You lose part of your body, they replace it with money. Lose part of your family, they wallpaper your house with fifties. Don't get me wrong—I enjoyed fighting the insurance instigators more than I cared to admit. Gave me a place to dump my anger. But once I had their checks in hand, the money made me uncomfortable. Here's your big-screen TV, Semolina, your three-bed RV. Here's your winter retreat on the Mexican Riviera. Tell me, Tank honey, what any of those things have to do with my Robert or Red or Garrick? You ever know a TV to tickle your belly? Ever snuggle up with a twelve-ton Winnebago?"

He waited some time before speaking. "So how was it you wound up at the Bulldog? That Colorado pair really just ditched you?"

"I expected this from the little princess," Semolina said. "But her father. I didn't take him for a weasel."

"The way I understand it, weasel only comes out of its hole when it's ready to show itself."

"Sounds like you've been watching the Nature Channel, sugar."

"Satellite dish. Up top where you can't see it."

Semolina coughed, holding what was left of the Marlboro Light away from her face. "There was always something odd about Danny's attraction to the girl, though it's not like he did anything that *wasn't* odd. He saw something in her the rest of us couldn't see . . . and now I know what it was. Little Mary Chambers is as duplicitous as he is."

"And just like that they were gone?"

"Vanished like smoke. While I waited in the restaurant. Kept some of my belongings, too."

"Well, they better hope to fluff I don't catch up with them."

"You're going to Minnesota?"

"Try and stop me," he said.

CHAPTER TWENTY-TWO

The snow was time's way of showing itself, of taking on physical properties. Frigid, indifferent, thorough—accumulating like the strata that buried the scent of his Liz, both sweet and stale, the first morning Scott woke beside her. Inches to feet to yards. Like the layers of ice-cold permanence that covered his learning to clip a baby's toenails, feeling lightheaded, or reading *The Return of the King* to a sleep-defying ten-year-old who looked up at his face through wide green eyes as if he were somehow crafting the sentences she loved. Minutes to hours to days.

"I sure could use a smoke," Susan said to him. "Too bad I quit last year."

"I'm almost ready to light one up myself."

"But . . . you're afraid you'd lose that edge of superiority?"

In the seat directly behind him, Mary laughed so hard she snorted.

He glanced over at Susan, puzzled. "I thought you liked the new Scott."

"Maybe I was talking to the old one."

Though it took him a moment to start, he laughed too. Without knowing why, he was glad for her sarcasm.

"We might as well relax," she said. "It's going to take some time to get there in this storm." She pushed a button on the compartment between the front seats. The lid popped open and a light came on. "You know, I've always wanted to see Minnesota."

"You're kidding," he said, looking at CD cases with names like Faith Hill and Reba McEntire printed on their spines. While he didn't know who they were, he was certain he wouldn't like their music. "You only live one state away."

"You have to remember," she said, "I went to Colorado once. It was a disaster."

"At last, our memories are in agreement," he said.

Susan looked over at him. "I'm pretty sure there's a tape in the player. Celine Dion. Dealer threw it in."

"The Dixie Chicks are fine," Mary blurted out. "CD's growing on me."

Everyone was quiet after that—and he saw Susan's suggestion to relax for what it was. An incantation. A powerful one. He could let go now. He could be as tired as he was supposed to be after a tumultuous several hours. *Cold, hot, down, up. Hawker dead, Hawker reborn. Held at gunpoint, holding at gunpoint.* It felt as if the snow was settling on his eyelids. *Mary gone, Mary back.* "You won't kill me if I fall asleep?" he said.

"I'll try to resist the temptation." Susan smiled, turning to face him again. She moved her lips in silence, but he was able to make out the message. *"We'll save that for Mr. Hawker."*

◆

Their headlights drilled through walls of white motion. The snowflakes dislodged by this process were shooting like sparks, millions of sparks, reproducing an effect from one of Eddie Jones's video games—space travel at the speed of light. This image was broken every few seconds by the windshield wipers, surrealistically silent. Mary yawned, stretched out her arms. Her dad was already snoring.

The *Wide Open Spaces* CD started for a third time; it couldn't have been very long, forty minutes at most. She studied Susan's profile, or what she could see of it from this angle. *Is this how Mom would have looked in her forties, a touch overweight, but still quite attractive?* Her mom would've dyed her hair most likely, going by everything Mary knew, losing the gray in an effort to fool those who care about time. The aunt pushed in the lighter on the dash, then dug a cigarette from her purse. Only it wasn't a cigarette. Once it was lit, Susan inhaled deeply, and an aroma as sharp as it was familiar tickled the finest hairs in Mary's nose.

After letting out the smoke, Aunt Susan said, "Medicinal marijuana. I hope it doesn't bother you. Though it's not strictly legal. Or medicinal really. Not in the strictest sense. I take it because my throat hurts. All those years of smoking. Don't ever start."

Mary could only imagine what her father would've said if he'd been awake to hear this. As for her, she could hardly deny that the bud smelled good. Really good. It would be easy as sin to ask for a hit. *Heaven is a river in the bright morning fog. You must see past the fog.*

"Can I use your phone?" she asked.

◆

Adrian volunteered to accept the charges before he realized it wasn't a collect call. "Where are you?" he asked.

"Two CDs closer. Problem is, it's the same CD. Just started again."

"At least one trailer's been set on fire," he said. "They're talking about it right now on CNN. The feds are keeping their distance. They think Hawker's just trying to provoke them."

"They're not going in?"

"Doesn't look like it," Adrian said. "But Hawker . . . he's sure painted himself into a corner."

Before clicking off the phone, she thanked him for the news and said they'd be there as soon as possible. No more stops.

"I'll be in the diner," he said.

After handing the phone back to Susan, she looked to her right. The wide open spaces, the little she could see of them, were uniformly white.

Daniel, we're getting closer. Wait for me.

She still thought about going before the press. *I've come to make you understand. I am to blame. I corrupted the Teacher.* But this had become a secondary concern. What she wanted most now was to apologize to her Savior—and to ask Him about the child she carried.

Daniel, Teacher, what does it mean?

She was staring at the windshield again, at the space between her sleeping dad and stoned aunt. The hole through the wall of motion was pulling Mary in. What was she seeing? A preview of death? A flashback to birth, from that time before language? The wipers kept moving, advancing, retreating. *Daniel, I'm getting close. Be patient.*

Smoke was taking the place of air. Susan cracked her window, but not enough to provide any real ventilation, like going after an oil spill with a paper towel. "Is that better?" she asked.

"You're not at all like Dad says."

"I probably was—once." She held the joint back toward Mary. "You want a hit?"

"Can't."

Susan asked why, coughing more than speaking.

"I promised God I wouldn't."

The aunt took another deep drag, bobbed her head almost imperceptibly—five times, as if counting silently—and released the smoke. "That's a pretty good reason."

"We each gave up something of consequence."

"Understood."

White from the snow, its headlights burning down, a pickup truck had ended its trip in the median. "People should pull off while they can do it voluntarily," Susan said coldly. She placed her bud in the ashtray's grooved ridge. "At least it seems to be letting up some."

For Mary, the smoke packed one powerful subversive effect. And if it wasn't making her high, it was opening doors in her memory, to other nights when that smell was in the air. Like that summer night a few weeks after graduation—the authentically fateful night that began in Di Johnson's Dolby-DTS Surround home theater basement. They were watching *Titanic*. It had been Cher's turn to pick the movie. In keeping with tradition, Di raided the stash that belonged to her mom—hidden as it was with all the finesse and imagination one would expect from a pothead parent. "Lighting the fuse to freedom," said Cher as she activated the bud, her words one more component of their private tradition.

"Just say now!" Di added.

The basement was air-conditioned and looked like an electronics store, making it the hideout of choice from the blistering clear days that had come to make up a Colorado summer—and which her dad blamed on SUVs and air-conditioned basements. These were the days that didn't want to end, where the sun was known to sneak back up when you were sure you'd watched it set. In exchange for being high all the time, Di's mom bought tons of DVDs from a mail-order club, whatever Di requested. Their "own personal Blockbuster"—that's what Cher called the basement, and she came from a full-package digital-cable home.

The bud had come out around eight, after Cher's favorite ship, ornery as a Colorado sunset, finally went down. The three friends started out giggling over stupid things, like mall safaris and Mr. Spellman's homework assignments, but Mary was soon sobbing uncontrollably. These were the tears of history, life, the world. The tears of breathing, waking up, having to floss her teeth every night. The everyday pain that compounded like interest. Like snow on the shoulders of an interstate highway.

"What's wrong?" Di said, putting her hand on Mary's arm.

Cher tapped her fingers on the coffee table. "Yeah, what the fuck is it?"

Mary had meant to say, "Everything," but she didn't. If her friends were surprised by the answer she gave, so was she. "It's my mother. She's dead."

The silence that followed seemed to last hours, though it was probably only minutes outside the Marijuana Time Zone. Then a voice called from the heavens, "Is everything all right down there?" Di told her mom that everything was cool, and Cher did an impression of Principal Bender addressing a packed assembly. "I tried marijuana and it was the biggest mistake of my life. Look what it can lead to."

Mary smiled, reaching for a Kleenex. Di smiled too, saying, "Let's get some pizza."

Cher ducked into the bathroom, saying, "Ten bucks the Paradiso is packed." Unlike her friends, Cher saw packed as a good thing.

"Parents are overrated, you know," Di said quietly to Mary. "Mine stayed together for the cat. When Mingus died, Dad split."

"I've got shotgun," Cher called out from behind the closed door.

They were about to meet Daniel Hawker.

◆

Scott's dream shoveled away great chunks of time, and soon he was talking with his mother, whose extended family, in her dusky final years, had come to include the cast of TV's *Touched By an Angel*. "You don't deserve this," he whispered to her, and she responded, seemingly freed from her Alzheimer's bondage, "No one does, dear. No one deserves any of this."

He woke—somewhat, his eyes didn't want to stay open—thinking about the only time he'd really defied his parents, when he was sixteen. He'd done this by hitching from Denver to Phoenix over Christmas break, just to see someplace different. Cows stared at him in New Mexico, followed his every move with dull, unflinching eyes. "Got any smoke?" two drivers asked. In the back of a Ford panel truck a naked blond woman slept. Her small, pale breasts caught the occasional light of passing cars. Her soft-featured face was cherubic in appearance, not of this world, but she snored violently, like a dangerous animal warning others to keep their distance.

By the side of Interstate 40 in Navajo country, at three in the morning, a semi pulled into the emergency lane. The door of its cab flew open, revealing a pistol aimed directly at Scott's face.

"Don't shoot me," he whimpered.

"Just wanted to make sure you didn't have any ideas about shooting me," the burly driver replied. "Climb in." He used his CB radio to get Scott his next ride, going south on 89, the other side of Flagstaff.

The recollection must have been turning into a dream as it unfolded, because this time, the driver kept pointing his gun at Scott, while physically transforming himself into a Wal-Mart security guard. With the face of Daniel Hawker. Scott turned to run, and in the process both jerked himself fully awake and pulled a muscle in his right shoulder.

"Oh God, where am I?" It hurt to breathe, as if the injured muscle were somehow connected directly to his lungs.

The snow had stopped. He was staring at the glass front of a convenience store. TRAPPERS POINT WELCOMES SPORTSMEN. PAY FOR GAS IN ADVANCE. Susan was inside, grilling the night clerk for information. Scott buttoned his coat.

CHAPTER TWENTY-THREE

Susan was looking at Mary as if her nose had grown fingers. "Do you always scream when you wake up?"

"It's just—" Mary was still trying to figure out where she was, and why. "You startled me."

"I don't think so," the aunt said, her face uncomfortably close, her breath smelling like tic tacs dropped in an ashtray. Mary's father stood beside her, looking in through the same open door on the car's left side. "We were inside the store. The clerk thought someone was getting stabbed. He would've dialed 911 if they had it up here."

Mary stared at the wall of light. The Gas 'N' Pass convenience store, the closest thing Trappers Point had to a supermarket. "You need to drop me at the diner," she told her dad and aunt. "I can't get you in."

She closed her eyes and was able to recall the subject of her night terror, the one that apparently had just caused her to scream. Those same five shrunken heads had returned to circle her father, more vivid and angry than before. Their flesh was taut, yet deeply wrinkled. It was the color of death, a color that wasn't constant. Like paint being mixed, stirred with a stick, it was orange and brown and sick-olive-green, merging, mottled, broken apart. "You really should go home, Dad. You too, Aunt Susan."

"We came here together," said Susan. "We're sticking together."

Mary took a deep breath, letting the cold wake her up the rest of the way. "Your mistake. I tried to warn you." She slid forward on her seat. "Could I get past? I just need to grab one thing from the store."

"Maybe you should buy some cranberry juice," her dad said.

She must have perfected her look of *I don't know what you're talking about*, because he continued. "Your bladder problem?"

The restroom was for employees only, but the employee didn't mind. "Sure. Be my guest. Just be sure to hold the handle down an extra few seconds." Mary did that, while using her free hand to start the ice-cold water—only one faucet worked—in a sink as gross as the toilet, with fingerprints ringing the basin. Still, she washed her hands for nearly four minutes, wasting none of that time on her worn-dead reflection in the mirror's smoky glass.

Her dad shouldn't have come—that's what she was focused on. He should've stayed where he belonged, with his TV and lamp, lifeless, harmless, another piece of furniture. But she hadn't given up on getting to Daniel without him. She had an idea, one last hope. With Adrian's help, there might be a way to ditch her tormentors. It wouldn't be much longer: she'd be standing with Daniel. She reached for a paper towel. The dispenser was empty.

No sooner were they back on the road than they attracted curiosity. "Mary, get down," her aunt blurted as a Humvee approached in the southbound lane.

"What's happening?" Mary whispered, now unable to see.

"They're definitely checking us out," Susan replied.

"Who are they?"

"Pick one," her father volunteered, "FBI, ATF, Homeland Security. Damn, they're turning around. We can't let them stop us now."

"And what do you want me to do?" Susan asked. "Outrun them?"

It took her dad a second to respond. "Maybe you should pull over, see what they do."

Mary braced herself as they came to a stop. "What's happening?" she asked.

"They're . . . still going," her father replied, "speeding up a little. Our family history must not have shown up."

"Shown up?" Susan asked.

"In their computer check. They don't know this car belongs to the aunt of a prominent cult member. We're just some curious Nebraskans who got tired of watching doomsday on TV."

Susan pulled back out and Mary pushed herself up, just in time to say, "Here. This is it."

"We've only driven a block and a half," said Susan as she pulled her Land Rover into the narrow lot that separated Main Street from the Trappers Point Diner. "This is where you're meeting him? It's awfully dark." They were facing the front entrance, with the reflection of one headlight burning like a sun.

Mary got out of the car and walked to the door, thinking she saw a note. But all she found was a decal: *Don't worry about this. Worry about the owner.* An illustration of a gun, pointing straight out, backed up the warning.

No wonder she jumped when a large woman appeared in the dark doorway.

"Semolina?" Mary whispered before the light came on and corrected that impression. "Oh, thank God."

"What do you want?" the woman asked.

"We're looking for Adrian C. Hummel."

"Government?"

Mary must have looked surprised, because the woman added, "Didn't mean to insult you. There's a lot of them around tonight."

She continued. "Adrian was sleeping in here. On the floor, with my front door wide open. It was colder than Hades. I couldn't do a thing to wake him. I dragged him back to his room. Lucky his keys were on this here table."

The woman pointed to a cell phone and laptop.

"I should probably take those to him," Mary offered.

"Adrian always complained he never slept, don't you know. Guess it finally caught up with him."

"His room?"

"Sorry. The motel. Room 17. I held onto the keys so I could check on him come morning."

Minutes later, Mary was standing over a pile of blankets in the shape of Adrian C. Hummel, whose snoring had not been interrupted by her dad turning on three lamps. "It smells like a hamster's cage in here," Susan whispered. She was facing a small round table near the dark green curtains that hid a front window, and she was holding a cassette tape. There were others on the tabletop. "What do you make of these?"

When Mary walked over she was handed a tape. It had a handwritten label, CHER BALSER-MIRACLE WITH THE DOG. "Shoot," she whispered, though it almost came out as something else. *So Cher was one of Adrian's contacts. What had she been telling him?*

The next cassette provided an answer to that question. Its title: CHER BALSER-SEX WITH THE SAVIOR.

"Ah, shit," Mary blurted, stopping before she added, *You exiled the wrong disciple*, a thought she'd been trying to suppress ever since Daniel had exiled the wrong disciple. *The Teacher does not err. The Teacher does not err.*

She was ready to slip the tape in her pocket when Adrian called out, "Hey, what's going on here?"

"SEX" hit the table's rim on its way to the thin, crusty carpet. Adrian was sitting up, pulling at a sheet to cover his stomach. "Mary?" he said.

◆

At first, Adrian thought he was seeing things again. There stood Mary, entirely angelic, alongside a strange woman and some homeless guy with trash sticking to his coat. When Adrian opened his mouth to speak, the Mary apparition said, "You fell asleep at the diner."

"And I'm awake now?"

"I'm Mary's aunt."

Which made the other person her father. There wasn't as much garbage hanging from his coat as Adrian first thought, but even so . . . What the hell was his story?

"You promised to take me back in," Mary said, her eyes pointed down. She seemed to be embarrassed by his state of unpreparedness. He adjusted the sheet to better conceal his doughy whiteness.

"You're taking us, too," the aunt added.

"We still have a deal?" Adrian said. "You'll get the Teacher to tell me his story?"

"We have a deal," Mary replied.

"I need a minute. Mind waiting outside?"

"It can't be any colder out there," said the father, already moving back toward the door. Soon, he and the aunt were gone from Adrian's sight.

He wondered why Mary was dawdling. Did she need to speak with him alone? Did she just need a break from the others? Whatever the reason, he wanted her away from the table—and the cassettes.

"Your dad," he said. "Quite the gentleman."

While bending down to pick up his underwear and socks, he caught Mary behaving strangely. Sliding her shoe sideways across the carpet, she seemed startled when he asked, "Is everything all right?"

◆

Mary leaned into his back to make the most of Adrian's wind-screening talents as he steered the snowmobile south into the alley. He smelled like motel soap, even through the coat, something she'd never noticed before. "Old Slick here belongs to Bev Larsen," he shouted. "The lady at the diner. You probably know her son. Gunt." This was Mary's first look at the fences and parking lots behind the Point's four businesses, five counting the Legion. A security light guarding the motel's dumpster also protected an old war-movie-type Jeep that had rusted uniformly. She wondered if the Jeep belonged to Adrian. During the warmer months, he'd always parked some distance from the Field of the Eastern Star. She never knew how he drove there.

Scott was riding with Susan in the Land Rover, a few car lengths behind the snowmobile.

"Your daughter's kind of sneaky," she said.

He didn't comment. As exhausted as he was, Scott couldn't believe how gullible he'd been when Mary told them the other snowmobile had a key in it. It didn't, of course, and for the second time that night he'd watched his daughter pull away.

"I'm not sure I got that," Susan added. "She has to be freezing on that thing, and we're keeping up just fine."

"We are keeping up," he conceded. But as much as he wanted to be put at ease, Scott felt sure that before this was over they were going to wish they had a snowmobile.

He'd already popped Celine Dion out of Susan's player before asking, "Do you mind if I play this?" He showed her the cassette he'd taken from the Hummel sty.

"Be my guest."

Hidden in dashboard and doors, the speakers hissed with dirty white noise, while—00:18, 00:19—stiff orange digits added up seconds on a black LCD panel. The tape must have been near its end. Scott looked for the rewind button—

"I talked with Mary Chambers again today. I learned a bit more about conflict in the compound."

"Where's the volume on this thing?" Scott asked, and Susan pressed the proper button.

"Mary talked about Cher Balser, the other disciple I've been meeting with. This marked a first. Though Cher can't stop talking about her sister disciple, Mary's never once mentioned Cher in conversation. Today she confirmed what Cher's been saying. There's no love lost between the two who started out best friends. And who came here together from Colorado."

"I didn't know about the friend," Scott said.

"Mary's worried about Cher. Worried she's lost all control. Only a few weeks back, according to Mary, God Boy caught a deprogrammer on his property. He assigned Cher to spend the night with him. Cher must have been persuasive, because the man decided to convert and stay—"

"That was *my* deprogrammer," said Scott. "Twenty-two thousand dollars' worth."

He tensed as the branch of an evergreen, heavy with snow, scraped the roof of Susan's car. "Doesn't sound like anyone told Mary that," Susan said.

The snowmobile took a right, a hard right best taken by an off-road winter recreational vehicle sitting close to the ground, but Susan kept up, barely tapping her brakes in deference to the dark, slick deathtrap that was rural Minnesota.

"I asked Mary about her family. She told me her mother died when she was young and that she'd never got over it."

This time, Scott kept his "She never talked about that either" to himself.

The Land Rover fishtailed. Scott's hand was on the dash, his arm a rigid beam. Susan hit the gas, bringing it under control.

"This appears to be true, but I didn't know what to think after I asked, 'What about your father?' Mary said he was dead as well, words in direct contradiction to Cher's account. When I told Mary I was sorry, she said it didn't matter. He'd never shown her anything but indifference."

As dryness tightened its grip on Scott's throat, the tape continued, *"I told her I knew about worthless dead fathers.*

"Hers, she said, led a joyless, godless existence—an existence without life. She called him the opposite of matter, a vacuum."

"Shit," Susan whispered. "Are you all right?"

He didn't answer.

"Scott?"

Fishtailing again, the car banged against a tree. But the SUV kept moving forward.

"Your car," he said.

"Fuck the car. Are you okay?"

He nodded halfheartedly, but his actions betrayed him. Scott was digging for his bottle of Maalox tablets.

"You're going to get her back, you know."

It took him a minute to notice that the tape was no longer playing. The last thing he'd heard was, *"So here lies the mystery. Cher Balser has told me she'd met Mary's father. At Mary's house, and at some school play. I've never questioned Mary's veracity. If anything, I'd take her word over Cher's in a moment. So why the lies about her father? Is it simple wishful thinking, or is the girl more complex than I've been assuming?"*

Still unable to recall Cher Balser, Scott whispered, "I might as well have been dead. I didn't even know who Mary's friends were."

"This is going to break her heart, you realize."

"What? Reality?"

"Come on, Scott. Weren't you going to be John Grisham the first time I met you?"

He didn't correct her. John Grisham sounded less ridiculous than Ernest Hemingway or Charles Dickens. He simply said, "I don't see the connection."

"Dreams," said Susan.

"Dreams?"

"You've got to admit, it seems silly now."

"That I could do something worthwhile?"

"That you were ever so innocent," she said with a laugh. "Not all that far from finding God and saving mankind. Though I've got to say, Mary's fantasy seems less selfish."

"I hadn't thought about it for years," he said.

"You numbed yourself."

"Circumstance. It wasn't self-inflicted."

"Exactly."

Headlights appeared in the mirror outside Scott's window—growing larger. He surprised himself by saying, "Kill your lights. Now. Make it harder for them to follow."

He added a "Yikes" when Susan obliged, transforming the road into a cavern's mouth, gaping and dark, incredibly dark. Not so for the inside of her car, the headlights were getting closer, and they were high off the ground, perfectly aligned with the Land Rover's back window. This made it hard to see. "I hope your vision is better than mine," he said quietly.

"They're not going to stop us," Susan assured him. "We've come too far."

The darkness exaggerated every jolt from a stone or dip. "We don't seem to be losing them."

No sooner had he said this than Adrian and Mary took an impossibly sharp right—and Susan followed suit. She must not have braked; her lights would have warned the other car to slow down, and the other car didn't slow. It took all of Scott's strength to turn his head to witness the collision between a dark-colored SUV and the snowy wall that Susan had barely missed hitting.

"Nice work," he whispered.

Susan's headlights came back on, and Mary turned her head to face them. It might have been Scott's imagination—his daughter's head was mostly obscured by a helmet, after all—but he thought she seemed surprised to see that Susan had kept up.

They were crossing the private land of someone who bred guard dogs that aspired to be wolves. Scott knew the land was privately owned from reading nine consecutive signs. These had ranged from the noncommittal NO TRESPASSING to TRESPASSERS SHOT ON SITE.

He popped two more tablets, taking the total to six.

"The clerk told me the compound was close to town," Susan said. "We must be taking the long way."

The road straightened out. Scott saw light in the distance, sifted through evergreens. It could have been the glow of an emergent moon, or the light pollution of a sprawling metropolis that had somehow escaped the attention of mapmakers and census takers. Scott, of course, knew what he was seeing; Hawker had not waited for Mary to return. The compound was burning.

A bright light cut across the road in front of them, just missing the snowmobile. "A helicopter," Susan said. "I don't think they saw us."

"With our headlights on? More likely they're in a hurry to get somewhere."

There was a clearing ahead, perfectly flat and free of plant growth. Scott now saw the actual flames, just beyond the open space, orange-red demons without solid form, dancing between old-growth deciduous trees. The blaze was reflected on the snow-covered field in patches of faintly glowing yellow and auburn—a radioactive spill.

He observed one more thing.

"Are you seeing what I'm seeing?" Susan asked.

"Fireworks?" he said, relieved to know he hadn't imagined the odd clusters of color.

"Nice," she said slowly, making him wonder if she was high. He'd thought he smelled pot back when he first woke up. "It almost looks professional." Dozens of red and blue stars fell from the sky, as out-of-sync blasts shook Susan's car like shallow potholes.

"Damn," she muttered, hitting her brakes. "This field's a frozen lake."

The snowmobile gave up no speed as its treads met the ice. Worse, Scott could have sworn that Mary was swatting the side of her driver's head, like a jockey demanding her horse move faster.

"They're trying to lose us," Scott said as they skidded to a stop, slightly off-angle.

"You think?"

The snowmobile's taillight grew smaller and dimmer.

"We have to keep going," Scott said. "Maybe if we stick to the edge?"

"Is that a good idea?"

"I don't know—it's the only one I have."

Susan clicked on her brights and put the Land Rover back in Drive. Then they were on the lake, *on the ice*, turning right to follow the shoreline. The carpet of snow seemed to give them some traction, better at least than exposed ice.

"This explains why she needed Adrian's help," he said. "The snowmobile. She wanted to stay *on top* of the ice."

"Just keep an eye out, let me know where they're going."

"I will, but I'm betting they exit near the fire." He rolled down his window to listen for spreading fissures, even while knowing that a few seconds' notice would only compound the terror. The temperature inside went into freefall, *69 . . . 52 . . .*, as documented by a digital thermometer at the base of the rearview mirror. A dark, crisp smell filled their nostrils. The outdoors had become a room with a fireplace, started by someone who didn't realize the flue was closed.

"They're almost across. I don't think the White Sea's planning to part and swallow us." But no sooner had he said this than a bass drum pounded from a point toward the center.

"More fireworks?" he asked.

"Just the lake."

"It's breaking up?"

"Nah," said Susan. "That much ice suspended on water. It's bound to make noise. You've never walked out on a frozen lake?"

These first sounds were joined by others, until an orchestra made up entirely of percussionists was producing a drum wall of thunder, building as it approached, yet eerily muted by the ice it moved beneath. "Mary, get across," he whispered.

The wave of sound passed. Scott opened his eyes. He was dry, he was looking out the windshield of a luxury SUV, and he was traveling forward. But that wasn't what mattered. The snowmobile had made it safely to land.

He rolled up his window and reopened the compartment where she stored her CDs. "I'm in the mood for some Reba Hill," he said. "Anything louder than that fucking lake."

CHAPTER TWENTY-FOUR

Mary understood his trepidation. But if Adrian had been whiny about driving onto the ice, it was nothing compared to his protests about navigating the narrow straits of this blazing archipelago. Smoke and flame lapped from all sides, ready to convert the snowmobile and its riders to fuel, something he clearly had issues with. The vehicle bounced as it grazed a deadly reef, hidden by waves of smoke. "We're dead," he cried.

"We're not dead," she shouted. "Now stop holding back."

"I'm going as fast as I can," he shouted back. "The snow's real thin in places. Stop hitting my head."

"I barely tapped it. Now go."

An oak to their right flared up as if it had been soaked for days in gasoline. Slinky flames leapt from the tips of branches, in search of fresh kindling. She saw a charred metal frame, falling in on itself, where her Life Ark Station should have been. Adrian moaned, "We're not going to make it." Then . . . Praise, Praise, they outran the fire.

Two rows of trailers had not yet capitulated. But this didn't mean she could ease up on her driver. "Faster, Adrian! Faster!" The advance troops, the heat and the smoke, were firmly entrenched, and she knew she wouldn't have much time.

She held her breath and leaned harder into his back. The last Stations blurred past, like the inside seams of a cannon's barrel, the very same cannon that shot them out into the clearing that circled the Inner Sanctum. Smoke still filled the air, but it was almost transparent. She saw others moving about. Holding cameras and microphones, these women and men looked dazed and lost, like the undead in a movie.

It hit her then that she no longer desired to speak to the press, with or without Daniel. She just wanted to talk with Him now, face to face, to make sure He was okay and to ask His personal forgiveness, "If I need it, Teacher." She'd add these last words because He still needed to clarify what it all meant. Her pregnancy? Was it good or bad?

Tell me, Teacher.

Adrian did as she instructed (he knew he'd be crazy not to), driving to the far side of Hawker's Inner Sanctum, to the circle, now hidden by snow, where old cars came to rust and stolen cars came to hide. But after all the swatting and prodding, Mary didn't even wait for him to bring his snowmobile to a complete stop. "Hey, come on," he shouted as she slid off the back and ran to the house. "I need to park in the clearing. Where the fire can't get it."

His words must have worked. Mary stopped by the door and turned to face him.

"That was rude of me," she said as she returned to where he stood by Old Slick. "It's just . . . it took so long to get back here."

She reached out to take his arm, but grabbed his keys instead.

"Wait a minute. No way."

"They'll be safer with me."

He was looking at her back as she said this. Once again, she was walking away.

"The guards, Adrian. They'll search you."

"I thought you trusted me," he shouted, wondering just how much damage the cassettes had caused. Not only had Mary seen the titles on their labels, he knew. She had taken one of the tapes, and it happened to be the last one he'd wanted her to see. "I thought we had a deal." Though he was powerless to do anything now, he wanted back his CHER BALSER-SEX WITH THE SAVIOR. He'd have to find a way. "At least wait up."

◆

God Boy's Inner Sanctum was even less impressive than he'd remembered. A simple ranch house with earth-tone brick, its trim needed paint. Adrian checked his pocket for the digital recorder. Then it was back to running. Catching up to Mary.

Standing on the concrete slab that passed for a porch while Mary opened a double-sash door with plywood in place of glass, he tore off his gloves, losing one to gravity. He pulled out his recorder and located the Voice Activate button. "Interview with Daniel Hawker, Real Thing, On Location, Inner Sanctum."

Adrian was ready. He wasn't going to miss a word.

But the next words on tape would be his own. "Hell's hole, it smells like a refugee camp in here."

Still trying to keep up with Mary, he added, "The front room is wide . . . and packed . . . and hot. It's a good-sized room, thirty, maybe forty feet on each side. It's bright in here too, with dozens of candles spaced about the floor. In saner times . . . in saner hands . . . a farmer would be sitting here with his family, watching TV.

"But the smell's still the thing commanding my attention. This place stinks of urine and sweat and other bodily emissions. It stinks of despair. And fear."

The fear, he conceded, could well have been limited to his own mind, the result of spotting Hawker's sentries. On the other hand, each of these mutants owned weapons, mistook violence for fun, and required as much room as any three young devotees. The cult members had to be frightened. The eight thugs he'd counted had taken off their shirts, with two going further to fully expose the tattoos and scars one could only acquire in prison. Though none of the monsters looked familiar, some were sleeping face down or sitting with their backs to Adrian. He couldn't see all their faces.

As for Hawker's followers, they just seemed spent. Their bodies were everywhere, crouched and slouched and sprawled about the floor, many quite close to flickering candles. They were, for the most part, clothed, though Adrian's eyes kept landing on the notable exceptions, like the couple sleeping on a foldout couch near the room's center. He assumed the pair had drifted off after sex, making him wonder if the three girls sharing their mattress had also participated.

206 ◆ **Tom LaMarr**

"I can hear someone playing bongos, determined, crazed, tapping out a series of super-fast triplets," he said into his recorder. "But that doesn't mean I can see him. There must be fifty people crowded in here. All through the room, bodies overlap, creating a single organism. And the mass seems to be buzzing. This is because the individual parts (the ones still awake) are mumbling incessantly." Prayer, he assumed, with each supplicant lost in her own world, unconsciously adding to the collective drone. He listened closely to confirm that each follower was producing a unique river of sound that never quite merged with the dozens of parallel streams. He caught few words, a splash of "surrender," a cascading "ever in the bright morning sun."

"Standing here, you'd swear they were speaking in tongues," Adrian noted. "Listen too long and you'll find yourself hypnotized.

"Wait, what's this? . . ."

Another guard entered through a door on the room's far end. "This particular homo-barely-erectus," Adrian said of the sentry, "wears both pants and a shirt, a feat that rises to the level of achievement here. But that's not the big news. That would be the toy on his shoulder, a bulky camera bearing a CNN logo . . . and actively seeking out naked bodies."

The camera's appearance helped explain something else that had captured Adrian's attention: a news crew cowering in a corner—one woman, two men, their jackets and caps sporting that same CNN logo.

"I cannot forget I have placed myself in peril," he said. "Incineration. Confrontation. Could be a question of which gets here first. As far as I can tell, no federal agents have made it inside. But we have to remember, this is only one room.

"Of course, the biggest thing I don't see . . . is God Boy."

Every so often he glanced over at Mary, to make sure he'd be right behind her if she slipped out in search of the missing cult leader. This also meant keeping an eye on the room's three exits: the one Adrian and Mary had come through, a hallway's mouth, and an opening to the kitchen. Adrian wondered why she stayed put. Was the rest of the house considered off limits?

"One more thing. There must be speakers everywhere, because the music is everywhere—and it seems to be getting louder with each passing minute. Vintage Hawker, sneaky and restless with its changes in tempo and key, it's providing the perfect soundtrack. I'm guessing that God Boy waits in the wings, holding out for the climax to announce his return."

The presence of these speakers made him question if Bev had, in actual fact, witnessed looting. Because the audio equipment seemed perfectly lootable. On the other hand, this marked the first time he'd stood in this room. It may well have been crowded with treasures before. There was also the nagging matter of what Adrian had—or had not—seen when he was outside, specifically, *anything in the shape of his Jaguar.* The possibility that his car had been stolen, *again,* threatened to erase an image he'd been holding onto for months, that of a soon-to-be-successful author escaping Minnesota's tundra behind the wheel of a cherry-condition XK8 Roadster convertible. Now, he could only hope that his car had been unable to get around a capsized school bus—and that the Jaguar remained somewhere close by. But he imagined worse scenarios, including one in which the car was already making that perfect, dreamed-of escape—on little-traveled back roads, with Hawker at the wheel.

Missing car. Missing savior. Adrian tried to push these thoughts away. Besides, how could Hawker have slipped by the United States government . . . and the press . . . even if he'd cut his hair and ditched the toy keys . . .

By driving across a lake with the headlights turned off, that's how.

Adrian looked across the room at Mary, and thought he sensed distress. Did she have reason to believe her messiah had fled?

He spoke in hushed tones the recorder wouldn't pick up. "God Boy is here. My Jaguar is here. I'm going to find both." He tapped his front right pants pocket—and cursed in silence. Mary had the key to his car, on the same chain as the snowmobile's. All he could feel was a bottle of caffeine pills.

There was movement from the CNN team. Specifically, they were crawling in single file toward the room's main entrance. As the woman passed beneath a poster of an actor he didn't recognize playing the role of a dead rock star whose name he couldn't remember, Adrian noticed the walls. What made these walls interesting were the pictures cut from magazines, now held in place by silver thumbtacks and glistening strips of Scotch tape. He saw dozens of disembodied heads, snatched from the shoulders of religious icons, historical figures, and enough disposable celebrities to fill an awards show. "Who decorated?" he asked his recorder. "Could it have been Hawker? Because it looks like the work of a thirteen-year-old girl with a strange sense of hero worship." By the time Adrian remembered the news team, they were gone from his sight.

He walked toward the room's center, and felt a hand gripping his ankle. "I know you," came a voice from the floor. When Adrian looked down, he saw the guard who had tortured him earlier that day.

"I'd suggest you don't mess with me," Adrian said. "I'm here at the Teacher's request. He's already upset with your not letting me in the first time."

The guard got up, though clumsily. He seemed to be having trouble with balance, and Adrian knew he was drunk or high. Unfortunately, the lumbering creature chose to steady himself by throwing his arms around the author from behind. *This is not good*, Adrian thought, expecting now to be raped or killed or brutalized in some fashion he didn't want to imagine.

But what he felt was a wallet slowly rising from his rear pants pocket.

"This all you got?" the thug asked.

Adrian tried to speak but no words took shape.

"Leave him alone," a woman's voice called out from the space behind the couch. "He doesn't have anything worth stealing."

It took him a second to recognize Cher. In addition to lying on her back, she was naked, painted blue, and shaved—everywhere. He thought of a Mayan ritual sacrifice. Or was this something he'd seen in an X-rated video? Whatever memories it was stirring, the haircut and paint didn't help her looks.

To Adrian's astonishment, the sentry released his grip. "Just don't go anywhere," the beast said. "I'm not done with you."

"Would you care for some illuminary essence?" Cher asked, waving her blue hand in the direction of a garbage bag spilling over with a spongelike, gray substance. He knew what he was seeing—the mushrooms distributed right before Hawker's sermons. Adrian had never partaken. He'd only pretended to swallow, wanting to keep his author's mind clear.

"Hawker?" he said now. "Is he here?"

"Instant enlightenment," Cher said as she sat up. "How can you refuse?" She gave him a broad smile, letting him see that she had not found a way to paint her teeth. He'd been wrong about the blue. It softened her features. The haircut too—at least the one above her waist—was growing on him. He imagined her repeating the things she said on his tape, where she betrayed the secrets of this house. All that sex. All those deviations. He fought to clear his mind. This wasn't why he came (though in point of fact, it *was* why he came most nights). He had business here, the business of his life.

"Please, I need to know. Is Hawker still here?"

"You'll feel better," she said, again directing his attention to the garbage bag.

He had a thought. Did the presence of the mushrooms mean that God Boy was present as well? It made sense. "So he got everyone high?" he said to Cher. "Any idea why your Teacher would want to dull everyone's senses?" Adrian knew the answer, of course. A good cult leader would have seen this action as a necessary prelude to the so-called mass suicide.

"Always thinking the worst," Cher responded. "Daniel didn't hand out the illuminary essence. One of the sentries found the stash in a closet."

Adrian started to ask if that meant Hawker had gone, but was cut short by the thunder outside, a whoosh and a crack that shook the house. The Inner Sanctum seemed to move on its foundation, if only a fraction of an inch.

This roused the other followers.

Bodies were shifting, and in some cases, standing.

A shirtless sentry rolled off his stomach and onto his back. Then, pushing himself into a sitting position, the ogre snapped, "Hey, what happened to the dancing?"

Almost immediately, there was dancing, and while Adrian thought all dancing was weird, this was more so. It was what people who didn't think dancing was weird called "expressionistic" and "experimental," and it was rarely in time to the music.

Five girls wiggled and jumped in the space before him. He paid extra attention to the three who weren't dressed.

"That's more like it!" shouted the guard.

The fear, Adrian could see, had not been limited to his own mind. These dancers looked scared. They wanted the sentry to go back to sleep.

A man joined their company, and Adrian recognized Gunt Larsen from his photo in the diner. Like Cher, Gunt had stripped completely down, though he'd apparently skipped the dye and shave cycles. His reddish-blond hair was still resolutely in place, including one place Adrian could have gone without seeing.

The music got louder.

After making sure Mary was still in the room, Adrian returned his eyes to the naked dancers. He noticed a new development. Gunt seemed to be trying to keep his attention on his partners—and away from the ex-con who stared at him while clutching a sizable erection.

Finally, Adrian thought, here was the craziness Bev had promised.

The music hit a crescendo, the dancing got wilder, and, easing the pressure in Adrian's chest, God Boy made his entrance. He came in from the hallway at the room's far end, taking his time, nothing urgent in his stride. "He's here!" Adrian exclaimed, nearly tempted to bend down and hug the only woman he'd slept with in two years. This would have been a mistake, of course, something he understood even before Cher narrowed her eyes and inquired, "What's wrong with you?" as if he were the one who had painted himself blue.

He held the recorder close to his mouth and said, "Interview with Daniel Hawker begins . . . now."

God Boy still smiled beatifically, walking slowly as if to make sure everyone got their fair share of smile. But when he came close to Adrian, the author could see just how disheveled he was. The long hair was uncombed, even tangled in places, and his face showed the shadow of beard growth, a few days' worth. And what was the deal with the bathrobe, worn over a loose-fitting sweater and pair of slacks? Looking down, Adrian glimpsed a pair of ancient Hush Puppies, the felt-exterior footwear of choice for a certain adulterous father in Tallahassee, Florida. And that, Adrian realized, was the impression he was getting from God Boy. Apart from the bathrobe and goofy toy-key necklace, Hawker was dressed like somebody's dad.

He didn't look like God.

And now that he was close, he didn't smell the part either. To Adrian's nose, Hawker more closely resembled the room, with its very human stench of urine and sweat. Two dogs followed the leader, a sheepdog and collie, while a third, smaller critter trailed several feet behind. Though Adrian had never seen one before (outside of photos), it had to be a potbellied pig.

He found one more thing of interest. Only he and Mary seemed to be reacting to God Boy's presence. The dancing, for example, continued without interruption. This made Adrian think that Hawker had been slipping in and out of the room for hours.

"Excuse me," Adrian said. "Adrian C. Hummel. The author. Could I have a few words?"

God Boy walked away.

◆

When Daniel paused by the foldout couch, Mary moved quickly to His side. Unfortunately, Adrian had been following the Teacher around the room, and he soon swooped in from the other side, all the while brandishing his small silver recorder like a cop's badge during a raid. "You need to give me another chance, sir," he said. "The world should hear your story."

Daniel looked the author up and down.

"When did you first realize you were the chosen one?" Adrian asked.

Without speaking, the Teacher took a seat on the arm of the couch.

"Why," Adrian persisted, "is the world still here?"

But Daniel just stared across the room, past the meddling author—and past Mary.

She could see it was time to speak up. "Sacred Teacher. I've come to seek your forgiveness, that or an answer."

Daniel closed His eyes, looking inward, as if receiving a divine communication from His Father. But whatever He was hearing, or seeing, or thinking, He apparently felt no need to share it.

"Teacher?"

He turned to face her, and she looked into His eyes. But while this should have brought comfort, Mary felt her legs grow weak—for all the wrong reasons. The blue, blue orbs were now glazed over. They seemed cold and unreal. Distant.

He needs my help, she told herself. *That's why I'm here. The women carried vinegar to Jesus on the cross.*

"What about the baby?" she asked.

"Baby?" Adrian echoed, his recorder now inches from Mary's face.

"Will this child be cursed or blessed?" Mary continued. "Who will it take after? Its mother or father?"

"It came to pass—"

"He speaks!" Adrian declared, and Mary was tempted to kick his shin.

Daniel started over, "It came to pass when men began to multiply on the face of the earth, and daughters of man were born unto them, that the sons of God took them wives of all which they chose."

"I don't understand, my Teacher. That's not an answer."

"He made darkness pavilions about him, turgid dark waters, thick clouds of the skies."

"The baby," she cried, and Daniel the Teacher who knew all things of Heaven and Earth turned to Adrian C. Hummel and asked, "What baby? Whose baby?"

Smiling again like a beautiful child on Christmas morning, Daniel walked away. Adrian followed, cutting ahead of the collie and sheepdog.

Seconds later, Mary saw Daniel leaning against the front wall, between the windows hidden by simple pull-down shades. There were faces around His head, illustrations cut from magazines and taped to the dark wood paneling. She saw Jesus, Satan, Buddha, Zeus, and—she didn't recognize the last one, but he seemed to be some ancient Egyptian. *The five shrunken heads. With Daniel, not Dad.*

At that moment, Mary made out something one of the mumbling disciples was saying from her place on the floor. "Father, Blessed Father, this is all my doing. I am the reason the world remains. I didn't believe enough."

Extending an arm toward the couch for balance, Mary shuddered.

"Sister, I was hoping you'd make it back." The tone of Cher's voice suggested she'd been hoping her sister would not make it back to Hallelujah City. "He hasn't slept for days. You should've seen Him at midnight, when it was supposed to happen. His insides crumpled like a ball of paper, you could just feel it."

Cher was naked—naked and blue. She sat cross-legged. The pose wasn't flattering, even from Mary's angle, looking down. "A few hours later he disappeared. We found Him this morning, in the woods, shaking from cold. He's been like this ever since."

"He wandered off? Into the cold?"

"I've been trying to get Him to leave. For His own safety, of course."

"Semolina thought He was planning to flee the country."

"You brought Semolina?" Cher craned her neck, looking past Mary to find Mrs. Bath.

"Is it true?" Mary asked. "Is He planning to leave?"

"I don't know. He's not big on decisions right now. I thought we were going hours ago—when the plane was here."

"*Was* here?"

"The pilot freaked when he saw the flames. That's my guess." Cher looked around the room, then lowered her voice to a whisper. "Did you hear what He did to the cows?"

Mary looked over at Daniel—and of course, His new Siamese twin, Adrian—just in time to see the Messiah pound His fist against the wall. Twice.

Cher shook her bald blue head. "He really needs some sleep."

Daniel dropped to His knees and clutched His hair, with one hand on each side of His head. He seemed to be pulling hard, hard enough to cause Himself pain.

"Sleep," Cher whispered.

This drew Mary's attention back to the disciple on the floor. "Sister Cher, what exactly have you told Adrian?"

"What do you mean?"

"I think you know," said Mary. "He's got a tape in his room called 'Sex with the Savior.'"

"He never interviewed me about any of that . . . Oh shit, that night he tricked me with liquor." Her face turned purple as her anger rose to the surface. Two parts red, one part blue. "That creepy . . . creep taped me."

"His tapes are a virus of sin," Mary said, enjoying the chance to throw back Cher's words. "It's up to you to stop the infection."

"I can't believe this. Adrian! Adrian Hummel! I'll tell you right now the only way you're getting your book out is posthumously!"

Cher rose to her feet.

"Slow down," Mary said, taking hold of her arm. "I've got something for you, but you might need a pocket." She held out Adrian's key ring. "His snowmobile. It'll get you back safely to his motel. You've got to destroy his tapes."

"But Daniel? What if He leaves?"

"We won't go without you. He'll want those tapes gone too."

"You'll really make sure He stays?" Cher said, before walking toward the kitchen on thin blue legs. She stopped, turning just long enough to say, "Sister, we came here as friends. It's only right we end the same."

◆

Adrian heard Mary shout from somewhere to his right, "No, no, no. You can't let him go in." She was blocking the room's entrance.

Her aunt was behind her, objecting, "And you can't keep God to yourself."

Adrian watched as Mary's father squeezed past her and into the room, and asked himself again, *What the hell is his story?* He seemed to have removed most of the trash from his coat, but the garment itself bulged with rags and boxes of cookies. Whatever the explanation, Mary's old man seemed right at home among God Boy and his collection of misfits. The dad looked around, displaying no reaction. "The music?" he asked. "What is that? Schoenberg? I know it. I've got it on vinyl. I just haven't played it for awhile."

God Boy shot him a piercing look.

"We need to get you out of here," Adrian told Hawker. "Somewhere safe. Where we can talk."

Hawker, of course, said nothing.

"You need to set the record straight," Adrian said. "Before it's too late."

"No one . . . is going anywhere." It was Mary's father. He sounded angry. "Because *it is too late.*" He was aiming a gun at the back of God Boy's head.

"Has Pilate found me at last?" Hawker turned to face his assassin. "Is this to be my Crucifixion?"

"Dad, stop!"

Two guards dove at the dad's knees, taking him down like a withered gray cornstalk. Hitting the floor, he lost hold of his gun. It bounced a few times, stopping several feet from his open hand.

They hoisted him to his feet, then held him in place like a condemned man in a movie. He looked small between the guards.

"Hawker," Mary's father demanded. "Release me now."

The guards responded by twisting his arms behind his back. It looked painful.

"You'll have to excuse their rudeness." Hawker was talking again, raising the question, Was he trying to piss Adrian off with the selectivity of his muteness?

"My daughter won't say it," said the man from Colorado, "but she knows you're lying."

"About what? The impossible perfection of a dragonfly's wings? The glory of Heaven?"

"Try, everything."

"Ah, yes." God Boy ran a hand through his hair. "And you, of course, believe in nothing?"

"I believe what I see."

"Then that makes your mind no wiser than your eyes."

"I believe—"

"That atoms are mostly space? That your material world is immaterial?"

"You're wasting your sophistry, Hawker. As you know better than anyone, it only works on kids too young to know better."

"And you, Scott Chambers, know better? How convenient after centuries of ignorance and myth to be born into a time when every riddle is solved. How fortunate to walk among men who know all things."

"My shoulders," groaned Mary's father. "Could you tell your goons to ease up a bit?"

"Please, yes, leave him alone," shouted the aunt. "You can hardly blame him for wanting you dead."

God Boy motioned to the guards to ease up, then waited, as if expecting a "Thank you." When that didn't come, he said, "I understand your conclusions, Scott Chambers. I do. What I can't understand is your pride in them. In a world without me, consciousness exists as a byproduct of cellular adaptation. The matter in your brain boasts no inherent superiority to that in your toenail. So where does the hubris come in? What is it that makes your intelligence so special?"

"Enough, for Christ's sake," said Mary's father. "You keep forgetting I'm not eighteen, keep forgetting that, just like you, I've heard it all before."

"Maybe if we'd stopped at toenails," God Boy continued. "We did well there. A toenail knows its place."

"It's over."

"A toenail never errs."

"Am I the only one here who thinks it's significant the world didn't end?"

"Your eyes can't tell you even this, Scott Chambers?" Hawker spread his arms, as if to say, Take stock of all before you. "We have overcome the world. From here on out nothing is familiar."

◆

Mary watched as the Teacher turned toward her. "My lamb," He said calmly as if nothing had happened, His smile warm as ever.

"Sacred Teacher, I think I messed everything up, but I don't know anymore."

Adrian's recorder hovered in the space between them. "The world needs to hear your story. To learn about your love . . . and mercy."

Daniel reached out to touch her shoulder. "Mary," He said, "you must come with me."

"Me, too," Adrian pleaded, just as her father muttered, "Don't— ow—go."

"There's one thing I need to do first," Mary told her Savior, and with that He withdrew His hand.

"Go on then, child. Conclude your business."

"And please go easy on my father. Don't let them hurt him."

Still holding Adrian's key ring, she walked over to her aunt. "Can we talk?" Mary asked, extending an arm toward the kitchen door.

"Of course."

Then they were standing beneath cold fluorescent lights. "Those tapes at the motel," Mary said. "I need them destroyed."

Susan didn't seem thrilled about returning to the Valfaard Inn. "You're in danger here, Mary. I think I should stay."

"I'm more frightened of the tapes. They could be harmful to me."

Mary knew it wouldn't help her case to add, "And even more so to Daniel."

"More harmful than a wall of fire?"

"I'll be all right. I promise."

"It's really that important?"

"I need one more thing. For you to get Cher Balser away from me. The blue girl—I'm guessing you saw her. She's kind of hard to miss."

Susan seemed more enthused, which would have been puzzling enough even if she hadn't asked, "That's Cher Balser?"

"You can take the snowmobile."

"No need," Susan said. "My car made it once."

They heard another blast outside.

"Poof." Cher was back. "One more trailer meets its maker." She wore a white parka that really brought out the blue. "I tried to get the others to remove the propane tanks, haul them far away from here."

"The fire must be close," her aunt said, staring at Cher. "Smells like it's already here."

This surprised Mary, because up to that moment she had somehow failed to notice the heavy, hanging fumes, the incense from things not meant to burn, like foam-rubber padding and plastic trim. Susan was right. The fire could have been in the basement.

"The snowmobile stays here then," Mary said, removing the key to Room 17 at the Valfaard Inn. "In case we need a life raft."

But Susan kept her eyes on Cher. "I'm going to help you with the tapes," said her aunt. "I can wait. If you need a minute to get that off."

"This is like, uh, real," the blue woman replied. "If the world had just ended when it was supposed to."

"You painted yourself with something that won't wash off?"

"I don't handle alcohol well. Guess I never have. Ask Needleknob there."

Susan took her arm and led her away.

◆

It wouldn't have seemed any stranger had Scott been underwater, looking up at the action through waves of helplessness and anger.

When Hawker herded Mary across the main room to the hallway, with the annoying author in slobbering pursuit like a dog keeping up with a jogger, Scott could still see the tops of their heads. But as they ducked through a door on the right, one of Scott's captors said, "Show's over," and the ruffians turned him to face left so that they could rejoin the party.

"Please," Scott said quietly. "You have my gun, I'm harmless."

He was lifted by his arms, still tucked behind his back. "Stop . . . sadists." The pain between his shoulder blades intensified. "Sorry," he grunted. "I'll be quiet."

A few seconds passed before they lowered him to where his feet touched the floor.

"Thank you," he whispered, even while knowing the gesture had resulted from a loss of interest and not a gain in empathy. A plump naked girl holding a bottle in her hand was dancing with the bony, red-haired man, and she put a great deal of energy into her jumping and dipping and shaking. Her breasts were enormous and fluid, exaggerating each shift in direction. When the man knocked over a candle, she doused the flames with wine from her bottle.

Stockhausen. Or was this von Webern? Even with his senses overwhelmed and adrenaline surging, Scott took note of the music again, and was still surprised that someone had created a bizarre sound collage of bits and pieces from what had to be the most obscure album in the record collection he no longer played. *Avant-Garde Discards: Twelve Rare Pieces from Experimental Modern Composers.* On the tape Scott now heard, soothingly harmonious passages followed twelve-tone extracts, resulting in a multicar pileup of styles. He was amazed that this patchwork succeeded—and even more astonished that the pastiche sounded good with synthesized keyboards and other electronic instruments layered on top.

"You have to let me go," he pleaded with the ruffians after several minutes had passed. "That young woman is my daughter."

"Tits here?"

"God no. My daughter is Mary. She went with Mr. Hawker."

"You're shitting me?" the keeper of his left arm said. "Mary's your daughter?"

Something hit the roof with a thud, a meteorlike thud. The music died, as did the overhead lights. The room was still bright, of course; candles weren't reliant on outside generators. Scott got as far as saying, "She needs my help," before the plump dancer shouted, "Fire!"

At once the bullies released their grip, and Scott looked to where he'd last seen his daughter. A room on the left side of the hallway was glowing. He saw the tips of flames. The dancer shouted again, but without bothering to form words. Her dance was more frantic now.

The ruffians, too, were on their feet and moving about. The candles cast shadows on faces that mimicked the terror of wild animals caught in steel traps. And then all at once, they were shoving as one toward the front entrance. This left it for Scott to push against the current. His ankles twisted as he jumped out of the way of some large shirtless men like the ones who'd restrained him, but he kept moving, fighting his way to where the fire burned. Feeling its heat, and hearing its rage, he turned right into the room that Hawker was in—or should have been in. In the pulsing auburn from the fire behind him, Scott saw no one; the chamber was empty. Smoke stung his eyes; the crackle of flames grew louder. There was a stampede in the hallway, a seismic free-for-all of screaming, cursing people who must have been in the back room. Adding one more distraction, a potbellied pig ran in behind Scott, sniffed at his shins, snorting, then tugged at the hem of his pant leg.

"Hey, stop that." Shaking the pig loose, Scott slouched toward the closet. "Scram now. Hurry. Before you start sizzling." The animal darted around him twice, then ran back out to rejoin the mêlée. Scott opened the sliding door with such force that it broke free of its grooved metal frame and continued across the floor, gouging an impressive crater in the bedroom's drywall. A wide sheet of plywood covered the closet floor, slightly crooked, slightly warped—and with light seeping out from under a corner. After tilting the sheet on its side, he looked down a simple wooden stairway, its hard right angles delineated by an eerie fluorescence.

He'd found the entrance to an underground bunker, one with its own power supply.

◆

A single row of hundred-watt light bulbs lit their way.

Everywhere Mary looked, she saw water coming through seams in the corrugated tin ceiling, some of it trickling, and some of it gushing. Melting snow. They were passing beneath the burning trailers.

She expected the tunnel to collapse and bury them. Soon.

Daniel was speaking. "The Lord went before them by day in a pillar of cloud, to lead them the way; and by night in a pillar of fire, to give them light; to go by day and night. Stay close."

Now leading the way, Adrian moved with an awkward sideways gait so he could best annoy Daniel with the recorder. Mary walked to the Teacher's left, which meant she kept brushing up against the uneven clay wall of the narrow passageway.

"Was Daniel Hawker originally a stage name?" Adrian asked.

"All things mutate in the fires of creation. He that descended is also the same that ascended up far above all heavens, that he might fill all things."

"I don't get it. Was that an answer?"

Mary wanted to say, *Shut up, Adrian. Show some respect for the Son of God.* But she couldn't deny that she, too, was baffled by His pronouncements.

They reached an opening on the right, a deep nook that served as a closet of sorts.

"Holy hell," Adrian said, gasping.

"Are we safe here?" Mary asked, taking in the propane tanks. Most of these were standing, a few had fallen onto their sides.

Daniel said, "Does a fish fear water? A hawk the sky? The ravens fed Elijah. They brought him bread and flesh in the morning, and bread and flesh in the evening; and he drank of the brook. The Lord protects all. A cockroach can survive up to ten days without a head." He stepped into the opening, while instructing Adrian and Mary to "Keep moving. You need to keep moving."

But Mary waited just a few feet ahead. When Daniel finally came back out of the recess, she took His hand and said, "Sacred Teacher." He didn't pull away. "There's no time left. We must get you out of here."

She felt shyer than ever before as she added, "You and I—we really need to talk."

"Sacred teacher, sir," Adrian interrupted. "Now that you've had a second wind and are talking again, what is this about a baby?"

"Mary," the Teacher said. "Your words show wisdom. Verily. You and I must talk."

He followed this with a sneeze, which prompted Adrian to ask, "Your allergies?"

"No, cold coming on," the Teacher said, smiling. "It's funny how nothing ever happens the way you picture it."

She heard a spurt of laughter: her own. Ragged, nervous, aching for rest. *Heaven is a river in the bright morning fog.*

A ladder stood at the tunnel's end. A house painter's ladder, poking through a hole in the concrete ceiling.

The Teacher puzzled Mary by gripping the second aluminum rung. But when He pushed upward she understood. He was using the ladder to open an escape hatch. She took hold of the bottom rung and heaved with all her strength. Unfortunately, whatever held that ladder in place showed no great desire to budge.

"Adrian," she snapped, "put that stupid recorder in your pocket and give us a hand."

The author took hold of rung number three and grunted. "This is impossible," he said moments later.

Mary suspected him of holding back. "All that propane," she whispered in his ear. "It could blow any second."

Adrian's grunt was louder this time. There seemed to be movement.

"Harder," Daniel commanded. "If we can knock the snow off the platform it won't be so heavy."

"Platform?" asked Adrian.

"Where He always started His Sermons by the Lake." Knowing where they were made Mary feel safer. She imagined the platform, imagined it tilting.

"Okay," she said, "this is it. One-two-three." Her arms burned as the "four" left her mouth. The ladder rose several inches and she heard what had to be friction, the sound of snow, crusty and dense from having sat there all winter, starting to slide. "Again. One-two—"

◆

Scott raced through the tunnel, finding all the incentive he needed in the combination of leaking water and electric lights, and stopping only once. For no discernible reason, he'd been drawn into a nook off to the right that housed a few dozen tanks of propane. It was there on the floor he saw the white poster-board sign that appeared to have been hastily embellished with a bold, black marker. The sign commanded, "FINISH IT." Next to that sign, he found his gun.

"Daniel Hawker," Scott said aloud, "who besides me wants you dead?"

When he reached the top of the ladder, he heard voices coming from a clearing to his left. The lake. Night wasn't so dark now: the snow, the trees, and shore existed as silhouettes, all gray, but with some more heavily tinted than others. He thought he saw figures on the ice, moving away from shore.

No sooner had Scott started walking toward the lake than a warm gust of wind hit from behind, giving him a slight push forward. He turned around slowly, shielding his eyes, and was fairly certain that a trailer on the far side of the house had exploded. He wanted to know if the others in the house had made it out alive, then smiled at the notion that he was anywhere close to being out of danger.

He patted the pocket of his coat to make sure the gun was still there.

"I sure as hell hope you know what you're doing," he whispered to himself.

The ground trembled again. He stepped onto the ice.

CHAPTER TWENTY-FIVE

C her Balser shifted in her seat like a twelve-year-old in church.
"CD?" Susan asked. "A little music to calm our nerves?" She pressed a button on the Land Rover's dash, which turned out to be the wrong one.

"Mary is a true believer," said the voice of Adrian C. Hummel. *"But I sense disillusion. Thanks to the actions of others in the compound. In particular, her ex-friend Cher Balser. Not too surprising with everything Cher's told me."*

The woman's blue fingers were drumming on the armrest.

"You came here with Mary?" Susan asked her.

"Who's she to you?"

"My niece."

"Oh." A break in the tapping. "We used to be friends."

"Could have fooled me."

Susan saw something odd in the convenience store lot, especially for the hour. A semi cab was pulling away from its jacked-up trailer, while a short, wide woman, bundled in fur and framed by a solitary streetlight, smoked a cigarette and supervised.

"That can't be good for business," Susan said. "Hiding the store behind a trailer."

"We are planning to destroy these tapes, aren't we?"

"I don't know, Cher. I thought it might be interesting to hear them. I still have lots of questions."

"You can't."

"And why not?"

"It's—" Cher looked down at the blue hands folded on her lap. "Mary and I weren't exactly getting along. I might've said some things."

◆

Then they were in the hamster-cage room.

"This place gives me the chills," Cher said. "If I could take back any two hours of my life."

"It's giving me something, that's for sure," Susan responded. "Wait, you didn't—"

Cher immediately busied herself by reading the handwritten labels on the cassettes and dropping them, one at a time, into the Nordstrom's shopping bag Susan had given her. "Shit, no 'Sex with the Savior.'"

Susan watched as the blue woman stormed over to Adrian's dresser and tore open its drawers, two at a time. "Nothing, nothing, nothing. Legal pads, batteries . . . a *Hunter's Guide to Northern Minnesota*. I don't see any tapes."

Cher dropped down onto the carpet and stretched out on her stomach to look under the bed. Something interesting caught Susan's eye. A small bronze key had slipped from a pocket.

Susan knelt down. "What's that," she asked, "way back in the corner?"

Cher slid forward a few inches. "Ugh, it's filthy down here."

Susan recovered the key. "Why don't I check the bathroom? I've got a hunch that's where we'll find the missing tape."

After pulling the door closed behind her, Susan turned on the overhead fan so she could take a small hit, to tighten her resolve. The fan was as loud as the heater had been, but at least it showed results. "Lord," she whispered to herself, releasing the last of her smoke, "give me the strength to finish this."

She popped in a breath mint, just as Cher surprised her by yanking open the door.

"Are you sure that's the name of the tape you saw?" Cher asked as Susan stepped back into the main room. "'Sex with the Savior'? You're sure that's the title?"

"Maybe it was more like . . . 'Cher Balser—Sex with the Savior,'" Susan replied.

"Damn. I can't find it. It's not here."

"Mary said he had tapes in the bathroom. Up above the ceiling panels. Maybe you should look there." *Or,* Susan said to herself, *in the pocket of my coat. Like, right next to that key you dropped, you backstabbing blue-skinned bitch.* "I haven't found the videos. Must be up there too. You did see a camera that night?"

"Fuck fuck fuck." Cher bolted into the bathroom as quickly as she must have that morning she woke up beside Adrian C. Hummel.

"I'll be right back," Susan called after her. "I think there's a flashlight in my glove compartment."

Back on the cool leather seat, she put her new car in drive. But she left her foot on the brake so that she could swap cassettes, place the Nordstrom's bag on the back floorboard, and pull out her reading glasses.

"Well, well, well," she whispered as she finally read the simple, cramped handwriting on the tiny paper tag taped to the bronze key. "Box C-2-1-6. Farmers Friend Bank of Can." The rest had been torn off.

"I've got a surprise for you, Mary."

She dropped the glasses and key into her purse and drove away.

"I get so sick of that mousy hypocrite with a halo," an inebriated Cher was saying on Susan's state-of-the-art car audio system. *"What kind of spell has Mary got over Daniel?"*

Susan was tempted to call the police in that Canterbury town they'd passed through on the way to Trappers Point, tempted to alert authorities to the blue-skinned space alien terrorizing the Valfaard Inn. But she let it go. Reviving her joint with the cigarette lighter—one of four in the car—Susan smiled. Cher Balser was her own punishment. Sometimes Karma comes from within.

By the time Susan reached the detour with all the signs and dogs meant to discourage trespassing, she was giving the police call more serious consideration. Cher-on-Tape had somehow managed to go downhill, and what started as disgusting was now genuinely disturbing. Susan liked her new niece, and did not care to hear her described as *manipulative* and *devious,* let alone as *Daniel's little sperm bank.* Mary seemed like a good kid—words that weren't going to turn up on this recording. It was just a matter of getting her away from this lunatic shit. Plus, she looked like her mom, way back when Liz left home to conquer the world.

"*Everyone thought she was just so sweet,*" the voice on tape was saying. "*But our little Virgin Mary planned to seduce Daniel from the moment she wormed her way into Zion.*" The blue woman had been right about one thing only: she didn't handle alcohol well. A three-legged wolf-dog dashed through the beam of Susan's headlights.

"Now . . . what to do about Adrian?" The Celine Dion tape went into a pocket.

The lake was vaguely orange now, reflecting the fire in the trees. Susan thought she saw people walking near the center of the smooth, unbroken expanse. Three, maybe four.

The sky was lighter, more gray than black, as she parked her SUV and jogged out onto the ice.

◆

The lake seemed noisier than before. Creaking, croaking, an occasional sigh. It made Mary think of the evenings she'd spent in Di Johnson's home theater basement, sitting too close to the rear speaker with the special effects. Daniel didn't seem to hear these sounds. They walked further and further from shore, while Adrian asked questions and Mary pleaded they turn back and use the snowmobile to escape danger.

This was all she knew anymore, that she had to get Daniel away from here, get Him to safety, get Him to sleep. He sounded so tired. He sounded so *human*.

"Rejoice evermore," He said. "Pray without ceasing. In every thing give thanks: for this is the will of God in Me concerning you." He clapped His hands twice.

"Why are we on the lake?" Adrian asked. "Wouldn't it better to walk toward land?" Mary saw apprehension in the author's face, exaggerated by the quivering light that came from the fires on shore.

Adrian persisted, "I can help you. If we can just get back on terra firma. I know how sleeplessness and stress can mess someone up. You just need to trust me."

"Prove all things; hold fast that which is good. Take nothing but photos. Leave nothing but footprints."

Mary thought she might cry. *Like a bird with a broken wing, there's just one thing I want—the impossible. It just happens to be something I always took for granted.*

As if responding to these thoughts of flying, a helicopter appeared above the Inner Sanctum. Mary saw a shaft of light, rigid and white, connecting it to the ground. But who was on board? The press? Federal agents?

Adrian was asking, "Why didn't you flee when you had the chance?"

The Teacher closed His eyes and hummed quietly.

"You knew the world wouldn't end—and you didn't want to die."

"Adrian!"

"Mary," Daniel said firmly, "let him continue."

"You had a plane."

Daniel ran ahead a few paces, then spun around twice. When he came to a stop he was facing Mary across eight, maybe ten feet of ice. "I wanted—" For the first time that night, the vacant look went out of His eyes. "I wanted to see if Mary would return."

She stopped too, just stopped altogether.

"But there's something no one here seems to have picked up," Daniel said. "The world did end. It's over."

"I could still get you out," Adrian said. "But you have to tell me everything."

"Mary. Will you come with me?"

"I—"

"You've done nothing wrong, my lamb. This was meant to be from before the beginning."

"From before the beginning?" Adrian said, his recorder still aimed in the direction of Daniel.

Mary's eyes, too, were fixed on His face. Breathing in slowly, she felt the smoky chill collect in her lungs. "Sacred Teacher," she said. "You never gave me an answer. What about the baby?"

"Time is a wall—"

"Teacher?"

"The trick is to look through that wall, to look through time. Look with me, Mary, to the other side where there are no sides, to that space without space, time without time."

"I don't see a wall, Daniel. Only time running out."

"Walls upon walls upon walls," He said with hoarseness in his voice. "Parallelograms, trapezoids. A trapeze through space."

Her voice was a teardrop, fragile and small: "I don't understand, my Teacher. You need to tell me, what about the—"

"Blessed," He said. "The child is blessed."

Adrian practically knocked her over. "The baby? The child? What am I missing?"

The ice seemed to move, dropping ever so slightly.

She heard a voice behind her. "Mary, stop! Wait for me!"

Looking back, she was surprised by what she saw. As the shadow took form, her dad looked vulnerable and slight, even in that stupid coat.

"Mary's special," the Teacher called out, His words hanging in the cold, a vaporous white. "You are not. Your life has no importance to anyone."

"Go home, Dad. You don't belong here."

The Teacher continued, "Not to me. Not even to your own child."

"Dad, it's not too late. Go back, please."

◆

Scott didn't know if he'd ever catch up. Hawker was moving again, with Mary and the imbecile posing as an author in tow, and running didn't strike him as a particularly sound idea.

"Mary, wait."

He saw someone approaching from the left. Running, of course.

"Adrian!" Susan had returned. "I have something for you!"

Even from a distance he estimated at fifty feet, Scott could make out some of her features, and this caused him to look up and see that the sky's grainy canvas had lost its gray to the faintest of blues.

Hawker stopped again, giving Scott one more chance to narrow the gap. Susan, too, stood still, though she was much closer to Hawker. She said, "Adrian, I listened to something interesting in the car." She must have been holding a small object in the white glove she lifted above her head, because Adrian shouted, "What is that? One of my tapes?"

"You're getting warmer," Susan replied. "Or should I say, you're getting hot? *Adrian, what am I seeing? Are you getting a little excited? You like stories with naughty girls and potbellied pigs, don't you?*"

"That's mine, goddammit," Adrian shouted. "The Cher tape is mine."

"*Wait,*" Susan continued her performance. "*That's it? You only get a little excited.*"

"Give it to me." Walking toward Susan, he slipped and lost his balance, breaking the fall with his elbow. "Oh Christ."

"Yes, my son, I'm here to help," Hawker answered.

"Those are my research materials." Back on his feet, Adrian appeared to be wiping snow off his coat sleeve. "Sacred, inviolable, you're not allowed to touch them."

The annoying author moved toward Susan, walking now with greater care.

"I'm warning you," she said. "Stop right there."

Adrian stopped. "All right. What do you want?" Steam poured from his gaping mouth. Scott thought of Chernobyl, ready to blow.

"You gotta be faster than that if you want to get your hands on Cher Balser." Susan smiled as she spoke, clearly in love with the moment. "Well . . . her tape anyway."

She curled back her arm, preparing to toss the sacred, inviolable object.

"If you think I'm going to kill myself chasing some worthless cassette tape, you don't know me at all."

"As much as I wish I could say it's not true, I do think I know you," Susan responded. "I've peeked inside your sick little world."

"Give me my tape."

With that she launched it, summoning the force and precision of a professional athlete who specializes in throwing cassette tapes. Achieving an impressive arc, the property in dispute flew far enough across the ice that Scott was unable to see it complete its first hard bounce. He only heard the chipping noise.

Adrian went after the tape, walking at first, then picking up speed.

Off to Scott's right, the fire was losing momentum, leaving smoke in place of flame. Two helicopters seemed to ride on that smoke, while aiming their searchlights at the smoldering compound. On either side of the haze, a pink band of sky rose to meet the pale blue.

Scott felt a vibration beneath his feet, a low-grade earthquake, as Adrian slipped in the distance, landing on his knees. But Scott's eyes were drawn back toward shore. With a building roar, flames shot from the tunnel's exit. There was a second blast from Hawker's house, and Scott could only assume the cache of propane had ignited.

"You've got to give him one thing," Susan said, surprising him with her closeness. He hadn't seen her walk over. "He throws a good End of the World."

"So tell me," Scott said, "what's on that tape?"

"The one Adrian's giving himself a heart attack over?"

"That would be the one."

"Celine Dion," she said.

"Celine Dion? The singer?"

Susan smiled again. "I keep Cher Balser in my other pocket. Don't ask me why, but I knew that cassette was important to him."

At that moment, a second blaze appeared on the horizon, just to the compound's right. Impossibly bright, it drew a laser's line across the snow. With just a hint of its power—this was only a speck of its corona—the sun had officially commenced yet one more dawn, the second to defy the End Time prophecy of Daniel Hawker.

"Whatever happens next," Scott told Susan as he pulled out his weapon, "I've enjoyed getting to properly know you."

Lifting his right arm, he was hit from behind, a solid burning blow. "Damn," he muttered, realizing it was simply where he'd injured himself in Susan's car, jerking himself awake. He steadied the arm, bracing it somewhat with his other hand. The gun was level with his eyes. His arms were trembling; his *body* was trembling.

"No, Dad. No." Mary spoke these words softly, more prayer than plea.

"I do this for you," he said.

But he couldn't do it, not for Mary, not for himself. His trigger finger would not comply.

Hawker extended an arm as well, stretching it out toward Mary. "Finish it," he said.

"*Finish it?*"

"I'm going with him, Dad." Scott's daughter moved sideways, placing herself in what should have been his line of fire. The top of her head came up to the madman's chin.

Hawker said, "The Spirit of my Father moved upon the face of the waters. He made two great lights; the greater light to rule the day, to divide the light from darkness. I *am* the Lord: that is my name, and my glory I will not give to another. I open the blind eyes, to bring out the prisoners from the prisons, *and* them that sit in darkness out of the prison house."

The sunlight gave his daughter's abductor a hard bronze mask, like something out of an ancient Greek play. Scott looked back over his shoulder, and what he saw was no less bold or mystical than the first dawn Hawker had been describing. As the greater light claimed its rule over the steam-white smoke now settling across the horizon, the lake was aglow with a gold honey warmth. The world seemed inexplicably peaceful. Everything made sense.

He let his arm drop back to his side.

"Dad, please. Just go home."

◆

"What . . . is *that*?" Scott heard Susan shout, letting him know he wasn't the only one viewing the new source of light, coming from a break in the trees ahead, on what had to be the lake's western shore.

The answer to her question came in brief installments, as a blue semi tractor pounded its way out of the woods, driving onto and into the ice, stopping in place, and sinking up to its headlights.

"Did that really just happen?" Susan asked.

Scott looked at his daughter; he had never seen anyone who looked so tired. She smiled faintly, and he saw her at every age of her life so far, the splotchy drooling infant, the twelve-year-old with the sweetly trusting nature she had somehow picked up on her own, and finally, the lovely young being who stood before him now, so like her mother, yet so remarkably different. This was the gift of parenthood, he realized then, to witness a life as motion, to be reminded—whenever we succeed in forgetting—that we are forces, not objects.

"I love him, Dad."

The ice shuddered as Hawker declared, "This isn't why you came, Chambers." .

Before Scott could speak, the madman added, "You came to be forgiven."

Scott laughed. "The last thing I need is your forgiveness."

"That may be true," Hawker said, pinching a toy key, the blue one, with two fingers. "You might start out a bit closer to home."

Scott looked deep into his daughter's face. What could Hawker possibly know?

"You lost your chance, Chambers." Hawker was rattling his Keys to Heaven. "When you lost her."

◆

From a semi tractor parked in four feet of water, Tank Matthews asked, "Semolina, gal, are you seeing this?"

Well, of course she was. The white sea was parting, the fracture extending maybe forty feet from shore. She saw other, smaller cracks branching out like tributaries. But for the most part, the lake was splitting in two—and sticking to the pattern Tank's cab had started. She thought of a red carpet being rolled out, something she'd never seen in real life. The blood-crimson color came from the sun, running like dye into the path of water.

"We're too late, Tank. I just know it." She saw four tiny figures, and wondered who was on the lake. "I'm sorry about your truck."

"I'm the sorry one here, Semolina. I was the one couldn't tell a lake from a field."

"But, Tank, it *looked* like a field."

"The break in the ice," he said. "Reminds me of a highway. Pavement after a downpour. Shiny and wet, holding the light."

The blue girl was sleeping in back, on Tank's wide bed. It had taken Semolina several minutes to recognize Cher Balser after she'd flagged down the truck, running wildly in the road, wearing a white parka and way-too-big sweatpants. At first, Semolina had considered the encounter fortunate, because the blue-faced girl had directed them to the lesser-known route. In return, Tank gave Cher the one thing she'd asked for, a pill to calm her nerves. The girl went down quickly, probably surprised by the potency of pills kept by long-haul truckers.

Semolina had still been feeling lucky when Tank instinctively swerved right to miss the black SUV half-buried in a wall of snow. The taillights were on, signaling a fresh collision. Of course, she didn't feel so lucky in hindsight, since hitting that vehicle might have been preferable to driving into a frozen lake. She recalled yet another odd thing about the last leg of this trip. Just after Tank avoided that accident, she thought she'd glimpsed two men hiding in a tree while dogs barked and clawed from below. The men seemed to be wearing suits and calling for help, but as she'd said to Tank, "There isn't time to stop."

Now, she reached across the space that divided their seats, and placed her hand on his relaxed-fit Levi's, just above a knee. "Thanks for the ride, Tank honey. Too bad it was over so quick."

"That's funny," he said. "I thought it was just starting."

Squinting, she smiled broadly. "That sun's really intense, sugar. You got a pair of shades I could borrow?" He leaned over and kissed her; his aftershave smelled sweetly familiar. Odd she hadn't noticed it before. It was the Old Spice her Robert once wore, applied with similar restraint.

"There's one thing I got to confess, Semolina Bath." Tank waited a few seconds. "What life insurance I got is all in my kids' names."

"That is a problem." She reopened her eyes to a sunrise that seemed even more dreamlike than before. "I guess this means I'm stuck with keeping you alive."

◆

No one was speaking, giving Scott the impression that time had stopped dead, with even the sun frozen in place.

His daughter got things moving again. "What happened, Dad? You used to like me." She paused, and he knew she was finding it difficult to speak. "Until you stopped . . ." He couldn't hear the next two words—Mary's voice had trailed off—but he knew what they were. Until you stopped *loving me.*

The ice heaved again, and he saw the water—a jagged river of metallic blue—cutting a swath away from the semi tractor. It was coming their way, moving with the momentum passed along by the truck. Sheets of ice were heaved aside, broken like saltine crackers, flipped at sharp angles, and he wondered how exactly one died from hypothermia. Was it painful or swift? Would Mary suffer?

Although it wasn't like her, Susan felt as helpless as the sun to intervene. Wherever she looked in this place stripped of all things familiar, including boundaries and rules, there was so much going on. She'd seen a truck crash into the ice, setting in motion a chain of destruction. She watched two helicopters approach, sweeping the lake's frozen surface with brooms of light.

Then Mary and her guru stood in a burning shaft. Mary seemed to be guarding the man, who still blabbered on about God knows what, and Susan witnessed the young woman's yawn as it yielded to terror, the ice breaking apart, coming her way. That was when Scott stepped into the light—and right before Susan heard the idiot author cry out that he'd been shot.

"I never stopped loving you," Scott shouted to her niece. "That was never the case."

"Choose right, Mary," Susan spoke aloud, though her words immediately shrank to nothing, lost to the mighty sound. "The baby. Your father." It was hard to say which Susan found more overwhelming at that point, the movie-projector brightness or the hammering blades. The roar seemed to come from every direction, with the ice providing an ideal conduit for angry pounding noise.

"Daniel Hawker," bellowed an amplified voice that seemed to be part of the light. A bullhorn, most likely. "If you are present, raise your arms."

Yet with all this going on, there was one image that registered most with Susan. This was the resolve in the face of her ex-brother-in-law. If anyone here was going to walk on water it was Scott.

◆

Suddenly, Scott was viewing it all in slow motion—the water's advent, the movement of others—the way a car crash unfolds, the effect of a human mind going into hyperdrive to process every piece of information that might prove helpful.

His gun had fired as it hit the ice, but the sound seemed muted, as if it were miles behind him while he ran toward his daughter. Now, he saw the look in her eyes, telling him to stop. He saw Hawker's lips, moving without rest like mechanical parts of a wind-up toy. He saw the hard silver water that—impossibly—looked colder than the ice it replaced.

And he knew he had waited too long. The lake would take his daughter. She would die of hypothermia, in Hawker's grip, stolen again by that monster. But at the last possible second, with the water at her heels, Mary started to jump—*to jump away from Hawker.*

It came too late. She'd missed her chance. Scott saw the ice breaking apart, still in slow motion, directly beneath her feet.

His daughter. His baby.

He took advantage of this relativity by leaping forward in regular time. His arm ached like hell where it connected with her elbow—he had never felt anything more satisfying. He watched her reel sideways, knocked through the air by the force of their collision, landing chin first on the greater shelf of ice.

Done, he thought, freeing time to regain its footing. And so it did. From all sides a huge buckling roar announced Hawker's descent—along with his own—the two locked in this together, just as they'd been from the moment Mary chose to leave home. Incredibly, irrationally, Scott wanted to find something profound in the face that had shown his daughter such hope and purpose. He wanted to see what she had seen—youthful innocence made flesh.

It wasn't there.

"Time's up," Scott whispered, and Hawker gave him a look that clearly said, "You're crowding my spotlight," as the world fell away from beneath their feet.

◆

Since he could no longer move, Adrian had been overjoyed to see he'd been spared by the break in the ice. Only moments before, he'd come to the astonishing conclusion that he would outrun it anyway—*Who would have thought he could go so far without a lung collapsing?* Hell, for a while there he thought he'd keep running till he hit the ripe red sun just above the horizon. But when he heard the gun go off, and felt his leg being torn apart, all he could do was fall forward onto the snow and wonder why someone had wanted to shoot him when there was at least one better target out here. Had anyone seen him go down? Would the chopper get him to paramedics while his muscle and bone could still be repaired? His leg throbbed. He didn't want to look at it, was afraid of it in actual fact. It felt as if the lake was heaving up and down in time to its beat. Without taking a break from wincing, he smiled, thinking that his leg needed to be put on ice—and knowing that, conveniently, there was no place else to put it.

He had new questions for God Boy. Was this chaotic drama his idea of a crucifixion, sending out a few believers he'd thoroughly screwed—physically, financially, or otherwise—knowing that someone would return with a weapon?

And was he, Adrian C. Hummel, simply playing a minor supporting role—and playing it poorly?

These thoughts were interrupted by the sky, exploding in brightness and noise. A blizzardy wind blasted straight out of heaven, originating from a point directly overhead.

"It's you," Adrian said to the light. "You were cut off back in the diner. After you said I'd finally write my book. After you said that millions would read it."

This time he saw no baby's head. The voice came through as a crunching, flapping tone that vibrated through his body and through the ice. "It won't exactly be *your* book."

Adrian started to speak, but the light continued, "You will live underground." Now, there was a word Adrian hadn't heard for some time. But the counsel made sense, seeing that this strategy had already presented itself as the only one open to him. "A disciple will help you write the Final Testament."

"Mary?" He wanted it to be Mary. "Mary Chambers?"

"No, the colored woman." *I knew it*, he thought. *This is a nervous breakdown.* "Colored woman" sounded like something the old man would have said, and more to the point, he'd never seen one in Hawker's compound.

Then, however, he understood. He would go underground with Cher Balser, the *blue* woman.

Amazingly, considering the combined intensity of the light, the noise, and the pain in his leg, he thought of a doomsday cult he'd read about online. The Millerites had rebounded after their "Great Disappointment," regrouping years later as the Seventh Day Adventists. All it had taken was some revisionist tweaking, the kind he was being asked to do. And what about Jesus? According to gospeltrooth.com, He once told the faithful, *This generation shall not pass till all these things be fulfilled.* Christianity had sure managed to survive the setback.

The light read his thoughts. "It can be allegorical."

"It?" He felt himself being rolled onto his back and lifted into the air, his very essence freed of gravity. "What *it?*"

"End of the world, genius."

He took a second to consider this. "About Cher," he said. "Mary Chambers would be much more helpful."

The blackness returned.

◆

Staring into the abyss, Mary whispered, "He that descended is also the same that ascended." The helicopter's searchlight seemed incredibly bright, creating the illusion that one great beam of light was coming from the water. "He that descended is also the same that ascended."

"*My lamb,*" Daniel said and she reopened her eyes. But all she saw was the river within a lake. No one was rising into the air—or even standing defiantly. A trio of plastic keys floated on the water. Like the petals of a lotus.

She saw one more thing, a dull gray balloon the size of two men, sinking then returning. "Dad's coat! I see Dad's coat!" A hand reached out and up toward the surface. But the more she looked, the less it seemed to be reaching. There didn't seem to be any push behind it, didn't seem to be any life.

A wide sheet of ice tipped at a twenty-degree angle. The end in the air was jagged, the bow of a sinking ship. But the image held for only a second. The slab cracked in half and the elevated section fell back to the water, violently slapping the surface before floating several yards to cover the churning chasm. "He that descended is also the same that ascended. He that descended—"

The slab collided with the main sheet of ice, right where she'd glimpsed the outstretched hand. Then she saw nothing but light. Pure light, empty light.

"We'll find the bodies." The booming voice in the sky was back. "You two proceed to shore. Slowly. *And separately.* The ice is breaking up. Take two different directions, to spread out the weight."

But neither woman budged from where she stood.

"Hand!" her aunt Susan shouted above the drum roll of blades. "There. There!"

Mary saw it too, pressed flat as could be between the colliding masses.

"Help!" she cried in unison with her aunt.

Instantly, two men in heavy winter gear rappelled down a ladder of metal and rope—and tore away at the ice with chisels.

Minutes later, a body was pulled from the breach they created. It looked bloated, an effect Mary wanted to blame on her father's coat.

"Daddy," she cried, while Susan shouted, "Scott, can you hear us?"

"Move to safety," the voice in the sky reiterated. "Now. Alone."

Mary couldn't move, which didn't really matter since she had no desire to do so.

"He'll be okay," one of the government agents shouted.

But he didn't look okay. He looked dead.

"Please move away."

The men slid the body onto a stretcher that seemed to have materialized from molecules of air. The stretcher was fastened to cords, which in turn seemed fastened to the pillar of light.

As the body rose into that brightness, her aunt spoke firmly, "There's nothing we can do here. It's out of our hands."

An icy gust of wind brought tears to Mary's eyes. Closing them tightly, she again heard Daniel's voice. "Mary Chambers, is this your choice?" The voice turned to a whistle, wolves howling in the distance, and faded completely when the gust died down.

"He'll be all right," her aunt said with even stronger conviction. "When this is over, lunch is on me at the diner. For you and your dad."

Mary felt a hand on her shoulder as Susan added, "I'm sorry about your leader. I really am. I know none of this makes sense. I know you feel worse than I can imagine."

"I . . . think I can walk now," Mary said, each word cracking with dryness.

Turning slowly, she felt the sun's faint warmth on her nose and cheeks. The world in this direction was white, new, buffed to a shine. She wondered briefly what heaven would have been like, and realized she had never really tried to imagine it. She just never got past that last hour on earth. There was movement in her belly, but she blamed her imagination, knowing it was months too early. One thing for sure, she really had to pee. The red-coal pinch. Did this ever let up?

Mary heeded the advice about moving slowly. But she stayed close to her aunt as they started off toward shore.

CHAPTER TWENTY-SIX

Strange, Scott thought as his eyes blinked open to a world saturated in light. *I couldn't have been conscious under the water.* Yet this was contradicted by an image, an image as clear as any in recent memory. Daniel Hawker: his hair defying gravity, twisting and tangling in a whirl of green bubbles. Daniel Hawker: returning his gaze. Equally strange, Scott remembered a dream of watching events on the lake's frozen surface. In this dream, he'd looked down from above, not up from the water.

"You were rambling."

This is how Scott was welcomed back. The voice belonged to Susan.

She rose above a snowy horizon of crisp white sheets. Mary stood closer on the same, left side of his bed. Their faces were slightly out of focus at first, as if a film of water still remained.

A doctor and nurse appeared to his right, each seemingly more interested in the monitors Scott now saw than in the actual patient. He coughed and cleared his throat. The tissue and muscle felt like leather left outside for years, like leather wanting to crack and tear.

"Did I say . . . anything about . . ."

Mary spoke softly, "You said you needed forgiveness for something I'd never understand. That I'd have to trust you."

"In that case I wasn't rambling."

"No, Scott." It was Susan again. "You were rambling all right."

"Dead?"

"You were. But no one fared too well out there. You should see the bruises you gave Mary where you pushed her. Where your hands hit her ribs."

He nearly asked if he'd been out long enough to have sustained permanent brain damage. Was thinking supposed to hurt this much? But the funny thing was, he didn't really care. It wasn't what mattered.

He felt fingers touching his own, and concentrated fully on squeezing Mary's hand. An IV tube trembled in response.

When he tried moving his other arm, the nurse stepped forward anxiously.

"What?" he asked.

"You have some adjusting to do, Mr. Chambers," the doctor said as she, too, moved closer. "The arm. We had to remove it."

He nearly cried out, "You can't be serious," but lacked the motivation.

"Mr. Chambers?"

"According to the agents who brought you here, your arm had been crushed between a few hundred pounds of moving ice," the nurse explained.

Scott still felt his fingers. He was bending them now. The phantom limb—he'd read about the phenomenon in a textbook at work.

"Everyone here was in agreement. We had no other choice."

He focused on the other arm, the one he actually had. Mary's touch—she still held his hand—felt like moonlight on a summer's night. It felt like a second chance, like a miracle he didn't deserve.

"No loss," he whispered at last. "I've been thinking it was time I gave up copywriting."

"That arm saved everything else," Susan offered. "It's the reason you're here."

"Then it finally did something right," Scott said.

"But it wasn't the arm," his daughter corrected them. "It was the coat with all its pockets of air."

He started to speak but Mary had already intercepted his thoughts. A cup appeared in front of his chin. Water, the substance of life, giver and taker. A plastic straw poked into his lower lip, which seemed to have turned to cork. It was the feeling of Novocain, of leaving a dentist's office after getting a filling.

Nearly frozen, the water delivered a familiar sting. He took a second, longer sip, then nodded in thanks. Mary pulled the cup away, just as he heard the doctor say, "We'll give you folks some privacy."

"What about that . . . Adrian?" Scott asked.

"They airlifted him here," Mary said. "Helicopter. Just like you. Seems he'd been hit in the shin by a stray bullet."

"He's here in the hospital?"

"Remember the blue girl?" Mary asked. "That was Cher Balser. From my school. She snuck him out in the middle of the night. Aunt Susan here saw them."

"Except for the blue paint, she seemed to be doing okay," Susan added. "She was driving a Jaguar. It looked brand new."

"I guess that's good," Mary said. "If any two people deserved each other."

He watched as she reached over to wipe his chin with a napkin. Unable to feel any pressure, he asked, "They didn't remove anything else, did they?"

"You had a visitor," Susan said.

"Semolina," Mary elaborated. "You remember our passenger? It was good she stopped by. I had something for her, a little key Aunt Susan gave me. I told Semolina to consider it payment for the flask."

He started to ask about the gun. Susan cut him off, anticipating the question. "No evidence," she said with the slyest of smiles. "And even if it hadn't mysteriously vanished, they'd need a victim to press charges."

He coughed again. "Mary." He felt tears on his cheek, and this reassured him. Given the room's watery brightness—and the weight of the air and bedding and light on his chest—he'd been harboring the suspicion he was still underwater and this was a dream, a last spurt of consciousness. "I want another chance. As a father. And grandfather."

"You know whose child this is?"

"Yes," he said, his voice and thoughts much firmer than before. "Yours."

"And that's enough?"

"I should probably go," Susan said. "Let you two talk."

Scott tried to laugh. "I thought you were buying us lunch."

"How could you have heard that?" asked Susan. "I mean, seriously, there's no way. And besides, that was three days ago."

"Three days?"

"You didn't miss much," she said. "Unless you enjoy hanging out with people who work for initials. NBC, FBI, etcetera, etcetera." Scott's ex-sister-in-law moved toward the door of the hospital room. "What if we made it dinner in Colorado? Someplace nice."

Scott was the one who replied, "I'd enjoy that."

It still hurt to think, but this didn't stop him from trying. There were things he'd have to say after Susan left the room, and for this he'd need words.

His brain wouldn't cooperate. It faltered. It wandered, going everywhere but where it could be useful. He felt an itch on his arm, the missing one, and wanted to ask the doctor or nurse, "What do you do with the leftover parts?" He heard crystals of snow pelting the hospital's roof, even while doubting this was possible. What floor was he on? No one had said. He heard something else, something considerably more distracting. Snippets of song, playing from nooks in his memory, took him all over time, a surface as fissured and slick as that of a frozen lake he knew too well. He endured a few lines from a Rod Stewart hit that Liz once loved, and enjoyed a Counting Crows dirge he used to hear coming from Mary's room. A few words from "Running on Empty"—*Running bli-hind*—segued into a more predictable chorus from "Wide Open Spaces" and an especially unwanted *Like a diamond in the sky*. But then he understood, remembering how "Twinkle, Twinkle, Little Star" had played over and over on cassette that long-ago night when Mary fought back a fever of 104. She had pneumonia, though the pediatrician had tempered his diagnosis with, "Thank God we caught it so early." Scott had been commended for bringing his daughter in on such a snowy day, giving him complete exoneration from Liz's charge that "only the world's worst father would drag a three-year-old with strep throat out in a blizzard." His wife had not seen the storm firsthand. She wouldn't be home for two more days, the evening after her conference in Miami wrapped up.

Sleepless on Mary's floor that night her fever broke, Scott had whispered above the pained exhalations, "My smart, beautiful daughter, I want your life to be an ongoing discovery. I want you to grow and flourish, to know passion and joy." He'd whispered above the Colorado wind and the snow spraying windows, above *'Tis your bright and tiny spark, lights the traveler in the dark*, "I want you to stay interesting and interested . . . loving and loved . . ."

Maybe that's what he'd say to her now. That he still wanted these things for her. That he was sorry for the way her dream ended.

"Mary?" He heard his daughter sobbing loudly. But then, she didn't look like she was sobbing. Or crying at all.

"Dad? Dad? Are you okay?"

"I might be," he said once he was able to catch his breath. "I think I just might be."